SUSPICION POINTS

A Detective Novel

By the same author

Vissi d'arte – a story of love and music

Eumeralla – a family saga about secrets, tragedy and love

The Doll Collection – a crime novel

SUSPICION POINTS

A Detective Novel

By

Joanna Stephen-Ward

Popham Gardens Publishing
November 2013

Acknowledgements

Special thanks to:

Annie Morris for reading the manuscript and giving me valuable feedback.

Richard Waters who provided the title and suggested the idea for the cover.

Peter Stephen-Ward who took the cover photograph, designed the cover and set up the book for publication.

Cover photograph taken at Lanhydrock, Bodmin, Cornwall. Front cover image with kind permission of the National Trust.

www.nationaltrust.org.uk/lanhydrock/

This book is also available in e-Book formats from Amazon Kindle.

Joanna's website:

www.joannaauthor.co.uk

This book is dedicated to three special people:

Kerry Conroy my sister

Ethel Curnow my aunt

Peter my husband

1

APRIL 2008

Saturday Morning

ROBERT

The phone began to ring as I opened the front door. Apart from a wrong number there would only be two reasons for a phone call after midnight – a family emergency or a crime. In spite of the grim options I was grateful for the distraction.

I picked up the phone. 'Trevelyan.'

It was a murder. There had been an arson attack on a house and a man and his baby son were dead. I wrote down the address and went back to my car to pick up Sharon. No, not Sharon anymore. Detective Inspector Richardson. Her recent promotion had destroyed any chance we had of being friends. It had changed her from being endearing and comradely to someone who was domineering and bossy. Four of us had applied. Sharon was the only woman. Despite the fact that I was sure she'd been given the job because of her gender, I'd tried to be gracious about her success, but she'd immediately made it clear that she was in charge and I had to obey her orders.

If neither of us had been promoted, we could have been friends even though our backgrounds were very different. When she'd told me she'd grown up on a sink-estate I'd been amazed. She wasn't ashamed of her East End background, and she spoke grammatically and clearly with a wide vocabulary. Her honesty was one of the reasons I had admired her.

We'd both moved to Cornwall two years ago. She'd moved three months before I had, and was well on the way to establishing herself where we worked. She had helped me settle in by introducing me to the rest of the staff, explaining the dynamics, and making sure I was included in the invitations to the pub after work.

When I got to the car I took the street directory off the back seat and looked up the directions to her house in St Austell. As I put the car into gear it struck me that even going to a murder scene with Sharon was preferable to spending a sleepless night in Dolphin Cottage. An empty house in suburban London or an empty cottage in Cornwall overlooking the sea – the feeling was the same. Until three years ago I'd never lived alone and had sometimes wondered what it would be like. Now I knew. It was depressing. No matter how attractive I had made the inside of the cottage and no matter how beautiful the view, the atmosphere of desolation was always present.

Sharon looked pale and exhausted when I arrived, but I knew any comment from me, however well meaning, would be met with an acerbic reply. Her house was small, and when we were on friendly terms she'd told me that it had two bedrooms and a patio garden and had cost less than her tiny one bedroom flat in Hackney. I wondered if she would buy something bigger now she was earning more money.

'I suspect this is a random arson attack,' I said as I started the car.

'Let's talk to the neighbours before jumping to conclusions,' she said sharply.

When we arrived at Farrier Way the ambulance was just leaving. The firemen told us that from the seat and spread of the fire it was clear that an accelerant had been used. Someone had pushed rags soaked in turpentine or petrol through the letterbox. The neighbours had all gone to the last house in the row. The street was attractive with terraced houses on both sides. It was surrounded by forest and looked as if the houses had been built in a clearing. Trees and hedges in the front gardens mostly screened the windows on the ground floor from the houses opposite, but anyone looking from an upstairs window might have seen something.

Sharon and I went to the end house to interview the neighbours. There were six of them in the basement kitchen. I could tell from Sharon's expression that she took an immediate dislike to them. I hoped she wouldn't antagonize them.

2

SHARON

In their luxurious dressing-gowns they all looked as if they were at a nightwear party. If we hadn't been in a kitchen in Cornwall the four younger ones could have been backstage at a fashion show in London or Paris waiting to parade on the catwalk.

I thought about how my mum and dad would look if they'd been dragged from their beds in the middle of the night. Dad wouldn't have his teeth in, he'd be smoking and have bad breath and a hangover. He'd have grabbed his cigarettes and left his teeth behind. Mum's dressing-gown would be shabby and too short and she'd either be barefoot or in flip flops showing her yellowing toenails and bunions. She'd have bad breath too, but not from smoking. It was from poverty and decayed teeth because she couldn't find an NHS dentist.

My parents were in their fifties. So was the woman who owned this house. And she looked twenty years younger than they did. She hadn't told us her age, but said she'd lived in this house since she got married thirty years ago. I tagged her as the socialite. Nicknames help me remember the witnesses and suspects. When we arrived she busied herself making tea.

'Sorry there's no coffee, but it gives me migraines. I love the smell so much if I made it for anyone else I'd give in to temptation and suffer agony for the next three days.'

I hate tea so I asked for a glass of water.

'Still or fizzy?' she asked.

'Just out of the tap, please.'

'Would you like a slice of lemon in it?'

As much as I felt like reminding her that this was a murder investigation not a party I made myself smile and say, 'No thanks.' I finally got my water.

She put a tin of chocolate biscuits on the table. Even if my mum had a packet of digestives in the cupboard she wouldn't have thought about the social niceties.

For the first hour I let Robert do things his way, so I could prove to him that his soft tactics were a waste of time. And as I had been deeply asleep when the call had come, I felt sluggish. I'm not one of those lucky people who can survive on four hours sleep a night. I need at least eight. A cup of coffee would have made me feel more awake, but I'd only had time to pull on my clothes, splash water on my face and comb my hair before Robert arrived.

'How did you get here so quickly?' I'd asked.

'I'd only just got home when the phone rang. Were you asleep?'

'Yes.' The admission made me feel boring. I wondered where Robert had been. Out to dinner with a girlfriend? With a group of friends? In his bottle-green cords, black brogues, tweed jacket over a jumper and thick cotton check shirt he looked like a country gentleman. I wouldn't have been surprised if he'd turned up in a dinner-jacket. He seemed the type to go to posh balls, parties and society weddings. He supported the ban on fox hunting, otherwise I would have put him down as a hunting, shooting and fishing type.

Robert started off with a friendly chat. We're just here to make sure you're all okay and not traumatized by the fire, approach. He maintained it was the fastest way to get information without asking questions. Treat them like innocents and their guard will drop. Once you've gained their trust they won't see the traps you set.

During that hour we'd learned that the two blokes, who looked about thirty, were clothes designers. That didn't surprise me. Their hair was perfectly groomed and they wore silk dressing-gowns and pyjamas and leather slippers. Neither had stubble on their faces. Were they so vain that they had shaved, combed their hair and slapped on aftershave when the firemen told them to leave their houses? One had lived in Cornwall all his life. The other one was French. They had a shop in town and were married to the two girls. That mystified me. I'd have sworn the two blokes were homosexuals. The socialite was a widow. I wondered what had happened. Cancer? Accident? Or had he been a lot older than her?

Robert looked at ease with them. They were his sort. All comfortable and smug. They'd eat their five portions of fruit and vegetables a day. They'd shun the smokers standing outside pubs and preach about lack of willpower and lung cancer. I bet this lot never had to worry about being evicted because they couldn't afford their mortgage repayments.

One of the girls called Robert 'Inspector'. His pause was deliberate and I cut in with, 'I'm Inspector Richardson. This is Sergeant Trevelyan.'

Even though there were eight of us in the basement kitchen it wasn't crowded. There was a table and chairs in the middle and units with granite worktops around the perimeter. Although the style was simple I knew it was expensive. I'd seen stuff like this four years ago when I was doing up the kitchen of my flat in Hackney. Even at heavily discounted prices I couldn't afford them.

The socialite started fussing over the pregnant girl who was French. She looked it too. Roses were embroidered on the lapels of her pink satin dressing-gown, and her slippers were burgundy velvet. Suspended from the pearls around her neck was a ruby and diamond cross. They could have been chips of glass, but she looked the sort who wouldn't wear fakes. The lace hem of her nightdress was visible. Her dark hair was cut in a gamine style and her ivory skin was smooth. Even at seven months pregnant she looked wonderful. Expectant mothers are supposed to glow, but she more than glowed.

I've never glowed in my life. If I was ever pregnant my hair would be sure to fall out and my skin would probably break out in a rash.

Even the old lady was glamorous. Her grey hair shone and her towelling dressing-gown was snowy white and looked new. She kept asking, 'Are you sure it wasn't faulty wiring?'

'Yes, Madam,' said Robert. 'The fire was lit deliberately.'

'What's happening to the world?' she moaned.

Same thing that's always happened, I thought. Hate, jealousy, human nature and greed.

No one looked upset. I wondered what Robert, with his passion for instinct, gut feelings and psychology, made of that. There were ten houses on this side of the street and I wanted to know where the rest of the neighbours were.

'The two places for sale,' I asked, after being told that two of the families were on holiday. 'Are they empty?'

'Yes,' said the socialite. 'They've both gone into homes – they were elderly.'

Thanks for that, I thought. Why else would they go into a home? 'Did you like them?'

'Yes. We visit them. We were terribly sad, but they're

7

better off in a home.'

'I meant the victims. The ones who burnt to death,' I snapped.

Robert winced. Before he could smooth things over I repeated my question.

'Well,' began the socialite. 'They hadn't been here long.'

Even Robert picked up on the evasion. 'What were they like?' he asked with a smile.

She bit her lip. 'They didn't really fit in.'

He looked as if he understood. 'In what way?'

'Well, these houses are . . . they wanted to do awful things. They were going to chop down the tree in the front garden because they didn't want bird mess on their car.'

Who does want bird mess on their car? I couldn't understand their outrage, but at least we were getting somewhere.

The socialite continued. 'And they were going to dig up the yew tree hedge in the front. We told them it was at least a hundred years old, and Bridget said, "It's about time it came out then".'

Bridget. Interesting. The fireman had told us that two bodies had been found. One was a man. The other was a boy aged about two. He had been in a cot in the smallest bedroom. The fire brigade had been called at thirty minutes past midnight on Saturday morning, so I'd assumed the man was separated or divorced, and had custody of his child at weekends.

'What was the man's name?' I asked.

'Declan Murphy,' said the socialite. 'I can't remember the baby's name . . . something Irish, I think.'

'Were Bridget and Declan a couple?' Robert asked.

'They are . . . were married,' said the socialite.

The pregnant girl yawned. Her husband touched her arm.

8

Something about the gesture struck me as being wrong, but I didn't know why.

The French clothes designer spoke. 'They have no taste. They were going to have that . . . LVC, is it?'

'UPVC,' said the socialite.

'Yes, that, and new doors and windows. We told them the houses were listed so they would not be able to put in one of those hideous doors.'

'They checked and found it wasn't true,' said the old lady.

Good for them, I thought.

'And they were going to concrete over their front garden so they had room for their cars,' said the French girl.

The old lady looked disgusted. 'They've only got one car, but they were going to get another one.'

'What a terrible thing,' I said.

They were unaware of my sarcasm. Robert wasn't, of course. He deplored my methods. I deplored his. It was one of the many differences between us.

'You said they were going to,' he said. 'Did they actually do any of it?'

'No, thank goodness,' said the Cornish clothes designer.

Was the motive for this murder because new neighbours, of the wrong class, wanted to modernize their house? Having doors and windows that didn't let in draughts made sense to me. I had bought a house that already had replacement windows and doors in UPVC. Who wants freezing wind blowing through cracks?

'We're all into gardens here,' said the socialite. 'We're members of the RHS.'

'RHS?' I asked.

'Royal Horticultural Society. We've tried to get the houses to go to people with the same interest.'

'My house belonged to my great-aunt,' said the girl who

was married to the Frenchman. 'Unfortunately the old man next door to us had no close relatives and when he died Bridget and Declan bought it before we could ask our friends or advertise it at the RHS.'

'We were terribly lucky with Phoebe and Stuart,' the socialite chipped in. 'We didn't know them before, but they're delightful – and they love gardening and nature.' She sounded as if this was a neighbourly gathering for morning tea.

'Who are Phoebe and Stuart?' I asked.

'They live next door to Bridget and Declan,' said the socialite. 'She's a writer and he's an artist.'

I tried and failed to sound friendly. 'And where are they now?'

'At a party.'

I looked at my watch. It was four-thirty in the morning. 'A party?'

'At the commune – it's not a commune really, but we call it that because – '

'Mrs . . . ' I checked my notebook. I'd forgotten her name already.

'Call me Alice,' she said, looking as if she was doing me a favour.

Robert said, 'Is that the commune at Pengelly House?'

'Yes,' said Alice. 'It caused quite an upset in the beginning, but that was before we got to know them. We were all at the party.'

'I wasn't,' said the old lady. 'I was invited, but it's my sister's birthday.'

'I left just before midnight,' said Alice.

'We left earlier,' said the Frenchman. 'At eleven. Fleur was tired so we came home.'

I wondered if all the information they were giving was

suspicious or if they were just people who talked too much. Perhaps they thought that every detail of their lives was fascinating.

'The party was for Phoebe – her first book's about to be published,' said the socialite.

Gritting my teeth and wanting to put a stop to all the social chat, I looked at my notes and addressed the Frenchman. 'You raised the alarm?'

'No, no. I was in bed asleep and the doorbell – it ring . . . like someone was needing help. They kept their finger on it until I answered. It was a man and he was shouting about the house next to us being on fire. Then he ran off and I ring the fire brigade. They came quick. They said to get out of our houses, the ones that were near the fire, so we came down to this one . . . it being the furthest away.'

The front door was open. One of the firemen called out. I ran up the stairs and went down the hall to the front door. He told me the fire was out and that it was safe for people to return to their houses. Before they left we gave out our contact details.

Then Robert said, 'If there's anything you remember please get in touch immediately. Because it's so late there are bound to be things you've forgotten. Even if you think it might be trivial, it could be an important clue.'

It was almost five o'clock when Robert and I went out to his car.

As we were doing up our seat belts I said, 'Married or not, those clothes designer blokes are poofs.' His expression was predictable. 'Oh dear. Have I offended your politically correct sensibilities, Sergeant?'

He didn't reply. His silence needled me. He needled me. He was a mystery. A well built, tall, gorgeous bloke with thick chestnut hair and hazel eyes. He rarely smiled and he never made conversation just for the sake of it.

I should have stopped, but I've got some of my dad's destructive habits. 'Don't you approve of the term poof?'

'No.'

'What about queer?'

'No. Have you got the cardkey?'

'Would you prefer me to call them gay? Would that make you happy, Sergeant?'

'No.'

I was taken aback. 'Why not?'

'I don't like the word used in that context.'

'What's wrong with it?'

'It's my grandmother's Christian name. She became so fed up with all the silly remarks when she introduced herself she changed it to her middle name.' He rooted through his pockets. 'Where the hell's the cardkey?'

'You had it last. So what shall we call them?'

'Craig and Yves. Or Mr Chenoweth and Mr Lefevre.'

Trust him to remember their names. His look of distaste made me want to redeem myself. 'I didn't mean to sound hard, but it could be a motive.'

'Motive?'

'Blackmail. Some people hate what they are.'

'Don't you mean – what you presume they are?'

Under his neutral tone I heard derision. He made me feel like a bigot.

'It's the way I was brought up,' I said. 'My dad hated that sort of thing. When we had sex education at school the boys were told it wasn't healthy because of AIDS. If I'm right they've gone to a lot of trouble to keep it secret. Didn't they strike you as being effeminate?'

'The French one perhaps, but I think that's more to do

12

with cultural differences.'

Even though Robert didn't look effeminate, I sometimes wondered if he was a homosexual. His gestures and walk were masculine, his voice was deep and his arms were hairy. It wasn't because of anything he did or said, but because of what he didn't do. I'd never seen him display a glimmer of interest in any of the girls at the station. And some of them were pretty and sexy. They flirted with him, but he never responded. He was aloof, lived alone and he'd never mentioned a girlfriend.

He found the cardkey and slid in into the slot.

'We've got plenty of suspects,' I said as he put the car into gear. 'Any of them could have done it. They all had motives. They're possessive about their houses, which are nice, but nothing special. It's not as if they're mansions or anyone famous lived in them.'

I'd expected him to disagree with me, but he said nothing. I got more irritated. 'Middle class respectability hides a lot,' I said as he pulled away from the kerb. 'We've got, what I'm sure are, two homosexuals who've gone to great lengths to hide it, and a couple who go to all-night parties at a commune. Artist! I bet he's one of those people who throw paint at a bit of paper and call it art, and some twit buys it because they think it's trendy. They're probably lying drunk or stoned in a gutter somewhere.' I'd just finished saying that when I saw a man and woman cycling towards us. 'Stop!'

Robert stopped immediately.

'What are you doing?'

'You ordered me to stop.'

'Not in the middle of the road!' I held onto my temper. 'Pull over to the side of the road. I think our party goers have come back from the commune.'

'Can't be them,' he said, sounding bored. 'They don't look

drunk or drugged.'

I itched to hit him. 'Sergeant Trevelyan, I refuse to tolerate your sarcasm.'

'Oh, look,' he said, 'There it is.'

'What?'

'They are drunk and drugged, but they're hiding it under the middle-class cloak of respectability. It's almost invisible, but I can see it because I've got one just like it in my wardrobe.'

I got out of the car and slammed the door, realizing as I did so, that I'd missed the opportunity of watching the couple's reaction to seeing the state of their neighbour's house. The bushes and tree hid most of the damage. In the light from the street lamps the crime-scene tape was visible, the front door was open and the forensic team were inside searching through the debris. The couple got off their bikes and turned to look at me. They were, I thought, in their mid twenties. Robert was right. They looked sober and did not appear to be under the influence of drugs.

I pulled out my badge. 'Detective Inspector Richardson.'

They looked startled.

'Do you live in this street?' I asked.

'Yes,' said the man.

'Next door to Bridget and Declan?'

They looked baffled. 'Yes.'

'There's been a fire in their house.'

The girl spoke. 'Are they all right?'

I shook my head. 'We're treating it as murder.'

Robert chose this moment to walk across the street. They turned to look at him so I missed seeing their expressions. Neither of them said anything. Was that odd? Or had the news shocked them speechless?

'This is Detective Sergeant Trevelyan. Can we ask you a

few questions?'

'Yes, of course,' said the girl. 'Come inside.'

'You're Phoebe and Stuart?' asked Robert.

'Yes,' said Stuart.

They wheeled their bikes though the gap in the neatly clipped hedge. I don't know what sort of plant it was, but the leaves were shiny. Robert would know and would probably be able to say its name in Latin. I looked at the yew tree hedge separating the two front gardens. Over a hundred years old or not it was nothing to make a fuss about. I couldn't see over it, but Robert would have been able to. He was looking up at a nesting box attached to the front of the house, high enough to make it safe from cats.

'Any lodgers?' he asked.

'Yes,' she whispered, as if they were babies and we might disturb them.

A bird-bath stood on a circle of lawn among the daffodils. Obviously these people did everything the environmentalists advised. Their window boxes were planted with geraniums. They left their bikes propped against the porch. Phoebe lifted a tote bag out of the basket attached to the handlebars. I watched Stuart put the key in the lock. His hands were steady.

They led us into the front room. She switched on lamps and one of those gas fires that look like a real fire. The walls were rose pink and the two sofas and curtains were burgundy. Books filled the alcoves on either side of the fireplace. There was a CD player, but no television. The piano was so old it had candle holders.

'Do you play?' asked Robert.

'We do, but not well,' said Stuart. 'It was my great-grandmother's. Would you like some tea or coffee?'

I was gasping for coffee. 'Coffee please,' I said.

15

Phoebe put the tote bag on the coffee table and took out two fancy tins. 'We've got orange cake, chocolate cake and cheese and spinach pastry slices – they're leftovers from the party.' She took off the lids.

There was half the orange cake and two slices of the chocolate, which was sandwiched together with a thick layer of cream. Both cakes were iced and beautifully decorated. The smell of chocolate made my mouth water. Phoebe and Stuart were treating us like unexpected but welcome guests. Was this in their nature or did they hope we'd be fooled into thinking they were too nice to murder anyone?

While Phoebe went to the kitchen Stuart excused himself to go to the bathroom, and we were left alone.

'Let them think Bridget's dead too,' I whispered.

Robert looked exasperated. 'Of course.'

I picked up the tote bag and sniffed it to see if I could smell an accelerant. I couldn't. Inside was a bottle of Miss Dior perfume, a tube of hand cream, a stick of mint flavoured lip balm, a packet of chewing gum and a man's white handkerchief with **P** embroidered in the corner. The two books made me curious. One was a tattered paperback of *The Thorn Birds* with its ripped cover fixed with sticky tape, and there was a hardback of War Poetry. I had a quick look at the poems that were bookmarked. The first one was, 'I Have A Rendezvous With Death.'

A wedding photo in a silver frame stood on the mantelpiece. I could tell from the bare trees and angle of the sun that it was winter. There was an ancient looking church in the background. Phoebe, dressed in a gown that looked like satin with her veil billowing in the breeze, stood with Stuart and four bridesmaids who wore crimson dresses and carried bouquets of pink flowers. Sensibly the gowns had long sleeves and high necks. A few years ago I'd been a

16

bridesmaid at my friend's wedding. Although it was January she'd chosen strapless, sleeveless dresses made of chiffon. I spent the day shivering. In the photographs that were taken outside my lips were blue.

Phoebe and Stuart returned. She was carrying a tray with a cafetière, mugs, sugar bowl and milk jug, and he carried a teapot and strainer. He explained, although we hadn't asked, that tea leaves were good for the garden and tea bags were wasteful and bad for the environment. The coffee was strong and excellent and the pastries and cakes were delicious.

Phoebe was wearing a superb outfit made of velvet. The jacket had wide stripes of dark-brown and amber, and the skirt, which came to just above her ankles, was amber. Her boots were the same dark-brown as the stripe in her jacket. Her white blouse had a high neck with ruffles down the front and at the wrists. Her golden-brown hair was swept up in a French pleat. She could have been the heroine in an Edwardian costume drama.

Stuart wore a navy suit and a pink shirt with a burgundy silk tie. His cuff links were gold. The clothes they wore probably cost more than my entire wardrobe. I'd felt scruffy and plain in Alice's kitchen. Now I felt even more scruffy and plain in my crumpled clothes that I'd hurriedly pulled on.

Phoebe was exquisite. Her eyes were green and large with clear whites and long lashes. She had one of those mouths that look as if she's smiling even when she's not. They both wore wedding rings. She looked serene. Well, so she should. She had a handsome husband, a lovely house and went to parties that went on till dawn. She was one of those lucky people who seemed to have it all.

Robert wandered to a painting hanging over the fireplace. He looked at Stuart. 'One of your neighbours said you're an artist. Are you Stuart Harris?'

17

'Yes,' Stuart said.

'I've got two of your painting in my cottage.'

The painting was, I had to admit, beautiful. If I bought art it would have been something I would have been proud to hang on my wall. The frame was simple and the scene was of a boy and a girl playing chess, seen through a window with all those panes and frames that would be hard to paint.

After Robert had done his socializing bit, he got around to saying, 'This might be a random arson attack, but we've got to rule out a few things. Did Bridget and Declan ever mention they felt threatened?'

'No,' they said together.

I saw faint blotches on the exposed bit of Phoebe's neck.

'Do you know where they worked?' Robert asked.

'Declan's something to do with cars . . . a mechanic I think,' said Stuart. 'She works at a hospital in Truro.'

'A nurse?'

Phoebe shook her head. 'The assistant manager of the medical records department.'

'Did you get on well with them?' I asked.

The blotches on Phoebe's neck darkened. Even so, I expected her to make the same evasions as the other neighbours had made. Her emphatic 'no' disconcerted me.

Robert had the knack of hiding his feelings the way I never could. 'Any particular reason?' he asked, looking as if he didn't care.

Phoebe and Stuart glanced at each other. Phoebe looked uncertain. Neither of them spoke. Robert was good at silence, but I wasn't. I was about to repeat his question when Phoebe chewed her lip and swallowed.

'I used to work in the medical records department too. The manager retired and we got a new one – she was a tyrant. Bridget slimed up to her and got promoted. They tried to get me sacked, but had to settle with making me redundant.'

Robert looked at her sympathetically. I wondered if he was attracted to her.

'Why did they want to sack you?' I asked.

'I refused to participate in the way they ran the department and their treatment of the staff. It used to be a fantastic place to work. We were all happy until Elaine came. I hated her, but I hated Bridget more. Tyrants need blindly obedient poodles. Bridget was perfect in that role.'

Robert pressed her for details, which she gave. She was brief and didn't wander off the subject. If Phoebe was telling the truth, Bridget and Elaine took pleasure in making their staff miserable and kept them from rebelling by threatening them with the loss of their jobs.

'The day Elaine started, one of the girls was on sick-leave,' said Phoebe. 'She asked what was wrong with her, and when she was told that the girl suffered from depression, Elaine said she should be hit on the head with a mallet. Our old manager had been kind and helpful so Elaine's attitude came as a shock. She immediately made it plain that anyone who cooperated with her would get special treatment. Bridget was the only volunteer. Everyone else resisted at first.

'But Elaine was more cunning than that. The rules changed to, 'Resist and you'll be punished.' Most of them stopped fighting her. In the end there were only four of us still resisting. Margaret, who still works there, and two chaps – Elaine and Bridget tormented one of them so much he had a nervous breakdown. The other one still works there, but is trying to find another job, and so is Margaret.'

3

ROBERT

It was light by the time we went back to the car. I was beginning to feel tired, but the coffee had revived Sharon.

'This is going to be hell to solve,' she said. 'We're not short of suspects. So many people hate Bridget. The people she worked with, her neighbours – '

'We've got to remember that Bridget wasn't the victim and we don't even know where she is. And apart from Phoebe, her neighbours didn't hate her, I'd say it was more dislike.'

'They were contemptuous of her because she was working-class.' She sounded resentful.

'No one said she was working-class,' I disputed.

We got into the car and put on our seat belts.

'They said she didn't fit in, that means working-class to me.'

I tutted. 'It was nothing to do with her class. She didn't fit in because she wanted to dig up hedges, chop down trees, concrete the front garden and rip out the original doors and windows and replace them with monstrosities,' I argued as I started the car.

'Thank you, Sergeant. Are you unobservant or just rude?'

'What?'

'I've got UPVC windows and doors. You must have seen them when you called for me just over three hours ago.'

20

I didn't know what to say so I said nothing, but I regretted my tactlessness. It had been dark and I hadn't noticed, but to attempt to explain would have sounded feeble.

'It's almost as if there's a rule that only glamorous people can live in this street.'

'Glamorous?'

'Yes, Sergeant, glamorous. You sound as if you've never heard the word. Didn't you think Phoebe was?'

'No.'

'What was she then?'

'Elegant. Glamour's more flashy – more obvious.'

'Trust you to nit-pick.'

'Apart from a wedding ring, she wasn't wearing any jewellery.'

'Is that significant, Sergeant?'

Although aggravated by her emphasis on Sergeant, I said casually, 'Only in the context of the word. I associate glamour with lots of jewellery. What about the man who raised the alarm? He might have set fire to the house and then had an attack of conscience. Why didn't he ring the fire brigade? That's suspicious. Why didn't he hang around? Why did he rush off? If he was in a car, depending on what direction he came from, the people on the other side of the street might have seen him.'

'But if he was driving on the other side of the street, would they have been able to see anything through the trees?'

I shook my head. 'I don't know. But it's worth asking.'

'He might not exist. We've only got the French bloke's word that he came to the door. What's his name?'

'Yves.'

'He might have started the fire, but not wanted it to damage any of the other houses especially not his own.'

I thought her suggestion was ludicrous, but I nodded as if I was considering it. 'It could have been one of the people Bridget works with.'

'Could be. If she's as loathed as much as Phoebe says. What about the man who had a nervous breakdown? He sets fire to the house then suddenly remembers she's not the only one inside and gets someone else to call the fire brigade. He might have forgotten about the baby. You'd have to be evil to deliberately kill a baby.'

'That makes sense. We'll have to interview the people at the hospital where she works,' I said.

'We'll go to the commune tomorrow to make sure Phoebe and Stuart's alibi checks out,' she said as I turned into her street.

'Do you mean tomorrow as in Sunday or this afternoon as in Saturday?'

'This afternoon. Is Pengelly House closer to your place or mine?'

I pulled up in front of her house. 'Mine.'

'Then I'll call for you. Dolphin Cottage? On the beach?'

'Yes.'

Before she opened the car door she said, 'Take a look at my windows and door. Monstrosities are they?'

I was too tired to appease her. 'In my opinion they are, but many people like them.'

She got out of the car and slammed the door. I waited until she was inside and then drove away.

Even though I was worn out I felt the same bleakness I always felt when coming home to an empty house. At my front door I wished I'd done things differently. When my cousin Vanessa and I had first moved to Cornwall we'd stayed with our grandmother near Mevagissy. For a while Vanessa and I had considered buying a place together, but the first sight of Dolphin Cottage had filled her with horror. The floorboards in the dining-room were warped, the walls weren't straight, and a lot of the glass in the windows was cracked. The kitchen and bathroom were derelict. But it was solid, the roof was watertight and there was no dry rot or woodworm.

'The whole place looks as if it's about to fall down,' Vanessa had said. She liked houses with character, but wanted them already renovated and ready to move into.

She tried to persuade our grandmother to talk me out of buying it, but my grandmother understood my need to have a project, although she didn't think I should live alone. Doing up Dolphin Cottage kept my mind occupied and focused. Before the work was complete Vanessa had bought a cottage about a mile away from me. Two hundred years old, it had been restored with its original windows and doors intact.

'It's probably best we live in separate places,' she said. 'My untidiness would drive you mad.'

I disagreed.

'Come on, Robert. If we both lived in Dolphin Cottage we'd have to share a study and you'd end up wanting to throw me and all my stuff out the window.'

I no longer contemplated suicide, but my thoughts about the future were pessimistic. I didn't expect to find happiness, but I did want to find peace. So far this had evaded me. The agony was not as intense as it had been in London, but it was still present and always would be.

I opened the front door wishing I'd persuaded Vanessa to stay with our grandmother until the renovations on Dolphin Cottage were complete and she could see how perfect it was. It would have been easier to cope with her untidiness than solitude.

I had just got into bed when I thought about the photos.

For three years I'd left them in a suitcase and had only put them out four weeks ago.

It was my grandmother who had said, 'Does it help . . . not having their photos on display?'

'I don't know.'

'Try putting them out. If it makes things worse, you can put them away again.'

Sharon would be sure to arrive early so she had an excuse to come in and look around. I was too tired to get out of bed. I'd put them away in the morning.

4

SHARON

Before I'd been promoted Robert and I had been, not friends exactly, we hadn't known each other long enough, but it was heading in that direction. But even then he hadn't told me much about himself. To be fair, I hadn't told him why I'd left London either. I had no idea why he'd moved to Cornwall, although he had told me that he'd been born here. I knew he liked quiet pubs and hated ones with TV or music playing. He liked beer, but preferred wine. Merlot was his favourite. Although he looked the sort who'd own a sports car or something posh like a Alfa Romeo, his car was a navy Renault Megane.

He'd told me about the old fisherman's cottage on the Roseland Peninsular he'd bought and was doing up, but we'd never got around to discussing our personal lives. I'd wanted to ask him if he had a girlfriend, but in a rare bout of common sense, realized it would be unwelcome. I had almost told him about my last serious boyfriend who'd got a green card to America, but it's hard to reveal yourself when your not asked and not told. And I guessed that he deliberately kept off private topics.

I wish I'd had a secure middle-class childhood that he must have had, although judging from his voice and his tastes he was more upper-middle than plain middle. My mum and dad spoke ungrammatically, but incorrect grammar and bad habits were drummed out of my brothers and me at primary school. I'll always be grateful to the headmistress for making us talk properly and for teaching us to hold our knives and forks the right way and other things that would, as she put it, 'ease our passage through life'.

'Most of you are cockneys,' she told us in her BBC voice. 'Keep your accent, because it's part of you and nothing to be ashamed of. But use correct grammar, because being ungrammatical *is* something to be ashamed of. Saying things like 'I done it' instead of 'I did it', will make you sound uneducated and hold you back.'

She shunned expressions that she called useless. 'Never prefix a sentence with 'to be honest'. Just say what you want to say. Ending sentences with 'you know' or 'know what I mean?' invites the comment, 'No, I don't.' And only ever use 'like' when referring to something you like or to point out a similarity.

'Peppering conversations with obscenities will make you sound lazy and foul-minded, and decent people will avoid you. If you want to refer to the ghastliness of something use the right adjective; ugly, hideous, filthy. Be concise. Think about what you want to say before you say it. I don't want to hear anyone here saying, 'er' or 'um'.'

So my brothers and I tried to educate my parents, but they refused to change. Dad thought she was filling our heads with rubbish.

'Me mum and dad talked like this,' he said. 'You can talk proper, but it's too late for us. And what'll happen when you bring Miss Posh or Mr Posh here to meet the parents? They think you're one of them and you bring them to a council estate!'

'No, Dad, she hates class and the way it stigmatizes – '

He laughed. 'Stigmatizes? Teaching you fancy words too.

Yeah, she's right to 'ate class, but she's wrong to think anything can change – it can't.'

Mum agreed. My brothers were ashamed of them, which wasn't what the headmistress had intended.

Saturday Afternoon

When I got home from Farrier Way I could have happily slept for twelve hours, but I set the alarm to make sure I got up in time to shower, wash my hair and put on make-up. Clothes were an important part of a detective's role especially for a woman. We had to look professional, but not intimidating, and authoritative without being overpowering. Robert's clothes had been perfect when we were called to Farrier Way, but I had looked like an untidy underling. It was hardly surprising that one of the girls had thought he was the Inspector.

I wanted to appear more elegant for our visit to Pengelly House. As I got into my flannelette pyjamas I compared their drabness to the silk and satin worn by the girls in Farrier Way. If I was rich would I buy things like that or would I opt for the comfort of cotton in summer and flannelette in winter? I fell asleep wondering.

As soon as the alarm went off I forced myself out of bed and into the shower, which I finished with a blast of cold water that made me shriek. Even after my shower, I still felt exhausted. I made a pot of strong coffee and ate two slices of toast, which I spread thickly with honey, hoping it would give me energy. As I blow-dried my hair I saw my eyes were bloodshot and had dark circles under them. Even the light make-up I applied did little to improve my appearance.

My black trousers were ironed and I wore them with a grey jumper, a black silk scarf and grey suede ankle boots. I looked better than I had last night, but it would take more than make-up, a good sleep and beautiful clothes before I could compete with people like Phoebe and the girls in Farrier Way.

I drove to Robert's with the windows down, which helped make me feel more sharp-witted. I'd told him I'd call for him at two. I arrived twenty minutes early. His cottage was on the edge of St Austell bay. The exterior was white with dark greenish-bluish woodwork and door. His black door-knocker was in the shape of a dolphin. The other two cottages in the row were called Mermaid Cottage and Anchor Cottage. I couldn't decide if the dolphin, anchor and mermaid door-knockers were pretentious or clever. Had the cottages had those names when they'd belonged to fisherman or had subsequent owners thought the names were quaint and original?

Robert took ages to appear. He was dressed, but his feet were bare and his hair was damp and sticking up all over the place. He'd obviously been towelling it dry. There were no dark shadows under his eyes. He looked cross. Typical man. I was the one waiting in the cold not him. If it'd been me I would have thought that I was running late and apologized for not being ready.

'You said – '

'I'm a bit early. Don't worry. Ah, is that coffee I can smell?'

Not bothering to hide his reluctance, he let me in. He'd certainly poshed up the cottage. The carpet was thick, the parchment coloured paint on the walls and the white gloss on the woodwork was so recent I could smell it. There were three bookcases, jammed tight with books. The sofas were covered in a cottage style print in dark blue and green that I recognized. A friend had chosen it when she was decorating her flat near mine in Hackney. It was a surprisingly feminine choice for a single man.

'Ah,' I said. 'Laura Ashley – Bramble.'

He stared at me.

'That's right isn't it?'

'Yes,' he said curtly. He was reacting to my innocent comment as if I was accusing him or scorning his taste.

There were no curtains, just white shutters, that judging by the dents in them, were original. Stuart's painting hung over the fireplace. This scene was in a cafe or restaurant with empty tables, and the windows had panes similar to those in his other painting. Outside he had painted the back of a woman in a long red coat and a hat with a wide brim which hid her hair. She was in mid-stride. There was a car parked at the end of the lane otherwise it could have been a scene from a hundred years ago.

I wondered what the first fisherman would think if he'd known that hundreds of years later his humble cottage, and those like it, would be desirable homes. But, weirdly, even without the television in the corner and the shelf of DVD's, I could see what the place would have been like.

'I can almost see them,' I said.

'Who?'

'The fisherman and his family.'

He looked at me as if I had said something idiotic.

A galley kitchen separated the front and back rooms. There was something classical playing on his radio. When I saw the view of the sea, the pier and the headland from the dining-room window I understood why such a sophisticated man had bought this simple cottage. The ground floor was at street level at the front but, because the land sloped to the bay, the dining room window was two floors above the beach.

'Wow,' I said.

He said nothing, making me feel like an intruder. If he'd called for me and come early I would have invited him in, made him coffee and even toast if he'd wanted. I wouldn't have stood there brooding. He looked like some tormented bloke in a Victorian novel. But if he'd come early and I hadn't been ready he would have been annoyed and waited in the car.

'I'll enjoy the view while you finish getting ready.' I spotted a full cafetière and a mug on the table and reminded myself that I was his superior. 'Can I help myself?'

He nodded, went into the kitchen and came back with the milk, which was full cream, and a mug. He plonked them on the table and left. Seconds later I heard his footsteps in the room above.

I scanned his CD collection. It was mostly classical, including Beethoven's nine symphonies in one boxed set, and Brahms and lots of composers I'd never heard of, but there were The Beatles, The Rolling Stones, Elvis Presley, Barbara Streisand, Piaf and musicals – *Evita, Cats, Phantom of the Opera, Chess* and *Jesus Christ Superstar*. The radio was tuned to Classic FM.

It was when I was looking at his books that I noticed a line in the thin layer of dust on the bookcase. It was not the only one. There were three lines of different sizes and lengths. There was a black and white photo of a couple wearing Air Force uniforms, which looked as if it had been taken during the war, and a wedding photo that was pure sixties. The man looked like Robert, so I guessed they were his parents. Alert for his footsteps coming down the stairs I picked it up to reveal a line in the dust. Photos. Why had he removed three photos?

When he came back I was sitting by the window gazing at

30

the sea and the children playing on the beach. His hair was combed and he smelt of some zingy, fresh aftershave or cologne. He picked up a navy Guernsey from the back of a chair and pulled it on over his pale blue and white striped shirt. Without speaking he poured himself a mug of coffee and added milk.

'Where's your bathroom?' I asked.

'At the top of the stairs. Straight ahead. You can't miss it.'

His tone should have warned me. The bathroom suite was white like mine, but I could tell that it was a lot more expensive. Doing up this place must have cost a fortune. Where did he get his money from? I used the toilet and flushed it. On the shelf over the basin there was one toothbrush, a tube of toothpaste, a stick of Chanel deodorant and a bottle of Chanel aftershave. No wonder he smelt so divine. In a small cupboard over the shelf was a razor, shaving brush and shaving-cream.

There was no sign of a woman's belongings or another man's. My ex-boyfriend and I had left things in each others flats when we stayed weekends, so I knew what to look for. I looked at my plain face in the mirror. I was always pale. Not interesting pale, but drained pale that made me look unhealthy. I sighed and stepped out of the bathroom.

I walked quietly to the door of the back bedroom, which I assumed was his because it overlooked the sea. A black iron double bed with a dark-green quilt cover and pillowcases faced the window. The quilt was thrown back, a red towelling dressing-gown lay carelessly at the foot of the bed and a pair of sheepskin slippers that looked so comfortable you wouldn't want to take them off, were on the floor. There were no curtains or blinds, just shutters that were open. Like the rest of the cottage the walls were parchment and the woodwork white. The wardrobe, bedside tables and two

31

chests of drawers were dark wood and plain. There were two bedside tables and both had matching lamps that looked old. There was a book and a glass of water on one.

The window was open at the top and I could hear the waves. A digital radio and an alarm clock stood on the deep window ledge. And something else. A photo frame that had been turned around and faced the window. What was it with Robert and photographs? What was he hiding?

His voice made me jump. 'Bathroom's at the top of the stairs.'

I didn't turn and look at him. 'I was just thinking what'd it be like to wake up to this view every morning.' I cringed and hoped he didn't think I was being suggestive. 'Is that why you don't have curtains . . . so you can wake up to the view?'

There was no reply. When I turned around he'd gone. I tried to reason myself out of my embarrassment. All I had been doing was standing in the doorway. It's not as if I'd been ferreting around in his wardrobe or checking his sheets. Too late I realized that looking at his bedroom had been intrusive. There might have been a woman or a man in his bed, although if there had been I'm sure the door would have been closed.

We drove to the commune in silence. Did Robert use silence as a weapon or was it his natural condition? But if he was comfortable with it I wasn't. I preferred rows and shouting. Is silence a middle-class type of punishment? Did Robert ever laugh? Did he ever roll round in bed gasping ecstatically in the arms of a woman – or a man? In one way I could almost believe he was asexual, but I sensed passion in him that he kept under control. But all that control hadn't got him the promotion. Even though I was a woman it had gone to me. The thing was, I could imagine his eyes glinting with amusement. I could imagine that he could flirt and make

32

risqué jokes or double entendres. Beneath his control I was sure there was warmth, sensuality and humour. I wished I could get him to show it.

Pengelly House looked like no house I'd ever been in. For such a huge place it was simple. There were no spires or turrets. It wasn't the sort of mansion where you'd imagine there was a mad woman hidden in the attic. Robert told me it was late Victorian. Wanting to see as much as possible I parked near the gates and we walked up to the house. I'm not sure what I expected. Certainly not the sweeping driveway, well kept lawns and shrubs or the tennis court where, in spite of the cold, four children were playing, what looked like, a serious game. One other child sat in the scoring chair.

A giggle added to the sound of birds, the whack of the tennis ball and the voice of the scorer. A little girl with blonde curls dressed in red dungarees ran out from behind one of the trees lining the driveway. Robert stopped and stared at her. I stared at him. At first he smiled then he closed his eyes. The child, oblivious, ran on. He opened his eyes. The expression on his face could only be called one thing. Longing.

'Oh,' I said, 'so that's what you like.' I regretted my words immediately. God knows why I said it. My dad's destructive streak again.

Robert looked at me in horror that quickly changed to fury.

'I'm sorry,' I said quickly. 'I didn't mean . . . '

He strode toward the house. I ran after him and put my hand on his arm. He stopped and looked at my hand as if it was a rotting piece of offal seething with maggots. I lowered it. He ran towards the house and up the steps to the front door and reached for the knocker. By the time someone had come to the door I was standing behind him.

'Robert, how lovely to see you.'

'Hello, Ethel.'

Robert? Ethel?

She kissed his cheek. 'Have you come about the fire? Phoebe and Stuart rang – their neighbours – how dreadful.'

Why was an old lady with an upper-class accent living in a commune? She looked late seventies or early eighties, too old to have been a hippy in the sixties. She was wearing a wool kilt in burgundy and dark-green tartan with a burgundy jumper and a bottle-green silk scarf, pearls, thick dark-green tights and black brogues. Her wedding ring, diamond engagement and eternity ring were conservative.

The tiled floor of the hallway was clean, the woodwork glowed and I could smell furniture polish. Why had I been so eager to prejudge? I'd seen Phoebe and Stuart and their house . . . all the essence of clean living.

'Mummy, this is the bit for here!' I heard a child say. Her voice came from the room on my right, which had floor to ceiling bookcases and a table in the middle where three children of varying ages and a woman who looked about thirty, were doing a jigsaw.

Ethel took us down the hallway and I glanced into rooms as we passed them. There was a grand piano in one that would have touched every wall in my lounge. The sofas and arm-chairs, in what I supposed upper-class people called the drawing-room, were covered in brocade. In a room filled with computers and office chairs there were two girls and three boys staring at the screens. Computer games or homework?

At the back of the house Ethel led us into the biggest kitchen I'd ever seen. I counted twenty chairs around the square table which was painted in daffodil yellow gloss. Two high-chairs stood along one wall. A young woman was tidying up and a man was sweeping the floor. Other people drifted in. Given the time their party had ended I expected everyone to look half asleep, but they were more alert than I felt. Coffee and tea were made, fruit juice, sandwiches, quiches, and slices of cake left over from last night's party, were offered. I had a glass of apple, ginger and rhubarb juice. It was cloudy and refreshing. I decided to buy some next time I went to the supermarket.

Half of my mind was on the case. The other half was on how I could explain myself if Robert reported me. I hadn't meant that he had sexual feelings for children. It's more that his expression surprised me. He was normally so neutral.

A woman called him Inspector. He didn't correct her. Neither did I.

We left Pengelly House with the confirmation that Phoebe and Stuart had arrived at the party at around eight on Friday night and left sometime after four on Saturday morning, no one was sure of the precise time. It could have been four-thirty or later. The party had been to celebrate the publication of Phoebe's first novel. People had been asked to bring along their favourite book or poem to read. Phoebe had read two extracts from *The Thorn Birds*. One where a child is beaten by nuns on her first day at school and the other where her father dies in a bush fire. Stuart had read the war poetry. How morbid. Why couldn't they read something funny?

Robert strode ahead of me. I tried to think what to say to him.

'A good idea to turn it into apartments, isn't it?' I said as I caught up with him. 'Much fairer than just a few people living in a huge house.'

Instead of going towards the car he marched through the gate.

I hurried after him. 'We can't let our differences interfere with the investigation. You got my meaning wrong. What I meant was . . . '

He broke into a run. I couldn't keep up so I went back to the car. By the time I caught up with him he'd almost gone a mile. I slowed down and said through the open window, 'Get in. You can't walk all the way home.' He stared straight ahead and kept on walking. 'Robert, we need to discuss the case.' He ignored me. I gave up and drove away.

To completely eliminate Phoebe and Stuart from the list of suspects I checked the mileage on the car and drove to Farrier Way. The distance was five miles and there were some steep hills. Even cycling at full speed either one of them would have been away from the party so long their absence would have been noticed.

As soon as I arrived home, I went into the second bedroom that I used as a study. I turned on the computer and wrote the e-mail I'd composed on the way back in the car. Apart from being genuinely sorry, I was worried that he'd refuse to work with me. Superintendent Venning, who'd had so much faith in me, would want to know why. My behaviour would disappoint him, and give ammunition to those who felt I'd got promoted instead of Robert because of political correctness. I doubted that Robert would snitch, but I wondered if I'd pushed him too far.

Robert,

What I said came out wrong. You're usually so solemn that I meant it's a little girl that makes you smile. I didn't mean your reaction was sinister. It was a throwaway comment that I meant as a joke. I know I'd be in serious trouble if I went round accusing people for no reason.

There'll be a team briefing on Monday morning. Could you fill us in on the set up at Pengelly House, please? How many live there etc.

I spell-checked it, put *Apology* in the subject box and sent it. I was about to switch off the computer when I had an idea. On Google Earth I zoomed in on Pengelly House. Hardly daring to believe that I'd got a breakthrough so early I stared at the screen, just to make sure I wasn't imagining things. I felt a thump of excitement. It was almost five o'clock.

I studied my ordnance survey map and drove to the front gates of Pengelly House and parked on the road. I got out of the car and followed the wall, which turned off the road into the forest. There was a path, but no access for cars. At the back of Pengelly House, there was a high wrought-iron gate leading into the forest. I could see an orchard and some greenhouses, but trees and bushes blocked the view of most of the house.

I turned away and followed the path through the forest. It took me half an hour to reach the wall separating the back gardens of Farrier Way from the forest. In each wall was a high wooden gate.

I needed a bike. I ran back through the forest and drove home. On Sunday morning I borrowed a bike from the old man who lived opposite me. He was excited about lending me his bike in the course of a murder investigation. It took me ten minutes to cycle to the back gates in Farrier Way. That was at a sedate pace. I started to cycle back to Pengelly House at full pelt, but the bike hit a tree root and I fell off. Even in daylight the forest was quite dark. I went back to the start and began again. Fast, but not too fast. It took five minutes.

5

ROBERT

Saturday Evening

I'd intended to be ready so that whatever time Sharon arrived we could leave immediately, but I'd overslept. Fortunately, I'd remembered to put away all the photos before I'd answered the door. I decided to pack them away for the duration of the investigation. I didn't want Sharon prying and asking questions. Her knowledge of Laura Ashley fabrics surprised me. She never wore patterns and told me she'd decorated her house in neutrals. I thought she would have loathed Laura Ashley. Her attitude toward life was unforgiving, hard, and clinical.

Judith had adored Laura Ashley. Not just the furnishings, but the clothes. She'd once said if she had a thousand pounds to spend in Laura Ashley she could spend it in an hour. We'd chosen the fabric for the curtains and upholstery together. I'd left the curtains in the house in St Margarets when I sold it.

The long walk from Pengelly House had tired me, but not enough. Raw from Sharon's words, I went up to my bedroom and stared at the sea. There were two boys fishing on the pier. I knew them both. One caught a fish. Yesterday I would have gone and bought it from him. We would have talked. Now I decided to stay away till they'd gone.

Angry with myself for allowing Sharon's insinuations to

change the way I lived, I picked up my wallet and went onto the beach. But all I did was buy the fish from the youngsters. I didn't stop to chat and ask them about school as I usually did.

'When are you getting your boat out, Robert?' one of them asked.

'Not yet. Too cold,' I said before walking off. Once I would have invited them to go out to sea with me when the weather warmed up.

Back in my cottage I grilled the fish and ate it without tasting it. I tried to think about the case. I went into my study and switched on the computer. I checked my e-mails. I deleted the one from Sharon without opening it. There was one from my Grandmother who was enjoying her holiday in Italy. She'd taken the digital camera I'd bought her for Christmas and had attached photos of Lake Como.

After switching off the computer I roamed restlessly round the cottage. I turned on the television. There was extensive coverage about the fire at Farrier Way. Alice, speaking on behalf of all the neighbours, said they were shocked and how dreadful it was that a baby was one of the victims. When asked about Bridget and Declan she said they had not lived there long, so no one knew them very well. The reporter did not press her. The old lady was in the background, but Craig, Fleur, Yves, Kate, Phoebe and Stuart were nowhere to be seen.

Then he asked, 'What's the feeling about this?'

This type of question always infuriated me so I was pleased when Alice snapped, 'Naturally, we're not thrilled about it. Innocent people have been murdered. What a stupid question.'

He recovered quickly. 'I mean, are you all worried about an arsonist being around? Are you fearful about your own safety?'

Alice looked apologetic. 'I'm sorry. I misunderstood your question. I hope most of us have smoke alarms. I have – in every room, so I'm not worried about myself.' She turned to the old lady. 'Have you got smoke alarms?'

'No, I haven't,' she said.

'Then we'll get you one first thing on Monday. Until then you'll have to borrow one of mine and put it in your hallway. You can have the one from one of my spare bedrooms.'

I watched the rest of the coverage, which ended with a lecture from a fireman about the importance of smoke alarms. I turned off the television. Alice had expertly parried the questions about Bridget and Declan. No one watching would have suspected that the neighbours had disliked them.

If the weather had been stormy I would have been tempted to take the boat out and lose myself in the wildness of the sea. I didn't care if the boat overturned and I drowned. I sat on the bed and put my head in my hands. I would have rung my cousin Vanessa, but she had gone to Yorkshire for a wedding and was staying the night with friends. My parents lived in London and a phone call from me in this state would worry them. On a Saturday evening my London friends would be getting ready to go out or having dinner parties. Something ruptured inside me and tears flowed like blood from a severed vein. I tried to stop, but couldn't. I fell asleep fully clothed.

When I woke on Sunday it was dawn. I was cold, hungry and thirsty. I sat in the dining room and drank two glasses of water. I made coffee. The phone rang at eight o'clock. I looked at the caller number. It was Sharon. I switched off the phone and considered my future. I'd never expected to be one of the innocents who suffered because of the suspicion that there were paedophiles lurking everywhere. Did I want to live in a world when a man's motives were misinterpreted when he looked at a child? Her comment reignited my thoughts of suicide. Was I brave or cowardly enough to end my life? I'd choose sleeping pills, painless and not messy. I'd write to Vanessa then go to bed and never wake up. But I was her only cousin and we were close. However great the temptation I couldn't do that to her. I couldn't do it to my parents or grandparents.

I was on my way to have a shower when the doorbell rang. Thinking it was Sharon I waited for her to go away. It rang again. I heard the rattle of the letter box.

'Robbie!' It was Vanessa. She sounded agitated.

I ran downstairs and opened the door.

She looked at me in alarm. 'Oh, Robbie.' She came inside and put her arms around me. 'Ethel left a message on my phone. She saw you yesterday – something about a fire you're investigating, and she said you looked a bit distraught.'

I told her about seeing the little girl and what Sharon had said. Then I began to sob again. Vanessa ran into the kitchen and came back with a whole roll of kitchen towel. She thrust it at me and started crying. By the time we had cried ourselves out, most of the roll lay crumpled on the floor. Vanessa put them into the bin, washed her face and made coffee and toast. She put butter, marmalade and honey on the table.

'Robbie, resign and join me. I'm so busy I need help and I'd rather it was you than someone I don't know. Please say you will.'

'What are you working on now?' I asked.

'Looking for someone's natural mother. It looks as if she went to Australia in the fifties with that forced child immigration scheme. She had a baby out of wedlock. I'm doing work for a solicitor in Truro who's searching for an heir. And I've just been asked to investigate what might be a miscarriage of justice in the 60's. A man was jailed for murder and was killed in prison. His daughter, who was only two at the time, thinks he was innocent. I've got to go to *The National Archives* and root through dozens of Metropolitan police files. It would be fantastic if we joined up together. Going to London would be easier with two of us to share the driving and we could halve the time it takes going through the files.'

'As he'd been killed in jail I'd hope that I'd find nothing to prove him innocent,' I said.

'Difficult to work out which would be better,' Vanessa said. 'Being the daughter of a murderer, or knowing he'd suffered for something he hadn't done.'

Our expenses would be minimal. Whenever we went to London we stayed with our parents. Mine lived in Hampton and Vanessa's lived in Chelsea.

'Okay,' I said. 'As soon as this case is over I'll resign and join you.'

I'd just poured the coffee when the doorbell rang.

'Do you want me to go?' she asked.

I nodded. 'If it's Sharon tell her to go to hell.'

I listened as she opened the door. I heard Sharon's voice. 'Oh, hello.' She sounded surprised. 'Is Robert in?'

'Are you Sharon?'

'Yes.'

'He doesn't want to see you.'

The door slammed.

On Monday morning I arrived at work at the usual time.

'Morning, Sergeant,' said Sharon. Her smile was confident

with no hint of apology, although she did look slightly wary. 'There's a team briefing in half an hour.'

I nodded and went into the incident room. Sharon had obviously been there for a while. The locations and the houses in Farrier Way were sketched on the whiteboard in green. Bridget and Declan's house had an orange cross through it. I was puzzled by a map of Google Earth projected onto the large screen.

After briefing the team about the fire she continued, 'People living on the opposite side of Farrier Way have been questioned, but no one saw anything. Last night, Sunday, Bridget turned up. She'd been in Bodmin for the weekend visiting her mother who was unwell. Otherwise she too may have been a murder victim. She's naturally deeply distressed and has been sedated, and is staying in Bodmin with her mother. Sergeant Trevelyan and I will interview her this afternoon.

'There are fingerprints on the door, brass letterbox and knocker, but, unless the murderer was especially stupid or careless, we expect these will belong to Bridget and Declan, the postal workers and any visitors they had. Forensics found a thread of material stuck in the letterbox, which may have caught when the arsonist pushed the material though, and the flap snapped shut. There's a slim chance that it may contain DNA. The murderer may not have worn gloves when they were handling the fabric or soaking it in accelerant. I'm not anticipating a positive result, but we can always hope.

'In the meantime,' she pointed to the screen of Google Earth, 'to begin with it seemed that Phoebe and Stuart Harris, who live next door to Bridget and Declan Murphy, had alibis because they were at a party at Pengelly House. Sergeant Trevelyan will fill you in about the set up.'

Taken by surprise I hesitated, annoyed that she hadn't warned me. 'You mean about the living arrangements?' I asked, forcing myself to sound courteous and trying to remember the details about Pengelly House.

She nodded. 'It was in the e-mail I sent you. Didn't you read it?'

Her expression told me she knew I'd deleted it. Feeling caught out I said, 'I didn't receive it.'

I stood up and went to the front. 'Pengelly House was an early Victorian stately home that fell into disrepair during the nineteen-eighties when the owner died without children. The closest relative was believed to live in New Zealand, but couldn't be traced. A group of writers, artists and poets bought it. They divided the rooms on the first and second floors into individual apartments. The largest has three bedrooms the smallest has one. All the rooms on the ground floor are communal and consist of a kitchen, formal dining room, drawing-room, music-room, library and several smaller rooms which are used as studies – mainly for the children.

'The ethos is that each family, although four single people live there, have their own private space, but with the advantage of doing whatever they want, whenever they want, with the others who live there. It appears to work very well. Originally there were six workers' cottages on the estate, but some of the land containing two of the cottages was sold when the group bought it. Three of the remaining cottages have been converted into holiday homes, which provide income. A gardener and his wife live in the fourth cottage. His wife cleans the cottages and does the laundry between lettings.'

'How many acres?' asked Sharon.

'Fifty.'

'Do any of the people go out to work?'

I nodded. 'Most of them. The ones that are retired do voluntary work.'

'Are they professional writers, poets and artists or just dabbling at it?'

'Some are published, but even those that are have to have a day job.'

'So most of them are dabblers,' she said dismissively. 'Do you know what their occupations are? Just a few examples?'

'A landscape gardener, an architect, a journalist, one is a property developer so he knew reliable builders, plumbers and electricians – a couple are nurses, I think there's a doctor, and a retired engineer. The architect drew up the plans – '

'Thanks, Sergeant. Sixty people were at the party on Saturday night. Not all of them arrived and left at the same time. Phoebe and Stuart didn't leave till sometime after four in the morning. No one is sure of the exact time. They don't have a car, they have bicycles.'

She recounted her cycle rides through the forest and I wondered if I would have thought of that. I should have. I knew Pengelly House had a back gate leading into the forest, but hadn't known that it led to the backs of the gardens on Farrier Way. It was a good piece of detective work and something I should have been part of. I felt a stab of unease. I knew I shouldn't feel like this, but I wanted Phoebe to be innocent. Sharon would say that it was because she was beautiful and well dressed and had class. Was it true? Would I have this gut feeling if she'd been plain, with a harsh speaking voice and bad grammar?

'The time it takes to cycle from Pengelly House to Farrier Way, along the road, takes thirty minutes,' Sharon went on. 'There and back one hour. To set fire to their neighbour's house would probably add another ten minutes. Overall, to do that one of them would have to be away from the party for over an hour. The cycling time from the back gate of Phoebe and Stuart's house through the forest to Pengelly House is five minutes – one way. Ten minutes both ways. Give them another ten to start the fire and we have a total of twenty minutes maximum.

'Phoebe admitted that she loathes Bridget who bullied her when they worked together. Revenge might have been her motive. Saturday night was cloudy and dry but cold. I don't know yet if people were outside, but I'm sure at least some of them went outside to smoke. There was no hint of cigarette smoke inside Pengelly House when we visited. Given the age range of the people who live there, it's highly unlikely that all the people at the party were non-smokers. If Phoebe was absent from the party and someone asked where she was, all Stuart had to say was, 'Outside talking, I think'. She might even have been acting alone and told him she was going outside to talk to someone. Any questions?'

There were none. Sharon, looking pleased with herself, continued, 'If either Phoebe or Stuart are the arsonists, it's possible they soaked the rags in an accelerant before they left for the party and put them in a plastic bag somewhere handy. That would cut down the time they were absent from the party even more.'

'We need to check on the man who raised the alarm,' I said.

'Yes,' said Sharon. 'Thanks for reminding me. I'll contact the TV news channels and ask them to make an announcement.'

Just after midday I drove to Bodmin with Sharon in the passenger seat. She asked if I wanted the radio tuned to Classic FM. It was her way of being conciliatory. She had a street directory and an ordinance survey map. She scorned satellite navigation systems and was an excellent map-reader. Unlike Judith. We had always rowed in the car. If I was driving and Judith was directing we'd get lost, because she couldn't work out where we were. Then she'd accuse me of driving so fast she didn't have time to see the signs. When she drove, and I navigated, she'd turn right instead of left.

'It's lucky you're not a surgeon,' I said on one occasion when we arrived at a party an hour late, 'otherwise you'd amputate the wrong leg or cut open the wrong side of the body.'

Even when we knew the route we quarrelled. I complained that she drove too slowly and was hesitant. By the time we reached our destination we'd be snarling at each other. Once when we were driving in France, on our way to a holiday cottage in Burgundy, Judith had thrown the map out the window. The memory made me smile.

'You're smiling,' said Sharon.

'Is it a crime? What deviant thoughts do you suppose I'm having now?'

She leaned over and turned off the radio. 'Robert,' she said softly. 'You've got to stop sniping at me.'

'And you've got to stop sniping at me.'

'We got on well before I was promoted.' She sounded regretful.

I didn't reply.

'We never talked about it.'

'About what?' I asked.

'My promotion.'

'I congratulated you.'

'You looked very sour about it. You think you should have got it, don't you?'

'Not necessarily. I just don't think you were the strongest

candidate.'

'Why not?'

'You don't think things through rationally. You jump to conclusions.' I saw her stiffen. 'I'm not saying you're not a good detective.'

'It's just that you think you're a better one?' Her voice wasn't as caustic as I'd expected. 'And you're older than me and more experienced?'

Sharon had spent more years in the police than I had, but she didn't know it. 'I've got a high success rate,' I said. 'You believe in facts and facts alone. I believe in combining facts, criminal profiling and psychology. And sometimes pure gut instinct . . . a feeling . . . '

'You don't solve cases with gut instincts and feelings.' She laughed. 'I'm the one who should be talking about gut instincts and you should be scorning me.'

'Why?'

'Because feelings and all that are supposed to be a female thing.'

'We're people first and male or female second. I don't believe in stereotypes.'

'Neither do I.'

'You were quick to stereotype Yves and Craig.'

'To me, it's obvious they're homosexuals. I bet you've never solved a case on intuition alone.'

'Wrong.'

'You have? Really?'

'Yes. It's one of the reasons I was promoted to Sergeant so quickly. How did you get your promotion?' I know my tone implied it was because of her gender.

She took a deep breath. 'Robert, we've never talked about our lives in London and our reasons for coming to Cornwall. There're things you don't know about me. I could tell you,

49

but I haven't told anyone. But believe me, my promotion was nothing to do with political correctness. Okay? Go left at the next roundabout. We're nearly there.'

Mrs Bradley, Bridget's mother, lived on a reasonably well kept council estate, which was nonetheless depressing in spite of the children's playground and areas of grass. I said something like that to Sharon.

'It's ten times better than the council estate I grew up on,' she said.

I decided not to say, 'That must have been bad,' because however sympathetic I sounded she'd think I was being patronizing. As we climbed the stairs, which were mercifully free from graffiti and the smell of urine, we could hear the hum of conversation. The door to Mrs Bradley's flat was open and full of people of all ages.

An elderly woman saw us. 'You the police?'

'Yes,' said Sharon.

'Right, we'll all go and let you get on,' she announced loudly. 'Come on, you lot!'

Obediently they began to leave. Sharon and I stood outside watching hugs and shoulder patting and hearing comforting words and promises to be back later or tomorrow. Judging by the intensity of the good-byes, Bridget had a lot of friends. It seemed that most of the visitors lived on the estate. Some went up the stairs. Others went along the walkway and let themselves into their flats. Soon only Bridget and her mother were left. We went inside and closed the door.

The flat was clean and tidy with white walls. A huge flat-screen television was fixed to one wall. The sofa and armchairs were covered in zebra print material and matching curtains hung at the windows. Sympathy cards stood on the window ledge. Straggly flower arrangements were stuck into glasses and jars.

Bridget was ashen, but ready to talk. Her leopard print sweatshirt emphasized her red and swollen eyes and tear stained face. Her brown leggings made her legs look like sticks and her white shoes had pointed toes and high heels that looked uncomfortable. She was so thin I wondered if she had an eating disorder. Her mother began collecting the plates and mugs. She said something to Bridget in a strong Irish accent. When she went into the kitchen Sharon sat next to Bridget on the sofa and told her how sorry we were. I sat in the armchair opposite.

'It were Phoebe who done it,' said Bridget before we had asked any questions.

'So stop looking for suspects,' said her mother as she came out of the kitchen. 'It were her.'

Sharon looked satisfied. 'Have you any idea why?' she asked Bridget gently.

'Revenge and she's jealous of me.'

I wondered how much Bridget's cadaverous appearance had to do with shock and grief. Even under normal circumstances she would have never been attractive.

'Jealous?' I said, trying not to sound incredulous.

'We used to work together. Then I were promoted and were her boss and she got jealous.'

Mrs Bradley went back to the kitchen nodding. Sharon wisely stayed silent.

'And I've got a baby,' Bridget choked on the word baby and tears streamed down her face. There was a box of tissues on the coffee table and Sharon pulled out a couple and gave them too her. Bridget wiped her eyes and continued. 'And she hasn't.'

'Does she want one?' Sharon asked.

'Want one! She's desperate – all she has are miscarriages. Her first baby died just after it were born . . . lack of oxygen. The cord got twisted or had a knot in it or something. Who collected money for a huge bouquet of flowers for her? Me.' She gasped for breath and began to cry again.

Her mother came out of the kitchen and stood over her with a glass of water and two tablets. Bridget shook her head.

'He said to take them. You got to help and you won't if you can't talk properly with all that crying.' She looked at me. 'From the doctor,' she said. 'He give them to us. Said they helped.' Her tone was defensive. Did she think we were going to accuse her of giving Bridget something illegal? She prodded Bridget. 'Come on, take them.'

Bridget took the tablets and gulped them down with the water.

'That Phoebe made my poor Bridget's life a misery, so she did. Just because she were the boss's favourite, it were. The stories I could tell you. When Phoebe worked there, poor Bridget used to come home every night worn out with the strain of it all, didn't you, Bridget?'

Bridget nodded, grabbed a pile of tissues and blew her nose. 'I tried to be friendly when I moved next door to her, but she wrote me a nasty letter. You should have seen the way she looked at my baby.'

'Jealous, she were,' said Mrs Bradley. 'Jealous. Sick with it. She had lots of reasons to be.'

'Elaine, that's the boss, didn't like her, but she liked me and Phoebe got jealous.'

'Tell them about them letters she sent to Elaine after she got made redundant,' said Mrs Bradley.

'Trying to make trouble between me and Elaine, she were,' said Bridget. 'Sent a whole lot of letters about how I was after the top job and said horrible things about her behind her back and that I hated her really. She never signed them or nothing, but I knew they was from her.'

'How did you know they were from her?' asked Sharon.

'Sort of thing she'd do. Her way of getting revenge.'

'Why was she made redundant?' I asked.

'Because she were useless. That's why Elaine liked me and not her. Her degree counted for nothing and she were bitter about it. But what use is a history degree in a hospital? She were made redundant eight years ago and she's still bitter.'

Mrs Bradley nodded. 'Wish she had of choked on it.'

'Fails at everything she does,' said Bridget. 'Wants to be a writer, but her writing was rubbish – full of big words – I couldn't understand it. She used to be a teacher, but gave it up because she couldn't control the kids. Blamed them, she did – made out they was savages. Well, that's what she said. More likely she got sacked because she was no good at teaching. I wouldn't know the truth, would I? I weren't there. She could of made up anything.'

I'd put Phoebe's age at about twenty-five. She certainly didn't look thirty, and yet the time line was wrong. She'd been to university, been a teacher and eight years ago she had worked at a hospital.

'How long did she work at the hospital?' asked Sharon, who was looking as puzzled as I felt.

'Four years,' said Bridget.

'She looks too young to have gone to university, spent – '

'What's her age got to do with her being a murderer?' asked Mrs Bradley.

'Thirty-six, she is,' said Bridget. 'That another thing she's got against me. Her time's running out.'

'Running out? What do you mean?' asked Sharon.

'For having a baby. I'm seven years younger than her.'

I felt like telling her she looked ten years older, but

reminded myself that she was the victim. Bridget was still talking, and I forced myself to look neutral. She was no longer tearful. Either the tablets had worked very quickly or her hatred of Phoebe had submerged her grief.

'She's one of them people that make excuses for everything. Instead of saying they never had enough money to get a car she made out they didn't want one and went on about the pollution. Lots of things she didn't have that I did – like a TV. Said she was too busy to waste time watching trash, but she couldn't afford one. And that's why they don't eat meat. They can't afford it. Nothing to do with cruelty to animals like she makes out.'

Having seen Phoebe and Stuart's clothes and furniture Bridget's idea that they were too poor to buy basics like meat, confounded me. 'Why do you think they didn't have much money?' I asked.

'If they could afford them things they'd buy them, wouldn't they?'

'Not necessarily,' said Sharon. 'Most vegetarians don't eat meat for ethical or health reasons – the ones I know anyway.'

'How can they afford things?' said Bridget. 'They don't work. Probably living off benefits.'

'Why do you think that?' asked Sharon.

'When I were on maternity on leave I never saw them going out in the mornings and coming back at night like they would of done if they was working. And when I'm home on annual leave it's the same.'

I decided that now was the wrong time to inform Bridget that Phoebe's book was about to be published and that Stuart's paintings were beautiful and he must make a lot of money from them.

'Was Phoebe popular with the rest of the staff at the hospital?' Sharon asked.

'Not when they saw that things would go badly for them if they didn't go along with all the improvements Elaine and me was making.'

Phoebe's allegations of bullying were confirmed. It struck me as odd that Bridget had no idea how she was depicting herself.

'Did all the staff in medical records turn against Phoebe?' asked Sharon.

'Most of them. The ones that didn't . . . one man went off his head, and there's Margaret Fox. Don't believe nothing she tells you. She's Phoebe's sister-in-law. Never liked me she didn't. She felt threatened by my friendship with Phoebe.'

Hiding my astonishment, I said, 'You and Phoebe were friends?'

She nodded. 'Good friends once. Margaret tried to turn her against me, even before Elaine came. She were jealous. She wanted to have Phoebe all to herself just because they'd been to school together and were – '

Sharon interrupted her. 'Bridget, there's something I need to tell you. You may be asked to give a statement in front of the television cameras. However convinced you are that Phoebe did it, please don't repeat your accusations in front of the cameras, because – '

'Why not?' asked Mrs Bradley. 'She were the one that – '

Sharon held up her hand. 'There are several reasons, Mrs Bradley. The first one is for your own good. Phoebe and her husband have got good alibis for the time the fire started. If you accuse them in public you could be leaving yourself open to being sued.'

'Can't get no money out of me, she can't,' said Mrs Bradley. 'I haven't got none.'

Sharon looked at Bridget. 'You and Declan owned the house in Farrier Way, didn't you?'

Bridget nodded.

'Won't be worth nothing now,' said Mrs Bradley.

Sharon silenced her with a cold stare.

I said, 'Bridget, was your house insured?'

'Had to be – part of the mortgage rules.'

'Then the insurance will pay for it to be renovated, so it will be worth – '

Bridget looked alarmed. 'Could Phoebe really get my money?'

'Yes,' Sharon and I said together.

'If she's innocent,' I said.

Mrs Bradley snorted.

'All of it? She could get given all my money?'

'Yes and you'd have to pay costs, so for your – '

'But it's not fair – I'm the victim and she's the – '

'The other reason is,' Sharon said, 'If you make your accusations in public it could compromise any trial.'

'What's that mean?'

'What does what mean?' asked Sharon.

Bridget looked exasperated. 'Compromise. What does compromise mean?'

I wondered how much effort it took Sharon to keep the scorn, she must have felt, out of her voice. 'Weaken, jeopardize, undermine. Any case against her might be dismissed if you voice your accusations publicly. We're grateful for your input and will investigate Phoebe thoroughly. Now, Bridget, how did you get on with the rest of the people in Farrier Way?'

'Would of got on with them alright, but Phoebe turned them all against me.'

'She's a spoilt brat,' snapped Mrs Bradley.

Sharon was looking impatient.

'What form did their dislike take?' I asked before she

decided we had enough evidence to bring Phoebe in for intensive questioning.

'The old crones looked at me like I was dirt. The queers were – '

'Queers?' asked Sharon innocently. 'Which ones are they?'

'Them clothes designers.'

I expected Sharon to throw me a triumphant look, but she didn't. Instead she pretended to look perplexed. 'But they're married, aren't they? Isn't one of the wives, the French one, pregnant?'

Bridget's face twisted with spite, turning her plainness into ugliness. 'Don't ask me how they managed that. I've seen them. I know.'

'Know what?' I asked.

'They might have a bit of paper to say they're married, they might own the houses in his and her names, but Yves and Craig are queers and Fleur and Kate are dykes.'

Keeping all trace of animosity out of my expression and tone, and trying to look as perplexed as Sharon, I said, 'But the girls are very feminine and pretty and one's expecting a baby.'

'Huh! I live next door to the house supposedly owned by Kate and Yves. But last summer they ate outside a lot, you know, when it were hot. One night I saw them all go out the back gate. I thought they must of been going to Fleur and Craig's house. But a few minutes later Yves and Craig came back through the gate – alone. That was the first time I saw it and it wasn't the last. Happens all the time. I'm onto their filthy secret.'

It was easy to imagine Bridget peering through a gap in her curtains with her eyes full of malice. No wonder she didn't get on with her neighbours.

'Do they know?' Sharon asked.

'Know what?'

'That you know about their living arrangements?'

'Not till one of the parties Alice had at her house. Yves was rude to me, so I told him I knew.'

'Does it matter nowadays?' I asked. 'It's legal. People can have civil partnership ceremonies. There's no need for – '

Bridget looked scornful. 'Yves is a Catholic. He and Fleur – she's supposed to be married to Craig – went to the same church as me every Sunday. What would his parents think if they knew?'

'Did you, er,' I was reluctant to use such a condemning word as threaten, but as I searched around for something more benign, Sharon chipped in with a brilliant piece of strategy.

'Did they live in France? His parents, I mean,' she asked.

'Yeah.'

'So it's not as if you were ever going to meet them, was it?' she said.

Bridget looked triumphant. 'I met them alright. They was over at Easter to visit. Yves was a nervous wreck when I introduced myself to them after church.'

'Yves,' Sharon said as we went down the steps. 'Another person with a strong motive.'

I nodded and made notes in my head. Much as Bridget repelled me I knew I'd have to keep my thoughts about her to myself, otherwise Sharon would accuse me of being a snob.

When we reached the bottom of the steps a door opened. A woman who had been in Mrs Bradley's flat stuck her head out. 'Hey!' she whispered. 'You got a minute?'

We went into her flat, declined her offer of tea and didn't sit down.

'I just want to tell you about Mrs Bradley – she's Bridget's mum. Evil bitch, she is. Never wanted Bridget to get married – threatened to kill herself and all sorts when she knew her tears wasn't working.'

'Didn't she like Declan?' I asked.

'She never liked no one Bridget took up with. But with Declan all her old arguments never worked. She said that Bridget must marry a Catholic – you should have heard the carry on if she went out with a Protestant. When she did have a nice Catholic boyfriend then Mrs Bradley complained he weren't Irish. But Declan were not only a Catholic he were born in Dublin to Irish parents. Poor Bridget, I think it was only then she caught on that her mum didn't want her to marry no one. Then she showed some spark. Even her mum's threats not to turn up at the wedding never worked. You should have heard it. His mum come storming over, lived over there, she did.' She made a vague gesture.

'On this estate?' I asked.

'Yeah, she used to. Anyhow there were such a fight – not fists, just tears and screaming from Mrs Bradley and shouting from Declan's mum.'

'Is there a Mr Bradley?' Sharon asked.

The woman snorted. 'Was once – not for long. He left when Bridget were a little girl. Got any suspects yet?' She didn't wait for an answer. 'Put Mrs Bradley down as one.'

'Does she have a car?' I asked.

The woman giggled. 'Don't need one – got her broomstick.' She saw Sharon's stern look. 'Sorry, yes, she has . . . a car, I mean. Think about it. Bridget's here with her. The son-in-law's in the house – '

'With her grandson,' Sharon pointed out. 'Would she kill her grandson?'

'Never seen much of him, she didn't. Spent last Christmas

59

and the one before that, alone. None of us round here wanted to ask her in, even if she give us enough hints and tears about how she'd be by herself. Bridget and Declan don't have to come here no more, see? His dad retired and got a good pension and then his mum retired a few months later – and she got a good pension. Lump sums too, so they bought a little house near St Austell to be near Declan and their grandson.'

'Did they like Bridget?' I asked.

Sharon gave me a 'what does it matter?' look.

'Adored her. Like her dad she is. Everyone adores Bridget.'

Except the people at Farrier Way and where she worked, I thought.

'Why did Bridget come to see her mother the other night?' Sharon asked.

'Ha! I were just getting to that bit. Mrs Bradley said she fell down them stairs. I come out of my flat because I heard her scream. I found her lying at the bottom. First I did think she's fallen, but after, I think it was a trick to get Bridget over to visit her. Staggered into my flat she did, wailing and carrying on. I done a first-aid course at my work and I know the more serious a hurt is, the less noise you make.

'Said she'd fallen all the way down, but I don't think so. Them stairs is concrete – she'd have broken bones and be knocked clean out, she would. But she wanted me to ring Bridget, so I did. She weren't pale neither. I didn't see no harm in it, but now . . . ask her if she's got any bruises. I bet she don't have none. And if she found out Bridget's been seeing her dad on the sly for years, that might just send her crazy – tip her over into madness – get what I mean?'

'I'm going to scream if we get any more suspects,' Sharon

said as we walked to the car park.

'Do you think the mother's a serious suspect?'

She frowned. 'Hard to say. But, if I had to, I'd judge not. Although her neighbour said she was evil, I don't think she is. Just lonely, bitter and possessive. While she might have killed Bridget's husband, I can't see her killing her grandson, even if she didn't see much of him. What do you think?'

'We shouldn't discount what she's told us and we'll have to look into it. Let's first find out if Mrs Bradley knew Bridget was secretly seeing her father.'

We were nearing the car when we saw four youths approaching us. They had facial tattoos and shaven heads. I saw Sharon tense. Her hand slid into her pocket.

'It's okay, keep walking,' I said surprised by her faltering pace. 'Look confident.'

We changed direction. They didn't.

Sharon expelled her breath. 'They looked like trouble,' she said as we reached the car. 'Sometimes I'd love to be a man. If I'd been alone I bet they would have had a go.'

I laughed.

'What's funny?'

'Nothing.'

'What would you have done if they'd attacked us?'

I shrugged. 'No idea.' But I was lying. I did know what I'd do. Even though it happened fifteen years ago my conscience still troubles me.

It was 1993. Vanessa and I had been twenty. I was living and working in Florence, and Vanessa was working as a temp at the *Public Record Office* in London. We were visiting our great-aunt in America.

'Rob, what did Judith do to upset you?' she asked as we were walking through a forest one afternoon.

'What makes you think she did anything?'

'You've avoided her since we were fifteen.'

To begin with I had avoided her. But it was because of embarrassment not because I disliked her. Our O levels were over. We were free. Eight of us had packed up a picnic and gone to Richmond Park. After eating we played silly games and chased each other. I caught Judith and something happened. I wanted to kiss her. She, unaware of my feelings, giggled and wriggled. My arousal was so conspicuous I was sure everyone could see. I let her go and ran out of the park. Later I told Vanessa I'd felt sick. I'd avoided Judith for a year, but I'd been unable to get her out of my mind and I missed her. Then, when I decided that I would see her again and bought baggy trousers to wear, she avoided me. That was one of the reasons I'd decided to go to Europe and study languages first hand instead of going to university.

So I told Vanessa.

She laughed and jumped up and down. 'Rob, she's crazy about you. She didn't realize it till you started avoiding her. She was so hurt.'

We'd both been laughing so much we hadn't heard anyone approaching. Suddenly there were six thugs surrounding us. Everything slowed down. I can remember every detail. One had the skull and crossbones tattoo on his arm. One was a skinhead. The one with red hair had multiple rings and studs in his ears and face. The shortest one was dressed in camouflage gear. The blonde was all in black. One was fat. They all leered at Vanessa.

'Better looking than the last one,' said Skull and Crossbones.

Skinhead said, 'What a beauty.'

The redhead, the blonde and the fat one unzipped their trousers.

'You can watch, lover boy,' said the redhead. He shoved

the blonde one out of the way. 'Me first this time!'

'We'll both have her,' shrieked the fat one. 'You do the front and I'll do the back!'

Vanessa's face was white. Skull and crossbones and the skinhead seized my arms.

By law I had to tell them. I said it in Italian.

The one in camouflage spat in my face. 'A wog! What are you saying? I don't speak French. You're in America now.'

I kneed him in the groin. Skull and crossbones and skinhead tightened their grip on my arms. I pulled myself free and spun round. 'Translated it means,' I said as I shattered their collar bones and knee caps, 'I'm a karate black belt.'

By the time I spun around again, Vanessa had thrown fatty and redhead to the ground. 'So am I,' she said.

I heard the tearing muscle as she wrenched their arms out of their sockets. I hurled Skull and crossbones against a tree and kicked him so hard in the groin he passed out. The one in camouflage was trying to get up. Vanessa broke his wrists and nose and kicked the hand that was clutching his groin. I heard his fingers break. The blonde ran off.

She swung her leg. 'We're going to make sure,' she said in an American drawl, 'that none of you can ever have sex, consensual or otherwise, again.'

Unsure about the laws in America about self-defence and concerned because skull and crossbones wasn't moving, I grabbed her arm. 'No,' I whispered. Having visions about us being arrested at the airport I called her by her mother's name. 'No, Mary.'

'We've got to stop them doing this ever again.'

'Then we'll ring the police.'

I had to drag her out of the woods. On our way back to our aunt's house we furiously debated whether to call the police from a public phone box. I wanted to. Vanessa didn't. The dilemma was solved because we didn't see a public phone box. When we got back to our aunt's she was out.

'We should have made sure,' Vanessa raged. 'They were all going to rape me. How many girls have they raped? We should have made sure they never could again.'

'When they're found they'll be taken to hospital. They'll say we attacked them.'

'I doubt it. Do you think they're going to admit that a girl and one man got the better of them? They're more likely to say they were attacked by a gang.' She laughed. 'And even if they do tell the police they'll be looking for an American girl called Mary not an English one called Vanessa. And they don't know what your name is.'

What she said made sense. 'Even so, there's a big difference between self-defence and causing severe injury. Remember the karate ethics. We defended ourselves. We escaped. To do more would have been – '

'Sensible. Justice.'

'Vengeance. We did more than defend ourselves. We caused multiple fractures.' I didn't want to tell her that I was frightened I'd killed one of them.

She started to cry. 'I wanted to kill them.'

'So did I. But we've got to have control over our actions.'

'We should have made sure. It's not like a miscarriage of justice, Robert. We were there. We knew what they were going to do.'

'And we stopped them. Karate's for self-defence not execution.'

'But did we stop them from ever doing it again?'

I didn't know. I've often wondered. Whatever scenario I imagine my conscience troubles me. What if skull and crossbones had died? I might have broken his neck. Was he dead or confined to a wheelchair? What if Vanessa was right and they were still gang raping?

Three days later, back in London, Vanessa still had a migraine. We told no one, not even our parents, what we had done.

I wondered what Sharon would say if I told her it wouldn't be the police we'd need, it'd be an ambulance.

6

SHARON

I shivered.

Robert looked at me. 'Are you cold?'

I shook my head.

'Are you all right?'

'Yes.' But I wasn't. He probably thinks he can add coward to all the other awful things he thinks I am, like bigot, irrational, nosey and lower-class. Maybe I should have told him when we were on friendly terms, but I didn't want anyone in my new life to know. My story, to anyone who asked why I'd moved to Cornwall, was that the gang violence, drugs, stabbings and shootings in East London were getting to me.

Once I asked him why he'd come to Cornwall.

His response, like mine, sounded rehearsed. 'My parents grew up here. We spent most holidays here when I was at school. I always regretted when it was time to leave. I got fed up with London and wanted a change.'

But Robert's London and my London were opposites. He'd lived in St Margarets. I'd never been there, but knew it was up-market. You only had to look at the house prices.

Moving to Cornwall was a last resort for me. At first I'd looked at other parts of London until I realized I wouldn't even be able to afford a studio flat. I thought about joining my brothers in Australia and persuading my mum and dad to come with me. But one of my colleagues had suggested simply moving out of London. I had plenty of leave so I booked days off in blocks of four and drove somewhere different each time. I stayed in bed and breakfasts. Wales was majestic, and I could have bought a small house with a garden, but many of them disliked the English. Wiltshire, Sussex and Oxfordshire were out of my price range. The flatness of Suffolk and Norfolk didn't suit me.

One long weekend I headed to Cornwall where I immediately felt at home. I drove around exploring areas and the major towns. I loved St Ives, Looe, Polperro and Charlestown, but they were too expensive. I decided on St Austell because it was an easy drive to the coast. It wasn't a tourist hot spot and parts of it were rough, so small houses were reasonably priced. Given my history the transfer was easy to arrange.

Robert drove out of the car park and I pulled my mind back to our growing list of suspects. I'd been wrong about Phoebe having it all. She was desperate for a baby. Or was she? Bridget might have been lying. Phoebe's motive would be revenge for being bullied and made redundant.

But, if Bridget was telling the truth, Yves had a stronger motive. Fear. Would he resort to murder to stop Bridget telling his parents about his sexuality? And he had been close by. The high hedges would have hidden him from sight. It would have been easy for him to creep through the front garden to Bridget's house. But I couldn't see him, or any of the other neighbours, killing a baby. They were snobs, but I didn't think they were evil. Unless he was so frightened Bridget would tell his parents that he didn't even think about the baby.

Was Bridget's mother a serious suspect? If she wasn't seeing her grandson, would she have baulked at killing him to get her daughter back? Bridget was seeing her father in secret, which probably meant he was also seeing his grandson and featuring in his life. Would rage and jealously have overcome her?

Before meeting Bridget all my sympathies had been with her. Not only had her husband and baby been murdered, she had neighbours who resented her. None of them had expressed any sympathy for her tragedy and they had wasted no time in telling us that she didn't fit in. Even Phoebe's account of Bridget's bullying, had done little to change my opinion. Now I had met her I understood why her neighbours disliked her.

'Bridget seems to have two personas,' said Robert. 'The people on the estate think highly of her and so do her in-laws.'

'Maybe she changes to suit the situation. She was friends with Phoebe before the new manager came. An odd friendship though, don't you think?'

'Why?'

I suspected Robert was too politically correct to say he agreed with me, although I bet he thought it. 'What did they have in common – apart from working in the same place? Phoebe's obviously from a different class – '

'If I'd said that you would have called me a snob, and quite rightly too.'

'Come on, Robert, I bet Phoebe didn't grow up on a council estate.'

'No, but they both ended up in the same street.'

'The neighbours didn't like Bridget and they liked Phoebe. Bridget and Declan had enough money to buy a house in Farrier Way, but they didn't fit in. Phoebe likes gardens – Bridget wanted to concrete over her front garden and dig up the hedge between them. I'm trying to work out why they were even friends.'

'Perhaps Bridget thought that being friends with Phoebe would be to her advantage,' said Robert. 'When it was no longer advantageous she dropped her.'

'Okay, but why would Phoebe be friends with her? Phoebe's lounge is full of books. There are no books at Mrs Bradley's that we could see. Just the huge TV and stacks of DVD's and TV magazines. Phoebe hasn't got a TV. They're so different. I would have thought that Phoebe would have looked down on Bridget – the way she speaks, dresses and she's not particularly intelligent, is she? She had no idea that she was portraying herself and Elaine as bullies, and the way she described Phoebe's book as being full of long words – '

'It might be full of long words – like compromise.'

I smiled. 'True, but to admit she couldn't understand it showed her lack of education. The ungrammatical way she spoke grated on my nerves, so I would have thought it would have driven someone like Phoebe mad.' I sighed. 'Maybe I was lucky.'

'But you said you grew up on an estate a lot worse than this,' Robert said. He sounded cautious.

I nodded.

'Then how were you lucky?'

'The estate was vile, but the primary school I went to was exceptional. The headmistress wanted us all to get on in life and every morning at assembly she'd give us an anecdote, and that used to set me up for the day. The teachers made the lessons fun – specially our English teacher. The first thing we had to do every lesson was look in our dictionary for a word at least six letters long and write a sentence using the word to show we understood its meaning then read it out to the class. It had to be a word we didn't know. She made a game of it. We had to take a letter out of the box – my first letter began with an S. I remember my very first word – it was substantiate. The teacher was impressed.' I smiled. 'I couldn't pronounce it – but she was still impressed. So I was lucky to have inspirational teachers – maybe Bridget's teachers didn't care – just taught the basics and didn't bother about anything else.'

'Did you work hard at school?'

'Not really. No more than I had to. I always did my homework and projects. I didn't want to go to university or anything, but I was an average student. Anyway, back to the case. Phoebe's clothes were divine. I know Bridget's grieving, but her clothes are so . . . '

'Common? Tarty?' he suggested helpfully.

'Worse – they're the sort of thing a prostitute down on her luck would wear.' I sighed. 'Can you think why Phoebe might have been friends with Bridget?'

'She might have been trying to help her because she felt sorry for her. I agree that they're unlikely soul mates. As you say they've got nothing in common except that they worked together. I've just had a thought – I can't remember Phoebe saying she and Bridget were friends, can you?'

I tried to recall the conversation. 'No. Now you mention it, I don't think she did. We'll have to interview the people she worked with tomorrow and the manager . . . Elaine. And as soon as forensics have finished with the house we'll look inside. I doubt we'll find anything useful, but you never know.'

We were heading towards St Austell when my mobile rang. It was Alice, the socialite.

'I'm not sure if this is important, but I've remembered something.'

'Are you at home?'

'No I'm at work.'

70

'What time do you get home?'

'About five-thirty. I'll be in all evening.'

'We'll see you then. Thanks for ringing.'

I put the mobile back in my pocket. 'Can we go somewhere quiet and talk? I need your background knowledge. Not a pub. We don't want anyone listening. You can't be anonymous here like you can in London.'

I hoped he'd suggest going to my place or his.

'Okay.' He looked at his watch. 'Let's go for a walk.'

So he was no where near forgiving me. He probably never would.

'A walk? It's freezing.' I was too afraid of rejection to tell him we'd go to my house. I didn't have a clue why I felt like this. I didn't even like him. All my ex-boyfriends had a sense of humour. It was my stupid hormones that fancied him. My brain disliked him. He made me uncomfortable. He made me feel intellectually, culturally and morally inferior.

Not only could he speak fluent German, French and Italian, he could write them too. Instead of going to university he had gone to Europe for four years, where he'd lived in apartments in Florence, Paris, Vienna and Berlin. He listened to classical music. He'd been to The Albert Hall and The Royal Opera House. He knew about art and who'd painted what.

Until I'd moved to Cornwall I'd lived in Hackney all my life. The only thing we had in common was that I'd been a girl guide and he'd been a boy scout.

He looked at the jacket I was wearing. Last year early April had been warm. This year it was cold. 'You'll need something warmer,' he said. 'I'll drop you at your place.'

I didn't invite him in. He could wait in the car. Aware of my UPVC door and double glazing that Robert and his sort despised, I grabbed my padded jacket and woollen scarf.

71

'You'll need a coat yourself,' I said when I got back in the car.

'I'll get one. There's a lovely cove a short walk from my cottage.'

While I'd been getting my coat he'd turned the radio on. I recognized the tune. 'What's that playing?' I asked.

'Beethoven's Emperor.'

He parked and I followed him to his cottage. At the front door he pulled out his wallet and gave me a ten pound note. 'See that fish and chip shop? They're the best in the area. I'll have plaice and chips. I'd recommend it. The haddock's excellent too. So is the cod. Tell him it's for me. I won't be long.'

What a neat way of keeping me out of his cottage. The man in the shop was friendly. He became even more friendly when I mentioned Robert. He took each piece of fish, dipped them in batter and cooked them individually.

'I'll have salt and vinegar, please,' I said as he began to wrap up my order.

'No. Not if you're eating this with Robert.'

When I began to protest he grinned. 'No. You'll see why.'

His smile was so warm I didn't argue. By the time I came out of the shop Robert was standing outside his cottage wearing a navy Barbour and a scarf, with a canvas bag slung over his shoulder. He was carrying a tartan rug. I insisted on giving him money for my share.

On a hot day the cove would have been a great place for a picnic. He spread the rug, which had insulated backing, over the sand. From his bag he produced two bottles of fizzy water, wooden salt and pepper grinders, a small bottle of white wine vinegar, a lemon cut in quarters and paper towels. I stopped myself from saying how posh he was. He was right about the fish and chips. They were delicious. I could taste the difference between the sea salt, black pepper and white wine vinegar and the ordinary stuff. But I didn't tell him.

'Our problem is,' said Robert, 'that all the neighbours could have done it. Only Phoebe and Stuart had alibis and you've shown that even they had time to do it.'

I tried to look cool, but praise from Robert was heartening.

'I've just had a thought,' he said. 'The baby.'

'What about him?'

'We'll have to check and make sure he was normal.'

'Normal? Oh, you mean Bridget might have killed him because he had Downs Syndrome or cystic fibrosis?'

He nodded. 'It wouldn't be the first time.'

'She could have had him adopted. I would.'

'Would you?'

'Yes. I'd want a healthy baby.'

To my relief he wasn't looking at me as if I was unfeeling or unnatural. He looked pensive. 'There's a lot of pressure to keep them . . . attitudes have changed,' he said.

'Yes, but the condition is the same.'

He nodded. 'An extra chromosome. They used to be put in special homes.'

'Whatever pressure was put on me I wouldn't keep it. I couldn't. But would Bridget kill her husband too?'

'They might have had an argument. We'll have to find out more about their relationship. How they met, were they happy?'

'We know already,' I said. 'They both lived on the same estate.'

'But how did they meet? Church, social club or – ?'

'Sorry, I see what you mean.'

He finished the fish and chips and took two apples out of his bag. 'Want one?'

I wanted a doughnut, but I took the apple and thanked him. 'Bridget had the car. What if one of the neighbours, or all of them, thought the house was empty because the car wasn't there?' I bit into the apple.

'The thing against that line of thought is why risk burning down a house and destroying things they valued . . . the front door, original windows – '

'Unless,' I said, 'the French bloke – '

'Yves.'

'Right, him. Was he lying about the man ringing his doorbell? Did he start the fire and make up the story about the man waking him? He raised the alarm early so the house wasn't destroyed.'

'But what would they achieve? Insurance would pay for the damage and Bridget and Declan would get the new windows and doors even sooner.'

'A warning? They hoped they'd give up and move?'

He stared out to sea. 'Yves might have been so frightened about Bridget telling his parents that he was driven to murder her . . . but again, while I can see him or Craig murdering Bridget, I can't see them murdering a baby.'

'No,' I said. 'Neither can I. The only thing that makes sense is if they didn't know the baby was inside.' We were discussing murder, but I was happy. Robert and I were talking like allies not enemies.

'And,' he said, 'I'm sure if any of them killed someone they'd feel remorse and none of them looked stricken.'

I thought back to the scene in the socialite's kitchen. 'One thing I think that's a bit odd, is that they all looked perfectly groomed. Both Craig and Yves wore silk dressing-gowns, their hair was combed – '

'Hang on,' said Robert. 'They hadn't been in bed very long. If they left the party at Pengelly House at eleven, they had to get home, maybe have a bath – '

'I would have thought they'd have a bath or shower before they went to the party,' I said realizing that they also would have shaved. 'No, forget what I said – I was thinking aloud. If Bridget's telling the truth then I guess that the two blokes were in one house and the two girls in the other – not that it means anything, I suppose.'

When Robert finished his apple he said, 'Although you've shown that Phoebe or Stuart could have done it, when we first saw Phoebe, she thought Bridget was dead. She didn't have to tell us about their animosity.'

'Yes she did, because someone else would have told us. And that would have looked bad for her.'

'Hardly.' He threw his apple-core into the sea. 'They thought they had an unbreakable alibi. They'd been up all night, she could have said she was too tired to think.'

'We've got to establish what the motive was,' I said. 'Once we know that it'll make things clearer. It could have been a random arson attack, but I doubt it. The only thing that points away from Bridget or Declan being the target is the fact that the murderer could have pushed them under a bus or truck. They would have at least been sure they killed the right person.'

Robert shook his head. 'Murder by setting light to a house is haphazard, but a confrontation is avoided. Most other methods require close contact with the person and that involves the risk of being caught in the act.'

'Poison?'

He shook his head. 'I doubt anyone we've interviewed has any knowledge of poisons. And it's risky. If someone gave their potential victim a box of chocolates with one of the chocolates laced with cyanide or arsenic there's the risk that someone else might eat it.'

'Bridget's so thin she'd be unlikely to have been able to put up much of a fight if she'd been attacked, so if Yves was desperate enough to kill her, he could have gone into her house during the day when she was at home and bashed her over the head or stabbed her.' I hurried on before Robert could argue. 'He would have run the risk of being seen from the upstairs windows, but if he wore camouflage . . . '

'Maybe they kept their back gate locked,' Robert said. 'But I agree that a direct attack would have got the right target. The evidence points to Bridget being the target, but we don't know for certain. There is also the problem of leaving DNA at the scene, no matter how careful you are.'

'What did you think of Bridget?'

He looked quizzical. 'In what way?'

'Did you like her?'

'No. Did you?'

I shook my head. 'She admits that she and Elaine were bullies – although, if asked, she'd probably deny they bullied anyone – the blame would lie with Phoebe and the others for failing to do what they were told. She'd say she was doing it for the good of the hospital or something like that. Why don't you like her?'

'For the same reasons as you.'

'She seems to have lots of friends on the estate.'

'The only reason she didn't betray them because she was never in a position to do so. I bet if they'd worked with her the friendships would have been broken.'

'How do you know Ethel?'

'She's a friend of my grandmother's.'

'Is that how you know so much about Pengelly House?'

'No. My grandmother used to live there.'

'What? At the commune?'

'No. She was born there, she grew up there.'

I should have guessed that his family were one of those aristocrats who moaned about taxes and raged when some chancellor in a Labour government in the seventies said he wanted to squeeze the rich till the pips squeaked. It's a wonder they didn't try and assassinate him. My dad was always going on about how great Harold Wilson was. He wouldn't have encouraged people like my mum and dad to buy their council house. My dad wouldn't have been made redundant and their house wouldn't have got repossessed and we wouldn't have had to move to an estate that was even worse than the place where we'd grown up.

Robert's family must have been forced out of Pengelly House. They must have been too proud to endure the thought of opening their home to commoners who'd come in droves and pollute the air with working-class accents. But I wanted to hear it from him.

'Why doesn't she live there now?'

'She left home when she was seventeen and became a nurse in London. When the war broke out she joined the Air Force.'

'Why did he sell the house?'

'Who?'

'Her father.'

He unscrewed the bottle of water too fast. It spurted all over me. 'Sorry.' He handed me a paper towel. 'Whose father?'

'Her father. Your great-grandfather.'

He actually smiled. It was only a little one, but it was definitely a smile. 'He didn't.'

I was puzzled. 'But you said the owner of Pengelly House died without heirs.'

'He did. He had three sons, but they were killed in the first world war. Well, that's not strictly true. One was a

77

conscientious objector. His parents disowned him and made him leave. He couldn't get a job and he was hounded by the people in the nearest village. He went to London and stayed with his sister – she was a lot older than he was. When he received a summons from the court he committed suicide.'

No wonder Robert was so controlled, having such awful ancestors. He must have been too frightened to smile for fear of doing it at the wrong time.

'His sister never forgave her parents and that's why she went to New Zealand,' he went on. 'In spite of a search the lawyers couldn't find any descendants she might have had. They were able to trace a marriage to an Australian, but his surname was Jones. It's possible that there are heirs somewhere who haven't got a clue what they've missed.'

'They might not have wanted a huge place like that with all the taxes and upkeep they'd have to pay. Still I guess they could have sold it to a developer.' As I spoke I wondered how I would react if I discovered I had a huge inheritance.

'And the house would have been pulled down – instead it's being looked after,' said Robert. 'And, as you said, it's better that a lot of people live there rather than just one family.'

Then something struck me. 'Hang on. If they can't find her or her children aren't you the heir?'

'The heir to what?'

'Pengelly House. Oh dear. Did your grandmother disgrace herself and get disinherited?'

'No.'

'Was she illegitimate or adopted or something?'

'No.'

'Then how come you're not the heir . . . if your great-grandfather owned the place?'

'He didn't.'

'But you said your grandmother was born there.'

'She was. Her parents lived in one of the estate cottages. Her father was the head gardener.'

When we were walking up the path of Alice's house in Farrier Way, Robert stopped and stared at her door as if was made of solid gold and the stained glass was encrusted with diamonds.

'What is it?' I asked.

'Nothing.'

But I knew something had struck him. Whether it was anything to do with her house or not I didn't know.

Alice, looking smart in a suit with perfect hair and make-up, took us downstairs into the kitchen. To my surprise the clothes designers, their wives and Phoebe and Stuart were sitting at the table, which was set for afternoon tea with a tea pot, mugs, cakes and biscuits. I was going to say we didn't want anything, but Robert said yes to tea and sat opposite Phoebe. Stuart looked as if he had been painting. His jumper was old and it had smears of paint on it. He smelt faintly of turpentine – an accelerant.

The pregnant girl fidgeted and looked uncomfortable. Just as I was trying to remember her name Alice inadvertently came to my aid.

'Are you all right, Fleur?'

She smiled and nodded. 'It just kicked me.'

'Kate, would you like more tea?'

Fleur's pink maternity dress flouted the current fashion of having her bump on show and her belly button protruding. Apart from the colour, it was the sort of style I would wear, and I guessed that Craig and Yves had designed and made it. Thinking back to Bridget's accusations, which I thought were true, I looked at the girl's fingers. Both wore wedding and engagement rings and the men wore wedding rings.

A door that had been closed the morning of the fire, was now open. It was a formal dining-room with an antique table and eight chairs.

Alice got to the point as soon as she had poured Robert's tea. 'Not long after Bridget and Declan moved in, there was an almighty row. Phoebe and Stuart had invited all of us to dinner. I could hear shouting as soon as I came out of my front door and started walking towards their house. Craig and Fleur and Yves and Kate had just come out of their houses and we all stood on the footpath. It was disgraceful.

'A woman was yelling in the front garden of Declan and Bridget's – some of the time I couldn't understand what she was saying, she had such a strong Irish accent. We did catch her saying, oh, something about, 'you can't stop me seeing my grandson'. But she was hysterical and crying. I assume it was either Declan's mother or Bridget's mother.'

Kate said, 'We weren't going to stand on the footpath waiting for them to finish so we walked past their house. We looked, of course we looked. All three of them were there in the front garden. Declan was shouting at the woman. Bridget was standing there looking upset.' She laughed. 'Then Alice, in her most superior voice said, 'Excuse me, do you think you could continue your appalling behaviour in the privacy of your own house?' There was so much yelling that Phoebe and Stuart could hear it and came outside.'

'Did you see the woman?' I asked Phoebe.

'No.'

'Declan had just grabbed her and dragged her into the house,' said Alice.

'Even when we were all inside we could still hear it,' said Phoebe. 'Though not as loud, fortunately.'

What sheltered lives these pampered creatures must have

led. Arguments of that magnitude, and far worse, were common events where I grew up. If Alice had said that on our estate she would have been beaten up.

'What did the woman look like?' Robert asked.

'Ugly,' said Alice. 'Grey hair.'

'Skinny,' said Kate.

Craig shuddered. 'Badly dressed. She looked as if she'd crawled out of a rubbish bin.'

His repugnance both amused and annoyed me. It was all right for people like him, who could design and make superb clothes, to sneer because someone was badly dressed. The royal-blue jacket he was wearing would sell for a lot of money in his shop, but had probably cost a fraction of the price to make. I wondered if he and Yves made their own shirts. They certainly looked bespoke.

'Sounds like Bridget's mother,' said Phoebe.

'We're no further forward,' I said to Robert as we got into the car.

'At least we've got confirmation about the bitterness between Declan and Mrs Bradley,' he said.

He was driving, but I saw him staring intently at the houses as we drove past.

'What are you looking for, Robert?'

'Nothing. Just looking.'

'Can you see something I should know about?'

He shook his head. We drove back to the station for an end of the day team briefing. I could tell Robert's mind was far away. He didn't respond to questions any of the others asked and didn't comment on their investigations. He looked as if he hadn't even heard them.

At the end of the briefing I threw down my marker pen. 'What's wrong with you, Sergeant? You're not on this planet.

You look like a maiden dreaming about love.' I had meant to make it sound like a joke, but saw by his scowl that I had failed.

'I'm thinking about things relevant to this murder.' He stood up and walked out.

When I got home that night there was an e-mail from my older brother in Australia. As usual he'd attached photos of him and his wife and baby son in their gorgeous house with its swimming pool and four bedrooms in Perth. While I was scrolling through the photos an e-mail from my younger brother came in. With photos of him and his pregnant wife in their gorgeous house with its swimming pool and four bedrooms in Perth. He'd also sent photos of a flat they'd been to see. Considering the beach location, its close proximity to the city and the size of the rooms the rent was astonishingly cheap.

> Look at the big rooms, Sharon. The Aussies call it 'God's own country' and they're right. Here Sharon's just a name. Not a working class label, but a name parents call their kids because they like it. I'm not looked down on because I'm called Wayne.
> Take the chance while you can. Don't let mum and dad hold you back. What have they ever done for you?

My brother's ingratitude towards our parents always made me angry. Bringing us up on a council estate in Hackney, keeping us out of trouble and guiding us along the right path when there were druggies living near, must have been hard. But they made sure we had lots of good influences. I was a Brownie and my brothers were Cubs. We loved it so much they went on to join the Scouts and I

82

became a Girl Guide. It was the discipline I got from the Guides that attracted me to the police.

It was our dad who advised us to get jobs where we'd always be in demand. 'Be a plumber or an electrician,' he said to my brothers just after he was made redundant in 1990. 'And, Sharon, you be a nurse. Always needed they are.'

But I hated biology at school. So I decided on the police.

'Good,' said my dad. 'Always in demand they are. Miners get laid off, factory hands get laid off, but when did you ever hear of mass police lay offs?'

When he was made redundant he was okay to start with. He thought he'd get another job. When he didn't and it became obvious that he wouldn't, he started drinking heavily. I dreaded coming home from school to my mum crying or pleading with him to stop. Things got worse when they couldn't keep up the mortgage payments on the council house they'd been so excited about buying. The romantic songs about money not buying love might be right, but they never sing about lack of money killing love. I saw it happen.

When my older brother qualified as an electrician he went to Australia. As soon as my younger brother qualified as a plumber he went too. Now they were always on at me to go. They sent photos of beaches, and links to the real estate sites showing flats I could buy or rent and jobs I could apply for. I looked at the screen at the flat one of them had photographed and sent. It was large and modern and had two bedrooms, a balcony overlooking a garden with bushes, trees and brown grass and a communal swimming pool. The sky was cloudless and the sun glinted off the water in the pool.

Could you afford a flat like this in the UK?

No I couldn't.

7

ROBERT

As soon as I left the briefing on Monday evening I drove back to Farrier Way. Something I'd noticed had made an idea jump into my head. Thinking I might have been wrong, I checked every house. I was right. I decided to test my theory on Vanessa. When I got home I rang her. There was no reply on her landline so I rang her mobile. It went to messages before I remembered she'd gone to London to *The National Archives* to check the Metropolitan Police records for the woman who believed her father had been innocent of the murder for which he had been convicted. She was only staying one night and was probably on her way back to Cornwall now. I left a message asking her if she'd be free at dawn tomorrow morning.

'Does it have to be dawn?' she asked when she rang back.

'Yes, sorry.'

She groaned. 'Why?'

'I don't want anyone to see us and I don't want Sharon to know what I'm thinking just yet.'

'Okay. Where?'

'Farrier Way.'

'Which house?'

'Park by the forest. I'll meet you there. How's the research going?'

'The evidence does firmly suggest he was guilty. Can't

find any anomalies. Now I've got to write a tactful report.'

Vanessa arrived first. I parked behind her.

She jumped out of her car. 'What's – '

I took her arm. 'We're going to walk down Farrier Way and you're going to look at the houses and describe what you see.'

'Which ones?'

'All of them.'

'All? Why?'

'Just do it. Come on. Observe and tell me in detail what you see.'

She looked baffled. We walked up the street and she looked carefully at the houses. When we got to the last one she said, 'Apart from the fact that there's a burnt house, I can't see anything significant.'

'Good. You're strengthening my theory.'

'Pleased to hear it.'

'Tell me what you did see.'

'All the paths are straight and tiled in variations of cream, terracotta, white and black with rope tiled edging. The front doors are all different colours. They're Edwardian, I think, with stained glass panels. Is it something to do with the doors?'

'Might be.'

'Original windows. Brass letter slot with curlicues. Am I looking for something unusual?'

'Yes.'

'Most of the gardens have things for birds – feeders, bird baths or nesting boxes – some have all three. Is that it?'

'No.'

'Robert, give me a hint.'

'No.'

'Some of the houses haven't got cars or room for cars.' Exasperation was creeping into her voice. 'No one's got net curtains. All the gardens are well cared for and have shrubs. Two have mini knot-gardens. There are no solid fences, just hedges. Some have gates, but most don't.' She frowned. 'I give up.'

I took her arm and we walked down the road and stood outside the house belonging to Yves and Kate. 'Vanessa, put yourself in the mind of the arsonist. It's night. Dark. He's looking for a specific house. What does he look for?'

'He?'

'Okay. Maybe she. If it's a targeted attack?'

'All the houses look alike.'

'Right. So how is he or she going to know which one is Bridget's and Declan's?'

'The number?'

'Correct.'

'Ah! You've found there's no thirteen?'

'What's the number of this house?'

The brass number was clearly visible on the white painted support of the porch. 'One.'

'So the next house should be?'

'Three.'

She yawned as she wandered to Bridget's where the door and windows were boarded up. There was no gate and no number on the porch. 'I can't see any number.'

'Let's go to the next house, which is Phoebe's and Stuart's.'

'I still can't see any number.'

'Look up.'

She looked at the glass above the door, where the number was patterned in white among the decorative glass. 'Oh. Three. Consecutive. The numbers are consecutive.'

'Yes. If the road was numbered odds and evens as normal, Phoebe's would be number five and Bridget's would be three. The murderer sees number one and assumes the next house will be three. And number one is one of the few houses with a number on the porch. Most make do with the number in stained glass over the door. And as it was dark and there were no lights on inside . . .'

'So the intended victims might have been Phoebe or Stuart,' she said slowly.

'Exactly. I didn't realize at first. We were just called to Farrier Way. No house number. When we got here there were fire engines so we didn't need a number. The fireman told us that everyone had gone down to the end house. I never even thought about house numbers. I just happened to notice yesterday. I saw the number ten above Alice's door. If the numbers were odds and evens her house would be either nineteen or twenty. And I started thinking what if the murderer was someone who knew Phoebe and Stuart's address, but had never been to their house. It looked as if Bridget was the target, but it could have been Declan. Now we've got Phoebe and Stuart – one of them or both.'

Vanessa looked at the other side of the street. 'Why are the numbers not odds and evens? Those houses look the same as these. Maybe it was once two streets.'

'Don't think so. It's not wide enough.'

We crossed the road. The street name was also Farrier Way, and the houses looked identical, although the gardens were more manicured and net curtains hung in some of the windows. The doors were more plain with etched glass instead of stained.

Vanessa nudged me. 'Let's go back to your place. You owe me breakfast.'

I looked at my watch. 'Can we make it dinner tomorrow

night? I've got to take the car to the garage to have it's MOT and Sharon's calling early. We're going to see the staff at the hospital where Bridget works.'

'Are you going to tell Sharon what you've found out?'

'I'll have too, but I want something concrete to go on before I say anything.'

While I waited for Sharon to arrive I debated how and when to tell her what I'd discovered. Trying to guess her reaction was difficult. Even if I had evidence that Phoebe or Stuart had enemies who hated one or both of them enough to kill, Sharon might scorn the idea and accuse me of trying to get Phoebe off the list of suspects because I was attracted to her. If she agreed with me, I suspected she'd claim the idea as her own. I didn't care about that, as long as the case was solved.

8

SHARON

On Tuesday Robert got into the car without acknowledging my, 'Good morning.'

'Sulking, Robert?'

'No.'

'You're very stony faced. What's the matter?'

'You.'

'So you are sulking.'

'I am not sulking. I am angry. We're a team or we're supposed to be a team. Calling me a dreaming maiden in front of everyone wrecks team spirit and makes me look foolish. Just because I'm thinking does not mean I'm dreaming.'

'It was a team briefing. You weren't taking part. I could tell you weren't listening to anything I was saying. You weren't, were you?'

He looked amused. 'I could hear your voice, but I wasn't listening. Doesn't mean I didn't know what you were saying. You were going through the days events and I had nothing new to add. There was no need for you to be insulting.'

'I didn't mean to be insulting.'

'What did you mean to be?'

'I meant to get your attention.'

We didn't speak again till we arrived at the hospital.

We were following the directions we'd been given at

reception for the medical records department, when a man cannoned into me almost knocking me over.

'Sorry,' he gasped over his shoulder.

Robert grabbed my arm to steady me. 'Are you okay?'

'Yes.'

We turned around and saw him running down the corridor.

'He's in a mad rush,' said Robert.

We saw a door marked *Medical Records* and pushed it open. A woman with black hair streaked with grey lay on the floor groaning. Two other women bent over her.

'What happened? I asked.

'She fell,' said one of the women.

The woman on the floor made unintelligible noises. Blood ran from her mouth. Some of her teeth had been knocked out. Behind her, four other women and two men were trying, and failing, to hide their glee.

Elaine, I thought.

'Who is she?' asked Robert.

'Elaine Dunn, the manager,' said someone.

After Elaine Dunn had been taken to accident and emergency, I introduced myself and Robert.

'She fell,' three of them chorused.

I told them we'd come about the fire at Bridget Murphy's house. We interviewed them in Elaine's office one by one. They were all dressed in tan suits with brown shirts and brown scarves for the women and brown ties for the men. The fabric looked cheap. The shirts were made of something that looked scratchy and uncomfortable. Their ugliness made my olive-green trouser suit look chic.

They had all heard about the fire from Margaret. In spite of the fact that a baby had been one of the victims, none of them appeared upset. No one expressed shock or horror.

Although, as it was Tuesday and Margaret would have told them about it on Monday, perhaps any shock or horror they had felt, had worn off.

Their alibis would be impossible to prove or disprove. They all claimed to have been in bed asleep, which given the hour the fire brigade had been called, was reasonable. Their stories about the bullying were the same as Phoebe's. Some said they were sorry about the baby and two were unwise enough to say it was a shame Bridget hadn't burnt to death, since the fire was almost certainly meant for her.

One thing I was learning about Robert was that he had the hearing equivalent of a photographic memory. It was why he let people ramble.

'It's like panning for gold,' he once told me. 'Precious specks among the dross.'

We interviewed Margaret Fox last. I was certain I'd seen her before, but couldn't think where. In contrast to the hideous uniform were her ankle boots that looked as if they were made of good leather and the pearls in her ears and necklace, which looked real. As if in defiance she had a pearl brooch pinned to the lapel of her jacket. Her wedding band was made with white and yellow gold and her engagement ring had a central ruby flanked by two diamonds. Her fingernails were well manicured and painted with frosted nail polish.

Robert smiled at her. Before he could say anything, she said, 'I saw you on Saturday afternoon.'

He looked surprised. 'Did you? Where?'

'Pengelly House. I live there.'

'Ah,' I said. 'I thought I'd seen you somewhere. So you were at the party?'

'Yes.'

I remembered now. Margaret had been in the kitchen

throwing used paper plates, serviettes and plastic glasses into bin bags when we arrived. Her yellow jumper had gone well with her auburn hair and her jeans had showed off her slim figure. When she had finished tidying she had put out the food that was left over and offered us a drink.

To my irritation she and Robert chatted about Pengelly House. I was about to interrupt when he finally got to the point and asked if there were any smokers at the party.

Margaret looked puzzled. 'Quite a few.'

'Are they allowed to smoke in the house?'

'Not in the communal areas. They can smoke in their own apartments if they want to – all the rooms have smoke alarms.'

'So the smokers at the party had to go outside?' Robert said.

'Yes.'

'Can you tell us about Bridget's relationship with the staff here?' I said. 'Phoebe said that everyone got on well before Elaine became the manager.'

Margaret, looking disgusted, said, 'Yes, we did. At first we felt sorry for Bridget. She often cried at work because of her ghastly mother who tried to stop her having boyfriends. Phoebe and I hadn't been working here very long when Bridget had two weeks holiday. When she came back we asked her what she'd done. She'd spent the two weeks helping her mother clean, tidy and rearrange the furniture in their flat. We didn't know what to say. The only social thing she'd done was go to church on Sundays – with her mother. When Phoebe and I went on holiday to Crete a few months later – eight of us stayed in a self-catering place near the sea – we felt guilty about saying what a wonderful time we'd had when we went back to work.

'As soon as Elaine came I knew, just knew, that Bridget

would change. I could see it in her face. She was all smarmy. It was terrible for Phoebe, she and Bridget had been friends.'

'Were you friends with Bridget?'

'No. I didn't like her.' Margaret looked thoughtful. 'There was something about her. I didn't trust her and I was proved right. She was ambitious – she was always applying for jobs of a higher grade, but never got anywhere. She asked Phoebe to help her, and she did. She advised her how to dress for an interview and helped her write her CV's. I thought, even then, that she used Phoebe.'

'Did you resent their friendship?' Robert asked.

'No, but it made me uncomfortable. Bridget felt she had exclusive rights over Phoebe. She resented our friendship. I think she even wanted to cause trouble between us, but we've known each other since we were at school. We went to university together and we're members of the same writing group. She's also my sister-in-law. It'd take more than a badly educated dimwit like Bridget to come between us.'

That Phoebe and Margaret had been lifelong friends made it more likely that Margaret would lie for Phoebe and leave out vital pieces of information to throw suspicion away from her.

'Bridget was possessive of Phoebe, but then when it suited her she dropped her. When Elaine came she got the promotion she craved, and not through merit either. It was a nightmare here till Bridget went on maternity leave – then Elaine no longer had someone to back her up. When Bridget came back, at first it was all the same friendly, friendly with Elaine. Then someone – I have no idea who – it might have been more than one person, started sending Elaine anonymous messages. She was furious and called a meeting demanding to know who'd sent them. No one admitted anything, of course. It was stupid of her to expect anyone to confess. We just stood there silently while she ranted and threatened.'

'What did the messages say?' Robert asked.

'The first one was something like, 'Bridget is only friendly with you because you're the boss. She hates you as much as everyone else does.' The next one was more stark. 'Bridget is plotting to get your job.' That's all it said. Another one said, 'You should hear what Bridget says about you behind your back, Elaine.' Then Bridget started taking lots of sick-leave. Don't know why she came back after she moved – money I suppose and she reckoned she could take lots of sick-leave and still get paid. I don't think she was really sick. She probably wanted to stay with the baby.

'Elaine's attitude to her changed. Bridget's shock was comical when she was reprimanded in front of us all about taking too much sick-leave. We laughed about that. Then another message arrived telling Elaine that Bridget was looking for another job. That caused a lot of damage to their friendship. I suppose Elaine thought there was some truth in them.'

'Were the messages sent from outside or internally?' I asked.

'Outside. Some were posted in Truro, others were posted in St Austell and Bodmin.'

'Were they hand written?' asked Robert.

'No. Printed – every message was in a different typeface. The colour of the paper was different too.'

I wondered if Phoebe had sent them, and if they had anything to do with the case.

'Bridget told us about them,' said Robert. 'She thinks Phoebe sent them.'

Margaret shook her head. 'Phoebe's not into revenge. She wouldn't waste her time with letters – she's got novels to

94

write, lots of friends and family to see and a writers' group to run – she's the president. And she'd left years before the letters started arriving. Elaine should have binned them and said nothing – not even to Bridget. But she festered in public. She actually held them up – all of them – and read them out. She even threatened to go to the police. If it was someone in the department sending them, she certainly gave them satisfaction.'

'How many letters were sent?'

Margaret thought for few seconds. 'About seven, I think.'

'How long had Bridget and Declan been married?' I asked.

'I can't remember exactly. After Phoebe left. I think she started going out with Declan when Phoebe was still here.'

'Was Phoebe jealous of Bridget?' Robert asked.

Margaret looked astounded. 'Jealous of Bridget? Of course not. Why would she be?'

Robert shrugged. 'Bridget claimed that Phoebe was jealous of her.'

'You've got to be joking. Bridget was jealous of Phoebe. Look, Phoebe was married – happily married, Bridget lived with her horrible mother – '

'I think Bridget meant after she was promoted,' I said.

'No, not even then. She was hurt and felt betrayed, but not jealous. Naturally she hated the change in the dynamics – we all did. And she didn't want a promotion or too much responsibility. She wanted to concentrate on her writing.'

'Bridget's very thin,' Robert said. 'Is she anorexic?'

'No,' said Margaret. 'She looks it, but she's got a healthy appetite. Whenever I've seen her in the canteen at lunchtimes her plate's been piled high with food. She always ate a pudding, and at morning and afternoon tea she'd eat a doughnut or cake. I'd say it's her metabolism and living with her mother must have been nerve-racking.'

'Did she put on weight after she married?' I asked.

'No. Although she was away from her mother, she still had Elaine to keep happy – that must have been tough. She was very demanding. And knowing how much we all hated her – '

'What about bulimia?' asked Robert.

'I don't think so. When I first knew her I did think she could be, but I watched her and she stays at the table after she's eaten. I don't know how long bulimia sufferers leave between eating and vomiting – '

'Thanks,' I said. 'It's probably not important, but we're just trying to build up a picture of her.'

'A number of your colleagues have said that they're sorry Bridget is still alive.' Robert let his statement hover.

I watched Margaret carefully. She looked guarded, but stayed silent.

'What's your feeling?' Robert persisted when it was clear Margaret was refusing to be drawn.

'Bridget brings out the worst in people, but I doubt anyone here hates her enough to kill her. Wishing her dead and killing her are different. I don't think anyone in this department would kill anyone – truly I don't.'

'Did you ever wish her dead?' I asked.

Margaret shook her head. 'If the fire had killed her I wouldn't have been happy about it, but I wouldn't have been upset either.'

We almost left without getting another vital snippet. It was Robert who asked, 'Did you ever see Bridget's baby?'

We'd asked all the others and they'd said no. I thought his question was a waste of time. I was wrong.

She nodded. 'He was a pretty little kid. Much better looking than her – he must have taken after Declan's side of the family, although he wasn't all that good looking either, but he might have been once – it was a bit hard to tell because he went bald in his early twenties. She flaunted the baby at Phoebe. Whenever I visited Phoebe and Stuart and the weather was warm, Bridget would be outside in the garden with the baby. She'd talk loudly to him, so Phoebe could hear.'

A mother playing with her baby in the garden seemed reasonable to me.

Margaret saw my look of doubt and said, 'She must have watched, because as soon and we went outside she'd come out with the baby. And guess what? When we went inside – so did she. Once I was standing at Phoebe and Stuart's bedroom window, we were looking at the view of the forest, and Bridget came in through the back gate. She saw us at the window – it was open – and she took him out of his pushchair and starting playing with him. We went downstairs to have lunch and I snuck back to look out the window and she was gone.'

'Why would that matter to Phoebe?' I asked. I knew the answer, but wanted to see if Bridget's story about Phoebe's miscarriages and the baby who died just after it was born, would be confirmed. It was.

Margaret had no idea she'd just given Phoebe another motive for murder.

Before we left the hospital, we went to the accident and emergency department and gave our details to the clerk to give to Elaine Dunn.

'What a cauldron,' said Robert as we went back to the car. 'Bullying, jealousy, anonymous letters – we're not even sure who the intended victim was. It may have been Declan.'

'I think we can be certain it was Bridget,' I said. 'Let's go through what we've found out. Her baby was normal. Phoebe had another motive. And she and Margaret are not just sisters-in-law they've been friends since they were children, which makes Margaret's defence of Phoebe suspect. And the smokers at the party had to light up outside, so all either Phoebe or Stuart had to do was tell someone they were going outside to talk to one of the smokers.'

'And,' he said, as I drove through the hospital gates, 'We've got more confirmation that Bridget's mother was possessive and bullying and didn't want Bridget to marry anyone. And Bridget was popular with most of her colleagues until she became Elaine's deputy.'

'Phoebe told us that. I can't see why it matters.'

'It gives us an insight into her character. She wasn't rotten, but she put money and power over friendship. She wanted to better herself – that's understandable, but the way she did it was underhand.'

I stopped at the traffic lights. 'Do you think the messages Elaine got have anything to do with the case?'

'Hard to say. If the aim was to cause Elaine to distrust Bridget, they seem to have worked. There's one other thing.' He paused and looked uncertain. 'It's about the baby.'

'What, Robert?'

'Can we discuss Margaret's assumption that he was normal?'

'Assumption?'

'She only saw him from Phoebe's bedroom window.'

'True, but – '

'Did you think there was anything odd about the way she described him?'

I shook my head. The lights turned green and I pulled away and turned right.

'A pretty little kid. He was almost two . . . it's an odd way to describe a male toddler.'

'You think Bridget wished he was a girl?'

'No, someone as astute as Margaret would have mentioned if she'd seen him wearing girly clothes or having longish hair. I mean . . . '

He looked strange suddenly.

'Robert?'

He swallowed. 'When I was in London . . . '

He was struggling with this. Something was wrong.

'Yes?' I tried not to sound impatient. 'What?'

'A, er, friend of mine was a paediatrician.' He took a deep breath.

'What happened to him?'

He looked startled. 'Happened? Oh, nothing. It's a difficult subject . . . I'm trying to remember what er, he told me . . . the right words . . . it's not as sad as it was years ago.'

I should have been irritated, but I was too curious. He was wandering off the subject in an un-Robert like way.

'No, sorry, I feel unwell . . . sick . . . something I ate . . . I can't talk about it.'

He couldn't talk about something he ate? I decided to go along with his excuse. 'Do you want to go to your place and I'll go back to the station and brief the others?'

'Thanks.'

When I pulled up in front of Dolphin Cottage Robert went inside without saying anything. I glanced at the window, but only saw him going towards the kitchen. He wasn't ill. It was talking about the paediatrician that had upset him. Had they been lovers? Even in these enlightened times most men I worked with despised homosexuals. Was Robert blackmailed? Had his lover died of AIDS?

I phoned him later. He apologized and said he was feeling

better. His car was still at the garage so I said I'd call for him in the morning.

'Would you like to stop for breakfast?' he asked. 'I've got something to show you.'

Amazed by the invitation, I accepted. I was just about to turn off my computer and go home, when an e-mail arrived from Bridget.

> I forgot to tell you – Phoebe's finances are not right. She wears clothes that Craig and Yves make for their shop in town. The prices are way beyond what I can afford and I've got a good job.

As I wrote a note to remind myself to check out Yves and Craig's shop, it occurred to me that Bridget didn't know that Phoebe's first book was about to be published. Although I knew I should be neutral, Bridget was the type of person I detested. Loyalty in a friend was important to me. Bridget had not only dropped Phoebe as a friend, she had bullied her when she was given a position of power.

Part of me felt the path she had taken was inevitable. Like her, I had grown up on a council estate, but my parents had been good people. Mrs Bradley was not only possessive, she was nasty, which is probably why Bridget's father had left. I had made my way up the career ladder on merit. Bridget had done it by colluding with a woman who sounded as nasty as Mrs Bradley. I would have never turned against my friends to advance my career.

The next morning Robert was his normal, unemotional self. The table in the dining room was set with a red gingham cloth and matching serviettes. There were packets of cereal and a carton of organic apple and blackberry juice on the sideboard. I hoped he'd cook bacon and eggs and he did. I'd never had such delicious bacon as the rashers he dished up on top of the slice of granary bread. He'd fried them in butter, and the sea salt and black pepper I ground over my egg made me want another one. He cut more bread, and I spread it thickly with butter, and marmalade, which he told me his grandmother made.

I'd only ever known one grandparent and she'd died when I was ten. I told him he was lucky. He agreed. He'd made coffee in a large cafetière. I sipped it in silence as I gazed at the view and heard the shriek of the gulls and the sound of the waves. It was a romantic room. I could imagine the two candlesticks on the wide window-sill and the ones on the mantelpiece burning in the evening and the table set with a more formal cloth. He certainly liked candles. There were two glass lamps with nightlights in them on the chest of drawers in the alcove. They were the sort that you see in spooky movies set in Victorian times with a woman carrying them up a long staircase.

A door at the side of the dining-room opened onto a small patio. An ornate garden table painted dark-green with four matching chairs was surrounded by pots of all shapes and sizes planted with bushes I didn't know the names of.

Stuart's painting was on one wall. Like his others it was lifelike and realistic. It was a night scene of a dining room with a table set for dinner. A woman, dressed in a white blouse that could have been Victorian or a Laura Ashley copy, was in the act of placing a pink rose in a vase. Again it was viewed through a window with small panes of glass.

'He's always got windows in his painting,' I said to Robert.

'Yes. He calls himself an inside outside artist. He's got a fascination with seeing things through a window or glass doors.'

I understood the attraction. When I walked down my street in the dark I always liked to glance inside when people had their lights on and their curtains open.

'Did you buy his paintings at an art gallery?'

'Yes. In Polperro. I was with my grandmother and there was an exhibition of painting by local artists. She bought me one for my birthday. I loved it so much I bought another one.'

How lucky he was that he had a grandmother indulgent enough to buy him paintings for his birthday. I thought about Bridget's theory that Stuart and Phoebe were poor.

I chose my next words carefully. 'I'm not prying – but I'd be interested to know how much they cost, because – '

'Five hundred pounds,' he said.

'Right. So if he sells a lot that would account for him and Phoebe being well off, wouldn't it?'

'Not necessarily. It would depend on how many he sells. If he only sold one a month that's not much. And he's got to buy frames, canvasses, paint and brushes.'

'And I guess he's got fees to pay for the galleries.'

'Yes, but Stuart, and other local artists, have also got other valuable exhibition sources. Several restaurants, cafés and pubs have their paintings hanging on the walls – they're for sale so the patrons can buy them. The artist gets free exhibition space and the venue gets free pictures to decorate their walls.'

'So Bridget's opinion that Phoebe and Stuart don't have much money, might be right.'

He nodded. 'Although neither of them look as poverty stricken as Bridget would no doubt like to think.'

'They don't look poverty stricken at all,' I said with a smile. 'More like well off. But I wonder, if like many people, they live on credit.'

'Yes,' he said. 'They might do.'

Being gracious made me feel awkward and I struggled to find the right words to thank Robert for the breakfast. 'Thanks,' I said when the cafetière was empty. 'That was a scrumptious breakfast. The best I've ever had.'

He looked surprised.

'Tell me about the case you solved by instinct,' I said.

He picked up the cafetière. 'I'll make some more coffee.'

I went into the kitchen with him. He filled the kettle, rinsed out the cafetière and poured more milk into the jug. His fridge was behind a false door. Was he being affected or had he wanted the kitchen to look ancient, which, apart from the microwave and electric kettle, it did. The oven and hob were black and looked old, but I knew they were brand new because I'd heard him telling someone when it was going to be delivered. He had a ceramic sink which added to the old-fashioned appearance. The units were an odd shade of blue, and distressed was the decorating term, if I remember rightly from the brochures I'd got when I'd been doing up my kitchen.

Apart from butter, eggs and cheese his fridge was almost empty. I wondered if, like me, he lived on microwave meals. He had tea caddies on the shelf over the sink, labelled Assam, Darjeeling, Earl Grey, and English Breakfast. There were two teapots, one large the other small. Another cafetière, larger than the one on the table, was on the window ledge. His mugs and the crockery in the sink were that blue and white striped Cornish stuff. I liked it, but thought it overpriced. Six shining stainless steel saucepans were stacked on a black cast-iron stand. It was too cluttered for me. There was a bread-bin and glass jars full of pasta, sugar, wholemeal flour and brown rice. Even if his fridge was almost empty it looked as if he had lots of visitors. I wanted to be one of them.

Shut-up, I told myself. You don't want anything to do with him outside work.

'Interesting kitchen,' I said.

'You don't like it.' He didn't sound offended. Knowing him he'd probably be insulted if I had liked it.

'It's just that I can't understand why people spend loads of money on getting a new kitchen and then bashing it about to make it look old.'

He smiled. 'The worktops and appliances are new, but the doors of the units are reclaimed. When the chaps painted them I told them to leave the cracks and bumps and be careless with the painting.'

I grinned. 'So the paintwork's not distressed it's careless.'

When we went back to the dining room Robert poured more coffee.

'The case you solved by instinct?' I prompted.

'I was a detective constable. An eight year old boy was missing. Parents were separated. According to his mother he hadn't arrived home from school. At first she thought he might have gone to one of his friends' houses and either he'd told her and she hadn't heard or he'd forgotten to tell her. When it began to get dark she rang around, but he wasn't with any of his friends. Then she rang his father. He wasn't there either. That's when she rang us.

'When we arrived she was distraught. She looked ill. As it was only my second case I didn't have a lot of confidence about questioning, so I was free to listen and observe. My reaction to her was the same as my reaction to Bridget's mother. I disliked her immediately. She lived in a large Victorian house in East Twickenham, but she was a ferocious snob. She had one of those accents that are so 'upper' they

104

sound fake.

'While we were getting the addresses and names of her son's friends she made comments about them. She said one family was terrible because the father owned a shop and people like him shouldn't live in nice houses.'

'I'm glad I wasn't on that case,' I said. 'I would have wanted to slap her. How can people still think like that?'

He shrugged. 'When the boy's father arrived there was such enmity between them. Neither of them made any effort to hide their animosity toward each other. I mentioned earlier that she was distraught, and that to me was not quite right. Do you know why?'

'No. Her son was missing. Why wouldn't she be distraught? Oh, wait. You mean she was putting it on?'

'No. It was genuine.'

'Then I haven't a clue what you're getting at.'

'Okay. I'll come back to that in a minute. When we went to see one of his friends the boy, who was his best friend, wasn't worried or upset. That was wrong. His parents were concerned, his sisters were too, but he wasn't. He was stubborn, but I kept on at him. The next day, under our questioning, he said, 'I promised not to tell.' Between us, his mother and I persuaded him to break his promise. He told us his friend was going to go and live with his father. The boy didn't know if the father knew, and then a few interesting things were revealed. I kept a note book and wrote down my thoughts.' He looked at his watch. 'I can give it to you if you're interested. It's getting late, we'd better get going.'

'What did you want to show me?'

'Come up to my study.'

He led the way upstairs. He had two desks in his study. Both looked like antiques. There was a large diary, a fountain pen, a bottle of black ink, exercise books and a mug holding pencils, biros and highlighters on the desk facing the window. A computer stood on the other desk.

He moved the mouse and the screen lit up. 'Read that and tell me what you think.' He sat at the other desk and began opening drawers. If he'd gone back downstairs I'd have been tempted to sneak a look at his favourites. He probably knew it and that's why he stayed.

I read the article twice before turning to him and saying, 'You think Bridget's son might have been a hermaphrodite?'

'Margaret's description made me wonder . . . do you think it's worth checking?'

'Yes, I said,' pleased he'd asked my opinion. 'Would Bridget have known about it from when he was born or find out later?'

'It depends. Sometimes the male organs are unusually small.'

'The post mortem's being done today. I'll ask them to check.'

He handed me a large note book. 'My notes about the case I solved by instinct.'

'Do you always keep notes?'

'Yes.'

'Are you making notes about this one?'

'Only in my head.'

We met a member of the forensic team at Bridget's house. The material used to light the fire may have come from an old sheet, but it had been so badly burnt it was difficult to tell. The thread found in the flap of the letterbox was being tested for DNA. If we were lucky the murderer wouldn't have washed the sheet, shirt or article of clothing. Would they have even though about DNA? I hoped that they had assumed the fabric would all be burnt. If the thread had come from an unwashed sheet, it would certainly contain DNA.

Forensics had opened the back door and all the upstairs windows, so the smell of smoke was bearable. The interior was much as we expected. Among the smoke and water damage was cheap furniture, a huge television, neutral walls and carpets. There were only two photos and they were in the main bedroom. One was of Bridget and Declan on their wedding day. Even then, Bridget had been painfully thin in her long strapless dress. I thought it would have been better to wear something that covered her skeletal shoulders and arms, but perhaps she was proud of being so thin. Declan looked at least forty, but that may have been because he was bald. The other was of their son, which must have been taken a few weeks before the fire.

Only the baby's room looked as if any imagination had gone into it. The walls were blue, the cot and chest of drawers were white and the curtains were yellow with a pattern of red trains on them. I gently pulled out a drawer in the chest. It was full of clean baby clothes in bright colours. A ruined mobile hung over the cot. A teddy bear, stained with water, lay on the floor. Around its neck was a red ribbon. It was here, that the sense of loss was acute.

Robert was staring at the teddy bear. He looked anguished.

'Tragic, isn't it?' I said softly.

He nodded and left the room.

We went downstairs to the basement. Unlike the rest of the house it was undamaged. To our surprise it was a separate flat, with a small kitchen and a bathroom, both of which looked as if they had been installed in the seventies. The bathroom suite was brown and there were worn cork tiles on the floor. There was a bedroom and a lounge with basic furniture. The bed had no quilt or pillows and all the drawers of the chest were empty, as was the wardrobe. We were about to leave when I saw an A4 sheet of paper on which FLAT TO LET was written in biro.

'Looks as if they were planning to get a lodger,' said Robert.

The post-mortem showed a normal, healthy, well nourished toddler with no bruising or signs of abuse. I crossed Bridget off my list of suspects. Phoebe, because she had the most motives, was top of my list. Yves was next. Bridget's mother was third. I didn't know where to rank the people Bridget worked with, or her other neighbours. When I got home that evening I sat at my desk trying to work out who had the most to lose. All the motives and losses were different.

I gave up, went downstairs and opened the fridge. I had a choice of three microwave meals – curry, lasagne or shepherd's pie. I wondered what Robert was having. Was he alone or with the blonde who'd slammed the door in my face? Perhaps he was with a man. I heated the lasagne, poured a glass of red wine and sat in the lounge. There was nothing I wanted to watch on the TV, so I decided to be civilized and eat in the dining room at the white melamine table I'd bought for my flat in London. This house was bigger and I'd bought furniture to fill it at a place a neighbour had told me about. Trago Mills was near Liskeard, and from the outside it looked like a tourist attraction.

The first time I went there I must have looked like an idiot. Every time I saw the price of something my jaw dropped. Whenever I had a day off I haunted the place. I bought a desk and chair, new pillows, duvets and towels. The carpet and lino I chose were offcuts. I bought things I'd wanted for the kitchen, but hadn't been able to afford in London – a six piece cutlery set in a wooden box, being the most extravagant. So far I was the only person to use it. My mum and dad had only been to visit once, and that was just after I moved in.

Friends from London had promised to visit at weekends, but gradually the e-mails stopped. In London I'd had lots of friends. Now my rank was an obstacle to friendship. The neighbours were pleasant, but they were either elderly or had children. I'd never been so aware of my single status.

Lonely and discontented I looked around the room at the white walls and woodwork, beige carpet and upholstery. Once I'd thought it chic, now it looked boring and sterile. The only things it had in common with Dolphin Cottage were lack of curtains and the bathroom, which, like Robert's, was white. I'd bought white shutters, preferring the added security and their clean lines.

His cottage said something about him. That he liked colour, books, music, and the photos showed his family was important to him. What did my house say about me? That I was tidy, clean, organized and – boring and sterile. What I'd rejected as clutter gave Dolphin Cottage character. I hadn't attended either of my brother's weddings, which were in Australia. The photos were sent as e-mail attachments otherwise I might have framed them, and given my place some atmosphere.

Early the next morning I went into the town near Farrier Way. It was too small to be a proper town, but too large to be a village. In spite of being off the tourist route it looked prosperous and probably served the farming, hunting, shooting and fishing community. I found Craig and Yves shop down a cobbled pedestrian lane with specialist food shops, a jewellers, an antique shop, two cafes, an estate agent, a pub and a wine bar. I didn't have to go inside. The prices were on all the clothes in the window display.

They were so expensive I wondered how they stayed in business what with the credit crunch. Even if Stuart sold a lot of his paintings, would he make enough for Phoebe to buy such expensive clothes? Robert would go through the possibilities. Phoebe or Stuart may have inherited a lot of money. Phoebe had big advance from the publisher? A lottery win?

The way the investigation was limping along was driving me mad. The only progress we'd made was being able to eliminate the man who'd raised the alarm from our enquiries. He had come forward. His story that he was taking his wife, who was in labour, to the hospital was confirmed by the hospital admittance records. He hadn't phoned the fire brigade because he'd left his mobile phone behind. It also told us that Yves was telling the truth.

9

ROBERT

Being in the baby's room had been disturbing. For the first time since meeting Bridget I felt pity. She had married, despite her dreadful mother's objections. Notwithstanding her poor education and lack of intelligence, she had been promoted. She and Declan had managed to afford to buy a house far removed from the council estate where they had grown up. She had played in the jungle that was life and won. Now her dreams and ambitions had been doused and she was back to where she had been before her marriage. I doubted that she would ever escape from her mother.

There are few things worse than going into a baby's room where the furnishings and toys had been chosen with love and joy, knowing that the baby will never be there again. I remembered standing in Hannah's room. Unable to bear it, I had only stayed a few moments, before going out and shutting the door. I had never gone in there again. It was Vanessa who had organized the donation of Hannah's clothes, toys and furniture to charity. The day they came to collect them I had gone out.

Vanessa and I had keys to each other's houses and she was in Dolphin Cottage setting the table when I arrived home on Wednesday evening. There was a bottle of Merlot on the sideboard. A saucepan of potatoes was boiling on the Aga, and I could smell mint. I immediately saw that she was

111

troubled, but she denied anything was wrong when I asked her.

'I've just thought of something else that makes Phoebe or Stuart the intended victims,' I said as I put lamb chops under the grill. 'Bridget and Declan had a car, but Bridget drove it to Bodmin to see her mother, so there was no car in their drive. Anyone who knew Phoebe and Stuart would be sure to know they didn't have a car.'

Vanessa thought for a moment. 'Depends how well he or she knew them. And quite a few of the houses didn't have cars parked in front – Farrier Way is so close to the town they don't really need a car for just day to day stuff.'

After dinner Vanessa asked me to draw a plan of who lived where in Farrier Way.

'I'm not sure,' I said. 'Two families are on holiday and two houses are empty – I don't know which ones.'

'Fill in what you do know. I went back and checked a few things today. Six and nine are the one with For Sale boards.'

We studied our finished list. I had also written the number the houses would have been if they had been numbered odds and evens.

1		Kate and Yves (Suspects)
2	(3)	Bridget and Declan (Victims)
3	(5)	Phoebe and Stuart (Suspects)
4	(7)	Owners on Holiday?
5	(9)	Craig and Fleur? (Suspects)
6	(11)	Empty. For sale
7	(13)	Elderly lady?
8	(15)	Owners on holiday?
9	(17)	Empty. For sale
10	(19)	Alice (Where the neighbours went when the fire was being put out)

'Listen, I've had an idea,' Vanessa said. 'I don't know what you think, but how are you going to find out if Phoebe or Stuart had enemies?'

'I'm going to have to tell Sharon and we can start investigating.'

'What if she scoffs?'

'I don't know. What's your idea?'

'Phoebe runs a writers' group, right?'

I nodded. 'She's the president. It's the same one Ethel goes to. We'll have to ask her if she knows anything.'

Vanessa looked smug. 'I rang her while I was waiting for you. She thinks Phoebe's terrific. This is my idea – Ethel said there's a flyer for the writers' group in the library, so after I'd been to Farrier Way to check things out, I went to the library. New members are welcome. I could go along.'

'Slight problem – what are you going to write?'

'Let's see if they've got a website.'

They did. A good one with plenty of information. They met weekly and they encouraged novelists, poets, playwrights and journalists to attend.

'Constructive criticism,' Vanessa read. 'New writers are welcome to come and listen and see if the group suits them. No obligation to read or comment.'

'That's good.'

She laughed. 'But I am going to read. A poem.'

'It's got to be original,' I said.

'It will be. It'll look more in character if I do.'

'Vanessa, your poetry is . . . it makes 'the cat sat on the mat' look like the work of a genius.'

'I'm not going to read anything I wrote, you idiot. I'm going to read one of grandma's poems.'

'Ah. Which one?'

'The one about the professional funeral goer.'

Vanessa and I had been twenty when our grandfather died. After his funeral the parishioners of the church held afternoon tea in the hall for the mourners. A woman came up to my grandmother and said, 'He was such a great man. I was so fond of him.'

To my horror my grandmother had replied, 'Well he detested you, so stop snivelling and get out of my sight, you hypocrite.'

Vanessa's face had turned scarlet with embarrassment.

I said to a woman next to me, 'I'm so sorry, my grandmother's not herself today. This is too much for her.'

The woman had chuckled. 'She's very much herself, my dear young man. What's more, she right. That woman adores funerals. She's a ghoul. She knew your grandfather and when he was alive she didn't have a good word to say about him.'

A few months later my grandmother wrote a poem titled *The Professional Funeral Goer*.

Vanessa was making a list. 'I'll go to the next writers' group meeting and e-mail you as soon as I get back. Even if I don't find out anything.'

On my way back to the station the following day I saw Alice, the woman from number ten Farrier Way, going into an estate agents. I crossed the road and opened the door.

'Good morning,' she said from behind a desk. 'Oh, you're the inspector working on the fire.'

I smiled. 'Sergeant. Do you know why the houses in Farrier Way are numbered consecutively?'

'Yes.' She gestured to a chair and I sat down. 'There used to be a big Victorian mansion opposite – nothing special, not like Pengelly House – a bit of a jumble of styles really. You could hardly see the house, it was set right back. It'd been

114

empty for a long time – just after my husband and I bought our place. Twelve years ago a developer bought the land and got permission to demolish the mansion, which was falling down anyway, and build houses. The regulations were strict and the houses had to be built like ours. When it came to re-numbering the houses we rebelled. We'd been living there for ages and the people in number seven didn't want to be number thirteen, so the numbers on the other side start at eleven.'

'Thank you.'

'Is it important?'

'No, I was just curious.'

'Have you seen Bridget yet?'

I nodded and stood up. 'Thanks for your time.'

'That's all right. Nothing much going on since the credit crunch started. Just people desperate to sell because they've lost their jobs or gone out of business. Very sad. Ah, there's just one thing. I don't know if it's important.'

'It might be.' I sat down again.

'It's just that I'm sure Bridget . . . no, sorry, I'm not thinking properly. It would matter if Phoebe was the victim, but of course it was Bridget – '

My senses on high alert, I smiled. 'Tell me anyway.'

'It's nothing much. Just that I'm sure Bridget was jealous of Phoebe, but it would only matter if Phoebe had been the victim, wouldn't it?'

'Why do you think she was jealous?'

'Phoebe's stunning and has a good figure. She's popular. She wears divine clothes. I hosted a garden party last summer. Phoebe wore one of Yves and Craig's creations; a white sun-dress in filmy cotton, discreet – she wasn't showing anything – and white sandals. She looked like a princess. Declan, and not only Declan, but other men too,

115

couldn't stop looking at her. I could tell Bridget was jealous. She looked awful. Old jeans and a blouse in a ghastly animal print that could have done with a wash. She looked common. Her hair was greasy too. Compared to Phoebe she would have felt a mess. She must have said something nasty to Phoebe, because Phoebe ignored her for the whole day and that's unlike Phoebe. She's normally friendly. None of us knew Bridget and Declan's plans for their house at that stage.'

'Would you have invited them if you had?'

'No.'

Jealousy. The word was being mentioned a great deal. Bridget claimed Phoebe was jealous of her. Mrs Bradley agreed. Margaret said Bridget was jealous of Phoebe and now Alice was saying the same. I wondered if Alice knew about Phoebe's miscarriages and the baby that died soon after it was born.

On Saturday afternoon Vanessa and I went to see Ethel. Her apartment at Pengelly House had one bedroom with an en-suite shower room, a sitting room and a tiny kitchen. She had given a lot of her furniture to her children and grandchildren and her bookcases and books were in the communal areas of the house. Her father had been the chauffer at Pengelly House and she and my grandmother had been born the same year and grown up together. Excited about helping Vanessa and me, she made tea and put cakes on a plate.

'Well, there are two people at the writers' group who dislike Phoebe,' she said. 'Olivia, who went to university with her, and George who used to be the treasurer. The writers' group was doing very well. We had lots of people attending the meetings. When the president resigned because he was moving to London we were upset. There are so few natural leaders. Phoebe didn't want to be the president, but we persuaded her. She took a while to decide she would take it on, and said she'd be the caretaker president till we found someone better. We weren't surprised that numbers increased under her leadership, but she was. She modestly didn't take the credit for it. Just said she'd built on the previous president's achievements.

'He was a good president, but Phoebe made the group more dynamic. She also got the support of the local papers, who gave us good publicity, which helped increase the membership. We'd had theme nights once a month, but as Phoebe said, the group was for serious writers and poets who wanted to get published, not for dilettantes. She cut the theme nights down to three a year – a love story or poem in February, a horror story near Halloween, and a Christmas theme for our last meeting in December. And she made those nights special with decent prizes for the winners and wine and food after the voting.

'We'd always been to the pub after the meetings, but Phoebe arranged picnics and dinners and she had parties in her house. Membership shot up. We went from an average of twelve members per meeting to twenty and once we had thirty.'

'Were Olivia and George members before Phoebe came?'

'George was. He'd been the treasurer for years. He was one of the earliest members. Olivia came just after Phoebe. They hadn't seen each other for years. I remember the night she arrived. Phoebe didn't recognize her, but she recognized Phoebe. They'd been friends at school and went to university together. I don't know what happened, but they must have had a terrific argument. Olivia's an amazingly good writer. You wouldn't think it to look at her – terrible clothes, she drinks heavily, probably an alcoholic, and she smokes a lot.'

'Is George a good writer?' Vanessa asked.

Ethel shook her head. 'He thinks he is, but he writes doggerel. His poems are childish and his prose is monotonous.'

'Any ideas why he doesn't like Phoebe?'

'No. They seemed to get on all right in the beginning. She'd been the president for a year when he resigned as treasurer. I said he dislikes her, but it's stronger than that – more like hate. Not sure if this is relevant, but he and Olivia tried to set up a rival group. It failed. George and Olivia fell out over it. I heard them arguing in the pub one night. He said she owed him money for the cost of the room they'd rented. Apparently they'd agreed to pay half each. She said it was nothing to do with her – that it was his idea and he'd promised her that there would be so many people attending that their money would cover the cost of the room rent. They blamed each other. Olivia came back to the group and told Phoebe she was sorry, but George had made it sound like they could make lots of money. I'm sorry, am I rambling?'

'No. I think this might be crucial.'

'I don't know why she let George come back to the group after that. After all he'd tried to destroy our writers' group.'

'How?'

'He held his group on the same night. He tried to entice members away from our group. He tried to get me to go. He didn't just ask either, he sent e-mails to all the members. I sent them to Phoebe, so she'd be warned.'

'What did she say?'

'She wasn't worried. Said anything he ran would be a disaster.'

'Did you delete the e-mails he sent you?'

'No, do you want to see them?'

'Yes.'

She went to her computer and switched it on. Like our grandmother she loved computers and was on Face Book. When the computer came on she searched through her e-mails. 'Here they are,' she said.

Dear fellow members,

Are you, like Olivia and I, fed up with the dictatorial way the writers' group is run? Yes? Well, you don't have to be fed up any longer! I am going to start another group, which will be run along democratic lines with you all having a say in how it's managed.
The current arrangement of meeting in the church hall is not conducive to writing, being too cold and us having to leave at 10pm so the caretaker can lock up, no matter that some of us have not read, but have paid our money.
At the last AGM I said we should move to the comfortable room above The Britannia pub. Phoebe refused on the grounds that we have a locked cupboard in the church hall where the register is kept. When I said I couldn't see what that had to do with anything, she said she would be the one who had to lug the register to the meetings and home again. A locked cupboard! The opportunity to meet somewhere more convivial is spurned for a locked cupboard! Poor Phoebe has the gross inconvenience of having to carry a register to the town centre and back.
Do we even need a register? No. I think not! I'll just ask who wants to read and they can. Keep it simple is my motto. Interested? I bet you are. Let me know what you think. Bombard me with ideas!

'Pity he didn't apply the simplicity motto to his prose,'

said Ethel. 'If I hadn't been so angry when I received that I would have laughed. I was going to tell him to go to hell, but I decided to let him think I might be a convert.'

George,

Thank you for your interesting e-mail. How much do you intend charging members per meeting?

Ethel

She clicked on his reply.

Not a problem, Ethel old girl. The pub charges £10 a night for the room. It's an extraordinary comfortable room with an open fire and loads of atmosphere. So if 20 people turn up that's 50p! A bargain! Better than £2 for the other group.

'Old girl. Did you feel like hitting him?' asked Vanessa.

'I felt like replying with, Hello balding, overweight, badly dressed, middle-aged man. But I restrained myself. I wanted information. When I went to the library I saw he had a flyer on the board.' Ethel smiled. 'I took it down when no one was looking.'

George,

Phoebe supplies tea, coffee and biscuits out of the funds. If we meet in a pub we won't be able to have that. And what if only a few people arrive? That will be more than £2.

Dear Ethel,

My group is going to be the best writers' group

in the country. I've got so many exciting plans –
a monthly magazine with the best short stories
and poetry from the members – you name it –
I'm having it! People will come flocking. Young,
old, girls and boys. Once things get going it will
generate tons of money and members won't
have to pay to attend meetings. What do you
think about that?
I'll see you at our first meeting. Do you want a
lift? I'll pick you up and I won't charge you this
time. I know you're short of money being a
pensioner. What's the address of that commune
place where you live now?
I'm going to have a reporter from the local
paper there, so wear good clothes and put
make-up on.

Ethel tutted. 'He makes it sound as if I dress in rags. I
didn't reply after that. But some members had fun at his
expense. Seven of them let him think they were interested
and that they might bring their friends along, which got him
excited. When no one turned up for his first meeting, he sent
them distraught e-mails.'

'What does he mean by not charging you this time?' I
asked.

'Before I moved here, we lived in the same street. He had
a car, I didn't. He insisted on giving me a lift to the writers'
group, even though I said I enjoyed the walk, which was less
than a mile. I didn't know him all that well then, and gave in.
He said he worried about my safety – if I got mugged he'd
never forgive himself. He drove me there and back and then
wanted to charge me two pounds.'

'Did you give it to him?'

'No. I said I didn't have any money left. I'd bought him a
drink in the pub after the meeting. He told me next time
would do. I told him I'd be walking next time. He kept

badgering me for the money. 'You don't get anything in this life for free,' he kept saying. Eventually I told him to shut-up.'

'Has he got financial problems?'

'If he has he could solve them by giving up smoking, drinking, and sell his car instead of driving everywhere.'

'Has he got a mortgage?'

'No. He rents. He's got a flat in a newly converted house. There are four flats. Two bedrooms, so I'm sure he could move somewhere cheaper.' She clicked on another of his e-mails.

> Where were you last night, Ethel? You promised you'd be there. Did you get lost? Are you ill? I put a lot of effort into the plans and now I'm out of pocket. I would have picked you up, but you didn't give me your new address. I don't like people who break their promises.

'What else can you tell me?' I asked.

'Lots of things. But I'm not sure if they would help. Nothing good. I sound so bitchy.'

'Do you think he hates Phoebe enough to kill her?'

'I don't know. I don't like him and my judgment might be skewed.'

'Tell us what else you don't like about him.'

'He makes up foolish names for people. It's as if he can't call anyone by their correct Christian name. Most people put up with it, but I refused to let him call me Unready.'

'Unready?'

'As in Ethelred the Unready. He thinks he's clever and was annoyed when I told him to either call me Ethel or Mrs Smythe. There's a girl he calls Dilemma. Her name is Emma. He Frenchifies their names or calls them by their initials.

There's a girl called Joan and he calls her Arc.'

'What does he call Phoebe?'

'Madame President – very sarcastically, but as annoying as this is I don't think it points to him being a murderer. He's one of these people who blame everyone else when things go wrong. Phoebe once said he was a member of the 'Blame it on everyone else brigade.' A good description. Whatever happens it's never his fault.'

'If you had to describe him in one word, what would it be?' I asked.

'Pathetic.'

As soon as Vanessa and I left Pengelly House, we drove to the street where Ethel used to live. It was impossible to tell which houses had been converted into flats and which were still houses. We parked outside her old house and looked at the map. Farrier Way was about half a mile away.

'Bells,' said Vanessa.

'Bells?'

'Door bells. They might have his name on them. We can find out which house he lives in.'

I hadn't thought of that. We walked up the street checking which houses had more than one bell. The third one we saw had four bells of which one was for G. Wilson. I remembered his surname from the e-mails.

'Do you think he would have driven or walked to Farrier Way?' Vanessa said.

'If he had any sense he would have dressed in dark clothes and walked. If someone saw him go to the front door and was suspicious they could have taken the car number if he'd been driving.'

We took the most direct route. The first house George would have come to was number one, the house belonging to

Kate and Yves. It was dark, but not late. The light in the hall was on, making it easy to see the number in the glass above the door. With the lights off it would have been difficult, perhaps even impossible, to see the number. The street lamp shone on the brass number on the porch. The door of Bridget's house was blackened. There was a board where the glass had been and the windows on the ground floor had been boarded up.

'Once the arsonist saw the number one, would they have bothered to make sure the next house was number three?' Vanessa wondered.

10

SHARON

The results on the thread caught in the flap of the letter box showed no traces of DNA. The sheet or article of clothing was clean. Although it was unsurprising, I was despondent and felt we were going backwards instead of getting close to solving the case. Scientific progress had deserted us. There were no fingerprints that could not be accounted for. We were back to motives. There were too many motives and no hard evidence.

This news made me more frustrated and tense. At this time of the month I was always bloated and irritable. I hated being a woman. Since puberty almost half my life was spent in pain. Three weeks into my cycle my breasts became so tender it hurt to touch them. I was short tempered, which I tried and failed to curb. I hated myself on those days, but when my temper flared all I could do was moderate it and not throw things or hit anyone.

When I started bleeding the pain transferred itself to my abdomen. I suffered agony for three days. When I was younger I ranted against the unfairness. None of my friends at school suffered like I did. Some felt mild pain or discomfort and a few lucky ones had no pain or discomfort at all. How I envied them. A doctor had put me on the pill, and while that helped the cramps, it made me emotional and weepy. I stopped taking it. A bad tempered detective was more credible than one that burst into tears. Bad temper could be attributed to the lack of progress we were making. Tears would be put down to instability.

'Who lives the other side of Bridget?' I asked Robert as we got out of the car in Farrier Way. 'Fleur and Craig or Kate and Yves? Are they the married couples? Or is it Craig and Kate and Yves and Fleur?'

'Kate and Yves.'

Phoebe came to the front door with a portable door bell in her hand. When she saw us she tried to disguise her apprehension. 'Come in. We're doing some gardening.' She was wearing a thick cream sweater with holes in the elbows, over an old pink shirt with frayed collar and cuffs. Her jeans, which were tucked into Wellington boots, had muddy streaks. Her cheeks were pink and her hair was loose and hung in those soft curls that I once spent a fortune trying to achieve only to come out of the hairdressers with a frizzy mess. She wore no make-up and looked younger and even more beautiful than she had the night of the fire. It was hard to believe that she was thirty-six.

We were walking down the hall when the phone rang. Phoebe looked at the caller ID and picked it up. 'Iolanthe, can I call you back? The police are here about the fire next door.'

'Was that your sister?' Robert asked when she put the phone down.

'Yes.'

I was surprised. Mrs Bradley had called Phoebe a spoilt brat and I'd assumed she was an only child. And how had Robert known it was her sister?

'Your parents like Gilbert and Sullivan?' he said.

Phoebe nodded. 'That's how they met. They belonged to a G&S group. Mum was a mezzo and dad was a baritone. He fell in love with mum when she was Phoebe in *Yeoman of The*

126

Guard. All of us are named after characters in the operettas.'

'How many brothers and sisters do you have?' I asked.

'Four brothers and three sisters.'

My surprise turned to amazement.

We followed her down to the end of the garden, where Stuart was turning a compost heap. Behind a hedge there was a paved area with a rotary washing line where a navy quilt cover, sheet and two pillow cases were hanging. Some sort of bushes with dead leaves divided the gardens.

Robert looked admiringly at them. 'Copper beeches make perfect hedges, don't they?'

They agreed and chatted about the plants. The wall at the back was covered with climbing roses that were just coming into leaf. The high wooden gate leading to the forest was painted the same colour as their front door.

Robert's socializing with suspects and putting them at ease was not solving the case, and I concluded that he was wasting time. Trying to sound polite I interrupted their conversation about Buddleias and their attractiveness to butterflies and bees. 'Can we go inside?'

Phoebe and Stuart pulled off their Wellington boots and gardening gloves at the back door and we went inside. This time I declined their offer of coffee.

'We need to check two things with you,' I said. 'On the night of the fire you came round the long way. Why didn't you cycle through the forest?'

'We did on the way to Pengelly House when it was light, but we'd never do it at night – too dark,' said Stuart.

'But it's a much shorter route.'

'Not if you fall off and hurt yourself,' he said.

'Presumably your bikes have lights?'

'Mine does, Phoebe's is broken. Would you like to check?'

'Yes, please.'

He was telling the truth. But his light was bright enough to see them both safely through the forest, although I could understand why they would have chosen to go on the road. I would have taken the road, even if there had been a man with me. If Phoebe or Stuart had lit the fire they would have known that by the time they arrived home there would have been someone official in the house next door to theirs.

There was the chance that no one would have discovered there was a short route to Pengelly House and their alibi would have held. If they had come through the forest they may have been seen. It would have been a small risk, because if they came through the back gate it was unlikely that anyone searching the house for clues would have seen them. But, as I reminded myself, clever murderers are too careful to take risks. Phoebe had been honest in telling us that she hated Bridget, but that could have been because she knew we'd find out anyway.

'Bridget said you wrote her a nasty letter when she moved in next door,' I told Phoebe, when we went back inside.

'Rot,' said Stuart. 'Considering all that had gone before, it was a civilized letter.'

'What did you say in it?' I asked Phoebe.

Robert shot me a warning look. I gave him a look back. Yes, I know I sound curt, but that's how I want to sound.

'I can show you – I've got a copy on my computer downstairs.'

Most of the basement was taken up by Stuart's paintings, easels, canvases and paints. There was a strong smell of turpentine. Phoebe took us into a small room. It was tidy with shelves of reference books and her computer and printer.

Turning on the computer, she said, 'Lucky I never delete anything.' While we waited for the computer to come on,

Phoebe continued, 'Bridget was promoted when I was on holiday in America for three weeks. When I came back she behaved as if we'd never been friends. She didn't even ask me if I'd had a good time, she just started giving me orders. When she moved next door, she acted as if we'd never been enemies.' She sat at her desk and found the file she was looking for. 'Shall I print it off?'

Robert said we'd read it on screen, but I said, 'Yes, please.'

Bridget,

I was shocked to discover you are our new neighbour. Your friendly attitude shocked me more, as if the Elaine nightmare and your bullying had never happened.
I refuse to socialize with you, but Farrier Way is a friendly street and we have parties to which all the neighbours are invited. Stuart and I will not tell any of the neighbours about our history and I hope you will also stay silent on the subject. It would be better for both of us if we pretend to be strangers.
I have no desire to turn them against you, but please respect my wish that when we do attend the same parties, a polite and brief greeting will be the extent of our contact. Do not seek me out or try to be friendly. If you do I will ignore you and that could be embarrassing. We will not invite you to any neighbourhood parties we host. When asked if you are attending, please say you can't as you are doing something else. I wish you no ill, and hope you'll be happy in your new home.

Phoebe

'Could you go back to the file,' Robert asked.

129

'Yes, of course. You'll want to see the date it was written,' Phoebe said.

The date of the file was two years ago, which corresponded with the time Bridget said she'd moved into the house.

'How did you feel when you discovered Bridget was still alive?' I asked.

Phoebe looked guilty. She blushed.

'I think you've answered my question,' I said.

'Don't put too much on the date,' I told Robert as we walked to the house the other side of Bridget's. 'Phoebe could have written a nasty letter, stuck it through Bridget's door, deleted it and then written a more benign one.'

'I'm aware of that,' Robert said as he rang the doorbell. 'But Bridget might interpret the letter we read as nasty.'

Craig answered the door and took us downstairs to the basement, where Yves was cutting out striped velvet material.

'Ah, a woman!' said Yves. 'We were just arguing over what to call the colours for our catalogue. I say sapphire and emerald, but Craig says navy and green. What do you say?'

'Sapphire and emerald,' I said. 'It sounds more classy and – interesting.'

Robert looked surprised. I suppose he thought I'd be aggravated or suspicious. I was feeling bad tempered and the effort to disguise it was colossal.

Yves looked triumphant.

'And it's more precise,' I continued. 'There are lots of greens, but emerald says it exactly.'

Craig smiled at Yves. 'You win.'

The workroom was tidy and looked organized. There were books of designs, two sewing machines, tape measures, two tailor's dummies, scissors hanging on hooks and pins stuck into cushions. Photos of young women, who looked familiar, adorned room dividers. I took a closer look. One was Phoebe, the other two were Kate and Fleur.

'Where are your wives?' I asked.

'Kate's working at our shop and Fleur's at her ante-natal class,' said Craig. 'You've come about the fire?'

Robert nodded. 'There are some things we have to ask you. Bridget's made some allegations.'

Both men looked uncomfortable.

'We're sorry to pry, but we have to ask,' Robert said.

'Yes,' I began. 'She said – '

'I know what she's said,' Craig interrupted. He looked at Yves. 'She's right. I'm only telling you this to get it out of the way. It's nothing to do with the case.'

'It might do,' I said.

They looked alarmed.

'Was she threatening to expose your homosexuality to your parents, Mr Lefevre?' Robert asked, sounding compassionate.

'Yves please, call me Yves. Er, she was, but, that is what I think at first. After I talk to Phoebe, I not take it so serious. She like the power of me being afraid. That's what Phoebe tell me. She knew Bridget before. They used to work together at the same hospital.'

'Phoebe knows?' I asked.

'Yes,' said Craig. 'She's the sort you tell your troubles too. She's kind – wise, not judgmental and we knew she'd keep our secret. Yves was desperate – so desperate he wanted to move. One afternoon when Phoebe was modelling for us, we confided in her. She said not to worry. And then – but this is Phoebe for you – so sensible. She told us it might be a good idea if we went to a different church from Bridget.'

'So we did,' said Yves.

'None of the other neighbours know?' I asked.

'No, I don't think so,' said Craig. 'Unless Bridget told them.'

'Bridget said you were rude to her,' Robert said to Yves.

'He was.' Craig laughed. 'She said she'd be one of our models. He told her we only used attractive women.'

'Why were you so cruel?' I asked.

Yves shrugged. 'I was honest. She look like a concentration camp victim. Even in designer clothes she would still be ugly.'

'If you'd been tactful you might have saved yourself the worry of being threatened about your lifestyle. Just because a women is plain doesn't mean she deserves a man's scorn,' I said aware of my own plain face and mousy hair.

'It wasn't just that,' Craig said. 'She was pushy and making snide comments about Phoebe.'

'What sort of comments?'

'Something about her being too plump to be a model. I don't remember exactly.'

I looked at the photos. 'Do you pay Phoebe when she models for you?'

'No,' said Craig. 'She keeps the outfits of her choice.'

'How many?' I asked.

Craig and Yves looked confused. 'Well, how ever many she wants, ' Craig said.

'She's never greedy – it's usually just one per season,' Yves added quickly. 'But we make her take more.'

I was about to ask why, when Craig said, 'Phoebe's got lots of friends – she does a lot of things – she goes lots of places. People see her wearing our designs and they ask where she bought them. People from Pengelly House come to our shop because of her. Her agent bought an outfit because Phoebe gave her our catalogue. She's a good advertisement for us, because she's so beautiful.'

'You do mail order too?' Robert asked.

Yves gave us both catalogues. I nearly told him we were investigating a murder, not shopping for clothes, but decided they might close up. I asked instead, 'The night of the fire and the party at Pengelly House Phoebe was wearing a chocolate and gold outfit. Was it one of your designs?'

'Yes,' said Craig. 'It's one she chose to keep. Is it important?'

'Bridget wondered how Phoebe could afford them.'

Robert looked annoyed. I realized I'd forgotten to tell him about the e-mail from Bridget.

Yves took a sharp intake of breath. 'Bridget is trying to make things bad for Phoebe?'

'Well – ' I began.

'At least she can't accuse her of setting fire to her house,' said Craig with satisfaction. 'She was at a party at Pengelly House to celebrate – '

'Yes, we know,' I said.

'If Bridget had told your parents, how would they have reacted?' Robert asked Yves.

'The shock – it would have killed my mother.' He spread his hands. 'My father – I don't know. He would be angry – worse than angry. It would have ruined my family.'

'You could have denied it,' Robert suggested.

'I can't lie – not to my parents – not to anyone.'

Robert looked at Craig. 'What about your parents?'

Craig's smile was cynical. 'I would have lied. I'm a good liar. My parents aren't Catholics, but they are conventional and wouldn't understand. They wouldn't disown me, but they'd be upset. It's why we went to lots of trouble to keep it hidden. And of course we want children.'

'And what about Fleur and Kate's parents?'

'Kate's family would be upset, not as upset as mine, but they would be unhappy and shocked,' said Yves. 'Fleur's family would be angry. They are Catholics. Very strict. Fleur went to a convent school. They might never want to see her again. It's better not to have anyone at all knowing.'

I was curious, but didn't know how to frame the questions about paternity and conception and how they had done it. I wanted to know how they were going to bring up their children. Were they going to pretend they were normal married couples?

After leaving Craig and Yves we stood in the front garden of Bridget's house. I studied the layout and saw there was a gap in the yew tree hedge. It was wide enough for a person to get through easily.

'Five minutes,' I said to Robert. 'That's all it would take. Phoebe or Stuart leave their bike at the back gate, run through the garden to the back door and unlock it, go to the front door and pick up the turpentine soaked material, which they'd left there in a plastic bag before going to Pengelly House, slip though the yew tree hedge, push the material through the letter box, light a taper and drop it through the letter box, wait a few seconds to make sure it's ignited and go back through the hedge. The gap is close to the house – it could have taken less than five minutes.'

Robert said nothing. But I was right. I know I was right and so, I think, did he.

11

ROBERT

Keeping my knowledge regarding the numbering of Farrier Way, and its possible significance, a secret, made me feel deceitful. I decided to tell Sharon and risk her scorn or accusations that I was trying to get Phoebe off the list of suspects. As we left Craig and Yves I decided to test her. It was possible that she had noticed the way the houses were numbered and not grasped the implications. 'Have you noticed – '

'Phoebe broke her word,' Sharon said as we walked back to our car.

'What?'

'In that letter she showed us she told Bridget that she wouldn't say anything about them having known each other before, but she told the, er, Yves and Craig.'

'Only because Bridget had threatened them,' I said. 'I'm not sure if this is relevant, but – '

Sharon interrupted me again. 'They've got a good set-up going,' she said caustically. 'It's another form of tax evasion – the free model gets free clothes – no money paid – no tax owed.'

'When did Bridget tell you about Phoebe's clothes?' I asked as we drove to see Bridget.

'She sent me an e-mail.'

'Thanks for telling me.'

'I'm sorry, Robert, I forgot.'

Of course you did, I thought.

'Bridget wondered how they managed it, and so do I.'

I didn't respond.

'How do you think they did it?'

'Did what?' I asked although I knew.

She sighed. 'You know what I'm talking about.'

'Enlighten me.'

'Do you think they overcame their revulsion of the opposite sex and did it?

'What?'

'Sergeant, I'll hit you in a minute.'

'Hit me and I'll report you. I refuse to speculate. It's not relevant to the case.'

'It could be.'

'How?'

That kept her quiet. I let five minutes pass before I said, 'I doubt that the revelation about Yves would have killed his mother.'

'You think he's lying?' Sharon said sharply.

'No. It's just that parent's reactions are often not as drastic as we anticipate. I was expecting my father to be . . . not angry, but very disappointed that I wanted to join the police, but he accepted it. I'm sure he was disappointed, but he – '

'A career choice is different to being a homosexual, Sergeant. How would he have reacted if you'd confessed you liked men?'

'I don't know. I've never thought about it.'

'If either of my brothers had told our father they were homosexuals he would have been furious.'

'What about your mother?'

'She would have been distraught and cried for days. So I do understand why Yves and the others wanted to keep it secret.'

We didn't speak again till we arrived in Bodmin and Sharon had to give me directions because I took a wrong turning.

Bridget's mother was out.

'Gone shopping,' said Bridget. 'For food.' She sounded as defensive as if we'd suspected her mother was robbing a bank.

To try and disguise my feeling of abhorrence towards her, I accepted her offer of coffee even though I knew it would be instant. It was weak and coffee granules were floating on top. I thanked her and took a couple of sips. Unable to drink anymore I put my mug down.

'The letter that Phoebe sent you when you moved next door to her – can you tell us what it said?' Sharon asked.

'Full of threats.'

'What sort of threats?'

"You'll be sorry you moved next door to me', sort of threats.'

'Could you be more exact?'

'How exact do you want?'

'The nature of the threats. For example, did she make you worry your life was in danger?'

'Yeah, but I weren't that worried. Thought she was just doing it out of revenge. To scare me, you know. If I'd of known, I would of moved.'

'Did she mention anything about burning your house down?'

'No,' Bridget admitted reluctantly.

'I know it's difficult,' I chipped in, 'but it would be useful if you can remember the type of things she said. 'Were her threats aimed at you or your whole family?'

'Just me, I think.'

'What did you do with the letter?' I asked.

'Tore it up. Sorry I did now. It'd be proof against her.'

'Did you tear it up as soon as you read it?' asked Sharon.

Bridget shook her head. 'Can't remember. Oh, yes, I think I did. She said things like 'I'll pay you back and don't think you can plot against me and get me made redundant and stop me from getting another job. I'll make you suffer for what you did.' Them sort of things she said.'

'How did you stop her from getting another job?' I asked.

Bridget sneered. 'She and that Margaret thought they was clever, but I knew what they'd do before they even done it. I'm not stupid. Thick as thieves them two are. Went to university together. Think they're so smart. Even Elaine didn't think of it, but I did. Phoebe gave Margaret's name for references when she were looking for a job. Letters from other hospitals arrived addressed to Margaret and calling her The Medical Records Manager. I took them in the mail room, before they got to medical records. And me and Elaine opened them and rang the hospitals and gave an honest reference, not the glowing fake ones Margaret would of given.'

'How did Phoebe find out?' I asked.

'She couldn't get a job – never even got asked for a interview. Margaret said she never got no letters asking for a reference. They caught on to what me and Elaine was doing and got one of Phoebe's relations, who worked for the council, to send a letter asking for a reference. It were bad luck Phoebe were there when I rang. Elaine were away so I done it and Phoebe recognized my voice. Wrote a letter of complaint to Human Resources, she did. But they never did nothing about it. Phoebe and Margaret was wrong to do it – that's what Elaine and me argued and they agreed with us.'

My loathing of Bridget increased. Even when Phoebe had

been made redundant, Bridget had felt no guilt, and had gone to the trouble of making sure she couldn't get another job.

'I see,' said Sharon. 'Why didn't you take the threatening letter from Phoebe to the police?'

'They wouldn't of taken no notice. And then she went and told all the neighbours horrible things about me. Lies. All lies.'

'Was the letter handwritten?' I asked.

Bridget shook her head. 'Typed.'

Sharon produced the letter. 'Phoebe printed out a copy of the letter she said she sent you.'

Bridget flushed a dark, ugly red. She reluctantly took the letter and read it. Her hands were trembling. She whispered, 'It's not true . . . this one.'

Sharon looked convinced.

'Did she send you one like this . . . perhaps after she sent you the nastier one?' I asked. 'Perhaps she was sorry . . . '

Bridget, though rattled, did not fall into my trap, by taking the escape route I offered. 'Never got this one. This isn't what she wrote.'

'It was on her computer,' I said. 'The date's about two years ago – that's when you moved to Farrier Way, isn't it?'

'I never got it. Just the nasty one. She was planning it back then. This is proof. She never sent me this one. It was another one.'

We let a minute elapse, while Bridget composed herself.

'Did your mother know you were secretly seeing your father?' Sharon asked.

Her flush, which had begun to fade, darkened again. 'Who told you?'

Sharon looked as if she was trying to remember. 'Sorry, I've forgotten. Did your mother know?'

Bridget looked at the door fearfully. 'No,' she whispered. 'I never told her. She'll be back soon. Please don't tell her.'

'Why not?' I asked.

'She'll be upset.'

'Did she like Declan?' I asked.

Tears poured down her face. 'She's all I've got now.'

'What about your father?' I asked.

'He's got a new girlfriend,' she whispered. 'Divorced – four kids – they like him and – ' Bridget jumped at the instant I heard keys in the door.

Mrs Bradley came in with two plastic carrier bags. 'Not doing no good in catching who killed me grandson, are you?' she said.

'Thanks for your time,' Sharon said to Bridget.

Wanting to know how true the allegations about Mrs Bradley being possessive were, I decided to test her. I turned to Bridget. 'Are you going to move back to Farrier Way when the damage is – '

Mrs Bradley glared at me. 'No she's not. She's going to stay here with me where she'll be safe.'

Bridget chewed her lip. 'I haven't – '

'You'll be safe here, away from that murderer Phoebe.'

'When we find out who did it, you can move back,' I said to Bridget.

'No she won't,' snapped Mrs Bradley. 'Them neighbours was horrible to Bridget. When the insurance has paid out we're going to move away from here to somewhere nice. We're going to buy a flat somewhere. We could even move back to Ireland.'

Bridget looked horrified. She was as trapped as she'd been before her marriage.

'Did you ever meet Phoebe, Mrs Bradley?' Sharon asked.

'Once. Come here for dinner, she did. Bridget were all

nervous, weren't you? Everything had to be just right, didn't it? Anyone would think the queen were coming. She hated being here. Beneath her, she thought.'

'What did she say?' I asked.

'Didn't have to say it – writ on her face. She were . . . what's the word, Bridget?'

Bridget shook her head. 'Acted as if she were doing us a favour just being here.'

'Acted like the queen, she did. Pretending to enjoy herself when you could see she couldn't wait to leave. Picked at her food like a mouse. And I'd gone to a lot of trouble because she were a vegetarian. Nervous she were of going out to the car in the dark – as if she were going to be killed by a gang. Wish she had of been – then she wouldn't have murdered me grandson. When are you going to arrest her?'

'When we've got sufficient evidence,' Sharon said. 'Thank you for your time.'

'Why haven't you got no evidence now? You should be looking for it, not coming here wasting time.'

'Murder by arson is difficult because most evidence is destroyed in the fire and by the firemen,' Sharon said. 'Footprints, fingerprints, DNA – '

Mrs Bradley grunted. 'Good excuse. That's all you police ever do. Making excuses is all you're good at. You should be questioning that spoilt brat Phoebe, not coming here upsetting my Bridget. And don't say you never upset her – I can see she's been crying.'

It would have been futile to explain to this woman the importance of psychology and criminal profiling in cases like this.

Sharon looked at Bridget. 'Did you know Phoebe has seven siblings?'

Bridget looked blank.

'Brothers and sisters,' I said with a smile to hide how appalled I was by her ignorance.

'Yeah. Never stopped talking about them. All had silly names too.'

'What's this got to do with her trying to murder my Bridget?'

'It's just that you, on more than one occasion, called her a spoilt brat,' Sharon replied.

'She is a spoilt brat, that's why,' Mrs Bradley snapped. 'Them brothers and sisters spoiled her.'

Bridget nodded vigorously. 'The reason she never wanted to wear no uniform was because she loved swanning about in all her fancy clothes. Always bragging that she had fourteen blouses and fourteen jumpers – one for every day of the fortnight. Seven skirts and seven pairs of trousers she had too – one for every day of the week. And it's not just jumpers she had lots of – she had jackets too – don't know how many – probably seven – one for – '

'Where did she come in the family?' I asked.

Bridget looked confused. 'What do you mean?'

'Was she the oldest, the youngest?'

'She were the fourth. Two boys was first, then two girls and then boy, girl, boy, girl. Never stopped going on about it, she didn't.'

Mrs Bradley looked furious. 'What's that got to do with – '

To my astonishment Sharon said, 'Criminal profiling and the way someone's mind works, Mrs Bradley. I associate the term 'spoilt brat' with 'only child'. Not only was Phoebe one of eight children she was a middle child – middle children are famously unspoilt. Thank you both for your time. Oh, did you like Declan?'

'What sort of a question is that?'

Sharon raised her eyebrows. 'Just a simple question, Mrs

Bradley. Did you like Declan?'

'Why shouldn't I?'

'I don't know.' Sharon's smile was sly. 'Why wouldn't you? Did you ever have disagreements?'

'What are you suggesting?'

'Nothing. Just asking if you and Declan ever disagreed.'

Mrs Bradley was looking so belligerent I said to her, 'We're trying to work out what Declan was like – because he might have been the target. So what was he like? Did he have any enemies that you know of?'

'He were all right, I suppose,' she said. 'Bridget could of done better.'

'Why were you staying here the night of the fire?' I asked Bridget.

'Mum had an accident.'

'Nothing serious, I hope,' said Sharon.

'She fell down the stairs.'

'Nasty,' I said. 'They're concrete. It's a wonder you didn't break anything. Are you badly bruised?'

'Yeah.'

'Have you been to the doctor?' asked Sharon.

'No.'

Sharon and I looked at each other.

'Why not?' I asked.

'Why should I? I'm not one to make a fuss – not like some people who go to the doctor when they've got a sore toe or a cold.'

'I would have thought that if you fell down the stairs, you would have at least needed to go to a doctor.'

She scowled. 'What's that got to do with anything?'

'Several people have informed us that you didn't like Declan. You didn't want Bridget to marry him and you hardly ever saw your grandson. You went to Farrier Way

143

and Bridget's neighbours witnessed you and Declan having an argument.'

'They shouldn't of been listening. Should of minded their own business.'

'According to them – '

'Are you accusing me of murdering me own grandson?'

'We're not accusing you of anything, Mrs Bradley,' Sharon said innocently. 'We are trying to establish if Declan was the intended target. We've been to your house, Bridget. Were you and Declan going to let the basement flat?'

She looked guilty.

Mrs Bradley glowered at her. 'What basement flat? You never said nothing about no basement flat!'

'The last owner had her daughter staying with her when she got divorced,' babbled Bridget. 'She were the one what made the basement into a flat. Not me and Declan.'

'You and Declan told me that it were full of rubbish when I wanted to go down there.'

'It were,' said Bridget.

'You never told me nothing about no flat. I could of moved in there and looked after me grandson when you and Declan was at work.'

'It wasn't ready for no one to move into,' protested Bridget. 'We wasn't going to get anyone down there – we was going to turn it into . . . '

'A what?' Mrs Bradley snarled.

Aware that Bridget had been keeping a great deal from her mother, we left.

I realized that Mrs Bradley called the baby 'me grandson' rather than Bridget's baby or son. And she often referred to Bridget as 'my Bridget' not simply Bridget.

'After that episode I think Mrs Bradley is more of a suspect than we thought,' I said as we reached the bottom of the stairs.

'Mrs Bradley would have had to get from her flat to the car park without being seen,' said Sharon as we walked back to the car park.

I looked back at the flats. 'Her flat doesn't overlook the car park. If she left the flat quietly – '

'Very risky.'

'Not if Bridget is a sound sleeper. And if her mother planned this she may have drugged her. It's easy to get sleeping pills from the doctor. All she – '

'But she ran the risk of being seen, if not by Bridget then by someone else,' argued Sharon.

'Shapeless clothes, a jacket with a hood. No one likes her. She's lonely.'

'Would she have murdered her grandson?'

'Difficult to know. She'd lost Bridget to Declan and his parents, and she was lonely and isolated. She must have known that Declan had life insurance – '

'How do you know he had life insurance?'

'Because – ' I stopped. 'I'd assumed Mrs Bradley had meant life insurance, but she could have meant house insurance. But if he had life insurance as well, Bridget will end up very well off. Mrs Bradley has the strongest motives so far.'

'Phoebe had lots more reasons – '

'Mrs Bradley will get what she wants – not just Bridget back living with her, but she's planning to move somewhere much better than a council estate. Everyone here seems to hate her, she might think it's all their fault and people will be more friendly somewhere else. Phoebe would have gained nothing, but a lifetime of guilt.'

'You're so anxious to turn suspicion away from Phoebe.'

'I'm anxious that we arrest the right person. And why are

you so keen to make a case against Phoebe?'

'I think Bridget could be telling the truth about the letter Phoebe wrote.'

I felt like telling her not to be a fool, but I made an effort to sound rational. 'To me it's obvious she was lying. Bridget's mother will gain not just emotionally, but she'll share Bridget's money too. Bridget's a bereaved wreck and her mother thinks she'll be easy to manipulate.'

When we got back to the station there was an e-mail from Elaine. She had addressed it to me with a copy for Sharon. Serve her right, I thought when I saw she'd called me Inspector.

Dear Inspector Trevelyan,

My jaw is broken and has been wired up, so I can't speak. One of my staff attacked me. Pity you didn't arrive slightly earlier or you would have witnessed it. He is deranged. He wasn't doing his job properly, and when I took him to task he punched me. The other staff are lying when they say I fell. I didn't. He attacked me. His name is Leslie Hooper. He's mad and hopeless at his job. This is an official report and I demand that he is arrested and charged with assault.

Elaine Dunn (Medical Records Manager)

Sharon came storming up to my desk. 'Hello, Inspector.'

'I was about to reply and, yes, I was going to tell her our correct titles.'

'What's the matter with these women? She's a manager. Why does she assume that just because you're a man, you're my superior?'

146

I clicked on reply and began to type. 'I have no idea. Ask her.'

Dear Ms Dunn,

Your allegation regarding Leslie Hooper will be
looked into. Thank you for letting us know.
Inspector Sharon Richardson and I came to visit
you at the medical records department because
of the arson attack on Bridget Murphy's house,
in which her husband and baby son died. Is
there anything you can tell us that might help
our investigation?

I hope you are recovering from your injuries.

Yours sincerely,

Sergeant Robert Trevelyan.

Sharon was hovering by my shoulder.
'Happy?' I asked.
'It'll do. This Leslie Hooper must be the one that nearly knocked me over.'

Sharon and I visited the medical records department in the morning. She rejected my suggestion that we go to casualty and ask a doctor if it was possible Elaine had fallen.
'Where's Leslie Hooper?' she asked the nearest woman, who looked startled, as she held up her badge.
Margaret came over holding a pile of files. 'Hello.'
'Where's Leslie Hooper?' Sharon repeated.
They all looked guilty.
'I don't know,' said Margaret.
'We want to question him about the attack on Elaine Dunn.'

'She fell,' said Margaret.

The others nodded. I noticed that none of them were wearing the brown uniforms. Some wore jeans. Margaret was dressed in a navy skirt and pale blue shirt. She looked younger and much more attractive. The uniform had made her look sick.

'Her injuries are consistent with being punched on the jaw,' said Sharon. 'Are you aware that lying to the police during an investigation is a criminal offence?'

No one spoke.

'Where is he?'

'I don't know,' said Margaret with a touch of defiance. 'Probably at home.'

'Where does he live?'

Margaret shook her head. The others followed her example.

'We'll find out from Human Resources. Can I remind you that this is a murder investigation.'

Margaret looked shocked. 'Elaine's dead?'

'No, but – '

'Pity,' someone, I didn't see who, muttered.

'Bridget Murphy's house was set alight,' Sharon snapped. 'Deliberately. Her husband and baby son burnt to death. A lot of people in this department have admitted they hated her. Leslie Hooper punched your manager in the face. He's a suspect. A murder suspect. Remember that before you lie for him. And remember that lying to the police does not go unpunished. Come on, Sergeant.'

We walked to the door, but before we could open it, Margaret said, 'He wouldn't have murdered anyone. He's not violent.'

Sharon spun around and glared incredulously at her. 'Not violent? A man who punches a woman, for whatever reason, is violent. It is a violent act.'

'She provoked – ' Margaret stopped abruptly.

Sharon smiled. 'You realize what you just admitted?'

Margaret turned pale.

We left. We went to Human Resources and got Leslie Hooper's address. He lived on the outskirts of Truro in an attractive terraced house with a steep front garden. A middle aged woman answered the door. It was obvious from her reaction that she knew why we were there. She was nervous and her voice was panic stricken.

'He moved out. I haven't seen him for months. We had an argument. I don't know where he lives now. He's not been in touch since he moved out.'

She was an unconvincing liar. I expected Sharon to ask if we could search the house, but Mrs Hooper, babbled on. 'He's not here. You can have a look for yourself if you don't believe me. Please, I'd rather you did, so you could see for yourself – '

'That's all right, Mrs Hooper. But if he does contact you please ask him to get in touch with us,' said Sharon giving her a card.

'We're going to see Phoebe now,' said Sharon when we left Mrs Hooper.

I said nothing. She looked at me as we marched to the car. 'You think I was harsh, Sergeant?'

'To Margaret, yes. You were okay with Mrs Hooper.'

'You approve of men punching women?'

'Of course not, but from what people say, Elaine Dunn is a nasty – '

'So you think she asked for it?'

'She provoked him,' I said as we reached the car. 'Probably humiliated him in front of all the staff. According to Phoebe and the others, another chap had a nervous

149

breakdown because of Elaine and Bridget.'

We didn't speak again until we were out of Truro. Then Sharon said in her most hectoring tone, 'Apart from me, how many people have you hated? People you knew, don't count politicians etcetera.'

'Not that many. And as I've never said I hated you, please don't – '

'Okay. Have you punched anyone or killed them?'

The honest answer would have been 'yes' and 'don't know', but Sharon was driving and might have run off the road. And Vanessa and I had sworn never to tell anyone about our encounter in America.

'Well, Sergeant, have you?'

'No.'

'Would you?'

'In self-defence – in a kill or be killed situation – '

'I would say you are one of the least likely people to thump a woman.' She made it sound like an insult. 'Have you ever been in a brawl?'

'No.' I was relieved to be able to tell the truth. The confrontation with the rapists in the forest could not be described as a brawl.

'I'm more likely to lash out in a temper than you are.' Her tone was even more derisory. 'If you had children would you smack them?'

I'd never smacked Hannah. Even if I had believed in smacking, Hannah had never behaved badly enough to deserve it. On one rare occasion when I was impatient with her because we were running late, I'd raised my voice, 'For goodness sake, hurry up, Hannah!'

She'd looked at me wide eyed with surprise. 'All right, Daddy, calm down.'

'Sergeant, would you smack – '

'No.'

'There you are then. You'll be saying next that Bridget deserved to be murdered.'

'She wasn't murdered and although it's probable she was the target, it could have been Declan.'

'We haven't found or heard of anyone who hated Declan enough to murder him.'

'That doesn't mean they don't exist.'

'Suppose that's true. Why would someone hate him?' Her tone became sarcastic. 'Could someone have been harbouring a secret passion for Bridget?'

'Unlikely. She's not the type that men would fight over – unless they were desperate.'

'But Phoebe would be, wouldn't she?'

Not caring how exasperated I sounded I expelled my breath.

'You think she's beautiful, don't you?'

'Please stop telling me what I think.'

That was when I decided to pursue the theory that Phoebe had been the intended victim and not tell Sharon. I'd do it in my own time.

12

SHARON

There was an e-mail from Elaine Dunn when I arrived at work. I printed out two copies, called Robert into my office and handed him the two pages.

Dear Inspector Richardson,

When I took over the Medical Records Department it was in the most frightful state. The staff thought it was a social club, not a place of work. My predecessor apparently encouraged this. I immediately set about correcting this state of affairs. Bridget was the only person who was willing to help me. She was an excellent worker so I promoted her. The rest rebelled and made their hostility towards me obvious.
The ringleaders were Phoebe Harris and Margaret Fox. Another ringleader was a male member of staff who had since left due to mental illness.
I like order and hate sloppy dressing. Many of the staff wore jeans to work, which is unprofessional. I introduced uniforms. Some of the staff were happy with this as it saved their clothes, but others, led by Phoebe, rebelled.

'Even with my lack of interest in clothes, I can understand why Phoebe rebelled,' I said. 'The uniforms are hideous.'

'They are,' Robert agreed.

> She argued that she was not in the public eye,
> did not wear jeans to work and that spending
> money on uniforms was a waste of NHS money.
> I took her and Margaret and four other
> members of staff to a disciplinary board when
> they refused to wear the uniforms I'd ordered. I
> won my case. Phoebe said they all looked like a
> bunch of refugees.

Robert smiled. 'A good description.'

> They looked professional and smart. When I
> first saw Phoebe she was wearing a pink blouse
> with a white stripe and a burgundy skirt, which
> is as unprofessional as you can get.

'If Elaine thinks Phoebe looked unprofessional, what did she think of Bridget's clothes?'

'Even the hideous uniforms would be an improvement on what we saw her wearing,' said Robert. 'Was Elaine wearing a uniform when we saw her?'

I tried to think back, but all I could recall was her lying on the floor with blood on her chin. I shook my head and we went back to the e-mail.

> Because Bridget and I were managers, I chose
> different uniforms for us. Phoebe had the nerve
> to say that if they had to wear uniforms then
> Bridget and I should wear the same ones.
> Again, I won. Human Resources agreed that as
> senior managers we were entitled to wear
> different uniforms.

I shook my head in disbelief. 'What was her motive? Did she want them all to look dreary and ugly?'

153

'Yes,' said Robert. 'I think that's exactly what she wanted.'

'Why?'

'Making them all look the same robs them of their individuality. Making them wear ugly clothes robs them of their confidence. If she and Bridget wore more attractive uniforms that would make them feel superior.'

'But Bridget's taste in clothes is dire. How would – '

'Take it from the viewpoint of the rest of the staff – Bridget wears an attractive uniform – therefore she looks better than they do,' Robert said.

The filing system at that time was straight numerical, but files where a patient had not attended the hospital for 10 years were stored elsewhere. I set about changing the system to the more efficient terminal digit system. If you don't understand this, it means that if a file number is 123456 it is filed under 56. To make this more clear number 123400 is filed in block 00.

'Does she think we're stupid?' Robert said irritably.

I smiled. 'She's probably so used to Bridget's ignorance she thinks everyone's the same.'

To implement this new system I needed people to work overtime. I thought that as they were working for the NHS they should be willing to work unpaid overtime. Only Bridget was willing to do this.

'I bet she was,' said Robert. 'It gave her an excuse to get away from her appalling mother.'

It was an enormous task. And to my annoyance none of the other staff were willing to work paid overtime either. When I tried to force the issue with Phoebe she said she had a rampant social life. This meant I had to go to an agency and pay for temps to do the majority of the work. Bridget and I often worked till midnight.

'Maybe Elaine's got a horrible mother too,' I said.

Because of the permanent staff's attitude the changeover took far longer and cost more than it should have. When the work was complete I set about trimming the staff. Fortunately some had already left, one I mentioned earlier, had a breakdown. I made Phoebe redundant.
Bridget had no idea that Phoebe lived in the house next door before she moved in. When they were friends Phoebe and her husband had lived in a smaller house. Phoebe ignored Bridget when they became neighbours and she must have poisoned the other neighbours' minds against Bridget too. It's not as if she'd lived there very long herself, but she behaved as if she'd been born there.
So I certainly think that Margaret, Phoebe, Leslie Hooper and the man who went crazy would have felt enough ill-will towards Bridget to kill her. Phoebe, due to her close proximity to Bridget's house, would be my chief suspect.
How is your search for Leslie Hooper progressing? Please keep me informed. I want to be in court when his case comes up.

Elaine Dunn (Medical Records Manager)

I hit reply.

Dear Ms Dunn,

Thanks for all the information. We went to the

155

address provided by Human Resources for Leslie Hooper, but his mother informed us that he no longer lives there. She does not have his new address.

Yours sincerely,

Inspector Richardson.

I laughed when she immediately replied telling us she was sure his mother was lying and to put a watch on his house.

'Does she think we've nothing else to do? Self-obsessed woman,' Robert muttered.

'But, as Elaine pointed out, he may be the one who set fire to Bridget's house,' I reminded him.

When Phoebe answered the front door and saw us she looked frightened.

'We need to ask you some more questions,' I said in my sternest voice. If she had set fire to Bridget's house I wanted her to crack. If we'd had any evidence against her I would have made her come to the station.

She took us into the kitchen. 'Would you like some tea or coffee?' Her voice was shaking.

'No thank you.' I outlined what Bridget had said.

'She's a liar. The letter I gave you was the only one I wrote to her.'

'It must have been difficult living next door to her. Not only was she your enemy, she had a baby. She told us about your miscarriages and the baby that died.'

Her eyes flooded with tears. Robert sat still. His face was blank. Phoebe got up and tore some paper towels from a roll. She wiped her eyes and sat down again.

'We've heard that she flaunted her baby at you.'

Phoebe shook her head. 'I didn't notice,' she managed to say.

I thought that was unlikely. If Margaret had noticed when she visited, then Phoebe must have noticed too.

'You've got plenty of reasons to want her dead. One, she betrayed your friendship. Two, she turned against you. Three, she sided with Elaine. Four, she used her power to bully you. Five, she helped get you made redundant.'

'I was – '

I ignored her. 'Six, she tried to stop you getting another job. Then she moves next door with her husband and baby. Not only that, but she wants to make improvements that you disagree with. Were you worried that it would devalue your house?'

Phoebe had recovered her composure, but was still pale. 'I am not a murderer,' she said steadily.

'You had eight reasons to want her dead.'

'No. I was glad when I was made redundant. It got me out of the snake-pit that medical records had become. Elaine and Bridget tried to get me to commit a serious offence so they could sack me, but it didn't work.'

'How?'

'They tried to provoke me into either hitting one of them or swearing at them. They were both taunting me. Bridget's a fool. She should have known it wouldn't work. She's never heard me swear and I don't go around hitting people.' She took a deep breath. 'I got put on three months special paid leave and my redundancy payment was good.'

'Still,' I continued, 'That's seven reasons.'

'It's not. I never resented the fact she had a baby.'

'Even if that's true, that leaves six reasons. I would have hated her if I was you. So would most people. Did you hate her?'

'Yes and I despised her too. If things had got unbearable Stuart and I would have moved. But they didn't get unbearable.'

'What would have made it unbearable?' I asked.

'If she'd turned all the neighbours against me.'

'The neighbours didn't like her. Did you turn them against her?'

She shook her head. 'She did that herself.'

'Not a good time to sell up now, is it?'

'We've added a lot of value to the house. We renovated it when we moved in – got the windows repaired, the whole place rewired and put in a new kitchen and bathroom. Even with falling property prices it's worth a lot more than it was when we bought it. And we've done up the garden.'

Phoebe and Stuart's kitchen was attractive in a different way to Alice's. The units were dark wood, the floors were slate and the worktops were granite. A coffee machine, in shining chrome, stood on the work top. Structurally the houses were all alike, but the ones we had been in all looked individual. Alice was the only one whose kitchen was in the basement and her units were cream.

Robert's silence was annoying me. 'When you and Bridget were friends did you visit her flat?' I asked.

'Yes. Once. She invited me for dinner.'

'Did you enjoy yourself?'

'No. Her mother was hostile and the food was revolting. No wonder Bridget's so thin.'

'Did you and Bridget have much in common?'

'Not really.'

'But you were friends?'

'I felt sorry for her at first, but she had an engaging personality, even if she does use people. We weren't good friends – just friends. She kept asking me for advice about how to cope with her mother.'

'What did you say?'

'I advised her to leave home and get a flat as far away from her mother as possible. She was going to. I went flat hunting with her. She found a place that she liked, but her mother said she'd kill herself when Bridget told her she was moving out.'

'Bridget seems to have lots of friends. Someone told us that everyone loves her. It seems as if you and your neighbours were the only ones who disliked her.'

'All the staff in medical records hate her, except Elaine. We used to like her, but that was before Elaine came. And the neighbours don't like her because – '

'Yes, we know. They said she didn't fit in.'

'She didn't.'

'Do you agree you have a lot of motives?'

'No. I had reasons to hate Bridget, but not motives to kill her. And even if I did, I would never kill an innocent man or a baby.'

'Did you like her husband?'

'I didn't know him.'

'Did you ever speak to him?'

'No.'

'But he was your neighbour. He'd done nothing to you. As you say, he was innocent.'

Phoebe started tearing up the paper towel. 'Before we moved here we had the chance to buy into Pengelly House. We decided against it because we were about to exchange contracts. We loved this house and looked forward to doing it up. Now I wish we'd moved into Pengelly House. This is supposed to be such a happy time for me. My book's published and I'm working on my second one. But instead of enjoying my success I'm living in fear that I'm going to be arrested for something I haven't done. Every time someone comes to the door – '

Robert stood up. 'I think we've covered everything. Thank you for your time.'

I knew he was furious. I also knew I'd sounded cruel. We drove for miles in silence.

'Thank you for supporting me back there, Sergeant.'

He didn't reply.

'Well, answer me.'

'I'll reply to any question you ask. But you made a statement, you did not ask a question.' His tone was icy.

I sighed. 'Do you want to solve this case?'

'Yes. Solve being the vital word. We won't solve it if we arrest the wrong person.'

'This may not have occurred to you, Sergeant, but as Bridget is still alive, the murderer might try again.'

'It did occur to me. Very early on in the case. That is if Bridget was the intended victim.'

'Of course she was. I think the only way we're going to solve this case is to get a confession. We've got no DNA, no fingerprints and no witnesses. I was trying to make Phoebe crack.'

'The best way to do that is to be gentle and sympathetic. You were brutal. If she did set fire to the house you didn't get the result you wanted, did you?'

'We'll have to keep at her.'

'You keep at her. I refuse to be part of any scene like that.'

'Then, Sergeant, you can do the questioning and I'll keep quiet. See how far we get. Think about it. Phoebe's highly intelligent. If she's going to murder someone she'd make sure she had an unbreakable alibi.'

'Her alibi wasn't unbreakable – you broke it,' he retorted.

'You wouldn't have spoken to Phoebe like that if Stuart had been there. And brace yourself for a complaint – '

'You're going to complain about me?'

'No. But Phoebe might.'

We were not far from St Austell when Robert slowed down the car.

'Are you in a hurry to get home?' he asked curtly.

'Why?'

'There's a farm shop nearby – I want to get something for dinner. It won't take long, but I can come back later.'

'No, fine,' I said. I was interested to see what sort of things he'd buy.

He turned right at a sign for The Lost Gardens of Helligan. He parked the car and looked aggravated when I got out. 'You can stay here. I won't be long.'

'I've never been in a farm shop.'

He shrugged and walked off. I followed him. The farm shop was rustic but clean with baskets of vegetables labelled organic. He picked up leeks, carrots, broccoli and potatoes. The customers had refined accents and the people behind the counter had refined accents. But at least I didn't look out of place in my khaki cords, jumper and Barbour. Since my promotion I could afford pure wool jumpers, good cotton blouses and silk too if there was a sale. Luckily, I liked the earthy colours favoured by the upper-classes. I wore little make-up and kept my fingernails short and unpainted.

'Hello, Robert,' said the man at the meat counter.

After debating over duck breasts and a large piece of fillet steak, he chose the steak. Then he bought cream, apples and a tub of expensive vanilla ice cream.

When the woman at the counter asked him if he was going to make an apple pie he said, 'Tarte Tatin.'

'Have you won the lottery?' I asked when we were

161

walking back to the car.

'No. Why?'

'You spent more on dinner for tonight than I spend in a week.'

'It's for two people.'

I longed to ask if it was a girl, but even if I tried to sound casual, it would come out like an accusation. It was probably that blonde who'd slammed the door in my face. Or it might be a man.

'Even so, it's a lot of money,' I insisted.

'But terrific quality. Better than anything you'd get in a supermarket.'

'Free-range, organic. It's a con.'

'How do you know?'

'I've read articles in newspapers. You spend more money so you have to convince yourself it tastes better.'

He pointed the cardkey at the door. 'Have you ever tried it or are you just regurgitating what you've read?'

'I wouldn't waste my money. I'm not a gullible fool.'

'Neither am I,' he said coldly. 'It's not just about taste either – it's about treating animals and birds properly. Hens in battery farms have a terrible life.'

I tutted. 'And the poor non-organic vegetables – do they have a terrible life too?'

'They're sprayed with pesticides and – '

'Poor things – does it hurt them?'

I could tell he was angry because he crunched the gears. 'No, but it can harm humans – but not me, because I don't eat them.'

We drove to St Austell in silence.

'You had free-range organic bacon and eggs when you came to breakfast the other morning,' he said as he stopped outside my house. He didn't look at me and his tone was cold. 'You told me it was the best breakfast you'd ever had.'

I managed to smile. 'It was better than the canteen food.'

'I hope so.'

'Have a nice dinner,' I said as I got out of the car.

'Thank you.' His tone was still cold.

As I ate the macaroni cheese I'd heated in the microwave, I thought of Robert and the blonde feasting on their overpriced food. Would they have wine? I guessed he'd light the candles I'd seen. I imagined them going upstairs and making love. Or would they be overcome with passion and do it on the floor or the sofa while one of his classical CD's was playing? They might squabble. The blonde I'd seen had been crying, but she was angry with me. Had they been fighting about his infidelities? Did she think I was a rival? It's more likely that she looked at me and wondered what Robert saw in such a plain mouse. Why didn't he flirt with the girls at work? Maybe he was too sensible.

Once I'd thrown a plate of food at a boyfriend who said my cooking was rubbish. Had anyone ever thrown a plate of food at Robert? I had a slice of treacle tart for dessert and thought about Robert and the blonde eating the apple tart with a fancy name. I imagined it smothered in cream and ice cream.

After cataloguing the days events, I made a mug of hot chocolate and took it up to bed, dispirited by our lack of progress. Phoebe was top of my list of suspects, because she was the one with the most motives. I was certain she hadn't intended to kill the baby, but finding proof was hard unless she could be coaxed or trapped into a confession. I saw her as a normal woman who Bridget had pushed too far. Although she didn't look it, she must be in torment over the baby and confessing would be a relief.

I started to read Robert's notebook about the case of the

missing boy he had solved when he lived in St Margarets.

> *The house is large with 5 bedrooms. It is dreary, with*
> *brown walls and woodwork, dull ancestral portraits,*
> *dark floor boards covered with brown rugs and brown*
> *velvet upholstery and curtains. There is a tiger-skin rug*
> *on the floor of the drawing-room and another in the*
> *dining-room.*
> *The boy's bedroom could be that of an old man. There*
> *are no toys, games, pictures on the walls or anything to*
> *indicate it belongs to an 8 year old boy. Again the*
> *colour scheme is brown. It is tidy and clean. His shirts,*
> *trousers and jackets hang neatly in the wardrobe and*
> *two large chests of drawers hold his jumpers and*
> *underwear – all folded and ironed. It is unnaturally*
> *neat for a child.*
> *I already suspect what has happened, but just to make*
> *sure I checked. There is no school bag. I was hoping*
> *there would be. I have no evidence, just instinct.*

I was interested in what Robert had written and understood how his psychology worked. Anyone who made their little boy sleep in a bedroom like that was weird. Even on my parents' limited budget our bedrooms, when we were children, were bright, with cheerful curtains and pictures on the walls. My mind was on this case and how he'd solved it, so I don't know why the thought came to me. But it did. I put his notebook down and turned off the light. I lay there tossing the idea around in my head till I fell asleep. When I woke up the next morning, I knew we had another suspect. I wondered what Robert would say.

It had been another frustrating day where we had made no

progress and Robert had been even more aloof than usual. I hadn't told him about my idea because I wanted to have everything clear so I could demolish his objections.

My next door neighbour came out of her house as soon as I got out of my car. She was holding a parcel. 'Sharon, this was delivered for you. I said I'd look after it.'

I thanked her and took the parcel inside. I knew what it was. A week ago I'd ordered two jumpers from a catalogue. With the unseasonably chilly weather I was running out of warm clothes. I didn't have a dryer and I'd washed some jumpers, but they were still wet. Without opening the parcel I put my other four jumpers in the washing machine.

The following morning I opened the parcel expecting to see an angora polo necked jumper in hazelnut and a crew neck wool jumper in mustard. Instead there was only one. A pale blue polo neck. There was a note apologizing that the other colour I'd ordered was out of stock. I was about to phone the company when I saw that instead of ticking the hazelnut I'd ticked blue haze on the order form. I thought of returning it, and searched through my wardrobe for something warm. My three winter jackets were at the dry cleaners.

'Bloody weather,' I muttered as I pulled on the blue angora jumper.

When I got to Dolphin Cottage Robert looked at me in surprise.

'Say anything about baby-grows and you'll regret it,' I snarled.

His eyes went to my stomach.

'No, I'm not pregnant! Trust you to think – '

He held up his hands in surrender. 'You're the one who mentioned baby-grows.'

'That's because I feel as if I'm wearing a baby-grow.' I

explained what had happened as I went inside.

He looked amused. 'Have you looked in the mirror? Since you put on the jumper?'

'No. And I have no intention – '

'I think you should.'

'Just tell me what's wrong, Sergeant.'

'Go upstairs and look in the mirror. The one in the bathroom.'

I dumped my bag on his sofa went upstairs. Expecting to see my hair standing up like a broom or blobs of mascara under my eyes, I stared at the mirror. I looked different. My cheeks were slightly pink and my complexion no longer looked sallow. To describe myself as pretty would be an exaggeration, but I no longer looked plain.

'Well?' said Robert when I returned.

'I look different.'

'A fortunate mistake. The colour suits you. You look attractive.'

His compliment amazed me even more than my new appearance did.

'When you were at school was your shirt white or pale blue?' he asked.

'White. Why?'

'Just something you said when we were both new here.'

'What did I say?'

'That you looked all right when you were at school, but your looks deteriorated when you left. I think it's because you started wearing browns and earthy colours.'

I'd worn those colours because I liked them and they looked grown up.

'Robert, could we sit down for a minute. I've had a thought. A startling thought. I need to know what you think.'

'Okay. Do you want some coffee?'

'I never refuse coffee,' I said, pleased that he'd thawed.

I sat on the sofa while he was in the kitchen. When he came in with the cafetière, mugs, sugar bowl, spoons and milk jug on a tray, I thought how like Phoebe he was in his habits. I would have poured the coffee in the kitchen, added sugar and milk and carried the mugs in.

He sipped his coffee and looked at me. 'Well, what have you thought?'

'I think we've got a new suspect.' I knew better than to wait for him to ask questions. 'Margaret. She lives at Pengelly House. She was at the party that night. If she's got a car, it would only take a few minutes to get to Bridget's. If she went by bike then the calculations I made for Phoebe would be the same. She hates Bridget. If she was out of the way then the Medical Records office would be a lot happier. She and Phoebe are not only friends they're sisters-in-law. She's said herself that Bridget flaunted her baby at Phoebe.'

I'd been afraid Robert would dismiss the idea, but he looked thoughtful. 'Wouldn't it be better to kill Elaine?' he asked finally. 'She seems to be the cause of all the misery. If what the staff say is true, it was a happy place to work before she came. With her dead the department would return to normal.'

I had thought of this and had worked out reasons for and against it. 'Maybe no one knew where she lived. She's got no friends there, so no one would be visiting her at home. The other staff knew where Bridget lived because Margaret would have told them she'd moved next-door to Phoebe.'

He nodded. 'You might be onto something. We'll have to find out if Margaret's got a car or bike. The difficulty is that if all the staff knew where Bridget lived, anyone of them could have gone to her house. No one has alibis – they all said they were at home in bed. Apart from Margaret who was at home, but not in bed.'

That night I went on the internet and ordered four new jumpers and shirts. I chose jumpers in navy, emerald-green, burgundy and royal-blue which would go with the two white, pale blue and green and white striped shirts I'd ordered.

In bed, I continued reading Robert's account of the missing boy.

Today we visited the boy's friends. The parents are delightful. They told us about an incident a few months ago that took place between them and the mother of the missing boy.

Their son, and another two boys who lived nearby, had been playing with the boy in his house when his mother was out. When she came home she told them to leave and not come back. She didn't want nasty, common children mixing with her son. Understandably upset, the children went home and told their parents. The two sets of parents confronted his mother, but she threatened to call the police if they didn't leave her house. She repeated her accusation that they were nasty and common and she didn't want her son mixing with them.

Feeling sorry for the boy, they left, but told their children that the boy was welcome to come to their homes if he wished. He did wish. We visited other parents who confirmed that he was the unhappiest child they had ever met. Well dressed, clean and polite at all times, but unhappy and nervous.

By this time I was convinced the mother had killed her

son. I tried to work out her motive. She found out he was still mixing with children she considered common? But Robert had said that she was distraught – genuinely distraught. Would she have been distraught if she'd killed her son? Maybe he hadn't been missing at all, but just hiding.

As soon as I'd heard that the missing boy was going to live with his father, I knew what had happened. Apart from instinct I had nothing else to back up my suspicious.

To my frustration Robert's notes ended there.

Next morning we found that Margaret and her husband owned a car and two bikes, but I knew this didn't prove anything. Unless someone confessed the case would remain unsolved. At this rate we'd never have anything substantial to take to court. We had no real evidence, just suspicions. By lunchtime I was hungry. We were driving out of Pengelly House when Robert said he was starving and hadn't had any breakfast because he'd got up too late.

'Do you know any good pubs near here?' I asked.

'Yes. Some excellent ones.'

We drove to a place called Blissland and went into a pub where we sat at a table in a corner. It was midday and there were only a few tables occupied.

'I finished reading your account of the missing boy last night,' I told Robert when we'd ordered sandwiches and cappuccino for me and ploughman's and tea for him. 'I think his mother killed him. Am I right?'

'Yes.'

'But I don't know why. Or how.'

'He was a child. He hadn't learnt to be devious. His

mother found him packing his case to take to his father's flat. She lost her temper and hit him. He fell and smashed his head on the hearth. Horrified about what she'd done she wrapped his body in bin liners and put him in the cellar. If her child was missing she would have been frantic with worry, but she was distraught, because she knew he was dead and that she had killed him.'

'Why didn't she say that he fell and hit his head?'

Robert grimaced. 'When I said she hit him, I mean repeatedly hit him. One of her rings had cut right into his face and made him bleed. Her blows had also broken his nose.'

I winced. 'Poor little boy. No wonder he wanted to live with his father. What a horrible woman.'

'His father was partly to blame. He knew she had a violent temper. It's why he left.'

I was incredulous. 'He knew she was beating their son?'

'No. He never caught her in the act and his son didn't tell him. She was beating him.'

'The father?'

'Yes. He was a battered husband. In his statement he said that her rages were sudden and unprovoked, but that she was always sorry afterwards. He wouldn't have left, but he fell in love with a girl he worked with.'

'Why the hell did he marry her?'

'Guess.'

'She was pregnant?'

'Right. And it's only after they got married that he experienced her temper. At first he thought it was her hormones making her like that. Before they married he said she was really sweet. He never admitted it, but I think the fact that she was wealthy had a lot to do with why he went out with her. Her parents were killed in a plane crash. It was

170

only a light aircraft – her father was flying it. So when she was twenty-one she inherited all their money and their house.'

'So it was her house and that's why he didn't make any changes?'

Robert nodded. 'Probably. He was a weak man.'

'I can understand why women get battered, but why do men let women batter them? Okay, they don't have to hit the woman, but they could hold her – or was he a skinny weed?'

'From what I can remember, he was thin, but you're right – he could have overpowered her till she calmed down.'

'What the hell is it with these men? Look at Bridget. Her father leaves her with a woman he knows is nasty. I can understand why anyone would want to escape from her, but he didn't think about his daughter, did he? At least if he'd been around he might have been able to dilute her mother's influence and damage. All the poor girl wanted was to get married and have children, and her mother tried to stop her. That's not love. And that poor little boy being left with a woman his father knew was violent. These men should at least stay in the home till their children are old enough to leave.'

Robert was looking amused.

'What?' I asked.

'I agree with you and, and from the expressions on their faces, so do the other customers,' he said softly.

I was sitting with my back to the room and hadn't noticed that the tables were filling up. I was too embarrassed to turn around and could feel myself blushing. 'Sorry, I didn't realize I was talking too loudly.'

'You weren't. You were speaking clearly, and as there's no music and not much background noise, your voice carried.'

I lowered my voice. 'I understand what you mean about

the differences between distraught and how she should have been. And I doubt I would have picked it up. Do you think anyone in this case is acting one way when they should be acting another?'

He shook his head. 'Unfortunately not. Unless one of the suspects is a psychopath who has no empathy or conscience, everyone is behaving as if they are innocent.'

'Psychopaths can be very cunning. Some are charming.'

'Yes, and that's why they're so hard to catch.'

Our lunch arrived. The Cornish Brie and homemade chutney on my sandwich was delicious and filling. The cappuccino was perfect and came with two chocolate mints. Robert's plate was piled with thick slices of brown bread, cheddar, pickle, butter in a dish, and an apple.

'All our suspects seem to be so normal,' he said as he buttered his bread and laid a slab of cheese on top.

'I disagree. Some are, but in my opinion most are far from normal.'

He'd just taken a bite of his bread, and couldn't reply, but he looked curious.

I continued before he could argue. 'Phoebe and Stuart – an artist and a writer – they're not normal occupations, and I don't mean that in a derogatory way. Perhaps unusual would be a better word to use. Put twenty random people together and how many would be artists and writers? And then we've got the clothes designers and their wives. Again an unusual occupation and that's before we consider their lifestyles. Most homosexuals are open about it these days, but they keep it secret. They've even gone to the extreme of getting married. Margaret's got a normal occupation, but living at Pengelly House is an unusual lifestyle, wouldn't you say?'

He nodded. 'But by normal, I meant psychologically

normal and I think they are. None of them have typical psychopathic tendencies. They all have friends – '

'Bridget's mother hasn't,' I pointed out. 'And I bet Elaine hasn't either.'

He looked thoughtful. 'Mm, but I'd say that's not their choice. They, especially Bridget's mother, want friends, but their negative qualities of possessiveness, spite and bullying have turned people against them. A typical psychopath tends to be a loner from choice. But, of course, there are untypical psychopaths.'

I sighed and sipped my coffee.

The story about the little boy haunted me so much I couldn't sleep that night. It also changed my perception of things. When I went to my first Guide camp I met girls from every class. I'd envied the rich ones who talked about their ponies, big houses and exotic holidays. Now I was thankful for my parents, who had been gentle with us.

My brothers had been thrashed by my dad a few times, and they deserved it. My mum had thrashed me once and that was for throwing stones at a friend I'd had a fight with. I knew I'd deserved it because, as my mother said, I could have blinded her. To reinforce the message, after she had thrashed me, she dragged me weeping to my friend's house, made me tell her parents what I had done and they all agreed that I was not to see her for a week. It took me a long time to get over the punishment, but I never threw stones at anyone again.

How many unhappy rich girls had I envied? I'd never know.

13

ROBERT

Sharon's transformation reminded me of the way Judith had made me realize that the colours I wore were wrong. She was at medical school and I had come home from Paris for Easter. Her mother had given her a book called *Colour Me Beautiful.*

'Robert, your shirts are the wrong colour.'

I didn't care. They were good quality, comfortable and pure cotton.

'You're summer or winter. Your shirts are for people who are autumn and spring.'

'What?'

How do you choose them?' she asked.

'By the size and the make.'

'Do you think about the colour? Do you really like brown and grey and fawn?'

'They're practical.'

'They don't suit you. I only realized last week when I was reading this book. You looked much more handsome when we were at school and you wore white shirts.'

'Colour can't make any difference to how you look,' I argued. 'A splash of spaghetti sauce on a white shirt and you look as if you've worn the same shirt for days. Worse, stains don't come out of white or pale colours no matter how much washing powder I use. White shirts look dirty even when they're not.'

A few days later she bought me a white shirt and a tube of stain remover. In her bedsit, she made me stand in front of the mirror in my brown shirt.

'Now turn around, take it off and put this one on.'

I took off my brown shirt. 'Why don't you take off your dress?'

She winked at me. 'Later.'

I put the white shirt on.

'Now look in the mirror.'

She was right. I did look better. I took her in my arms. 'I like the colour of your dress, but I'd like it better if it was on the floor.' I kissed her.

That was the night I asked her to marry me. That was the night she said, 'Yes.'

Vanessa was going to the writers' group on Tuesday night.

'Whatever time I get home, I'll send you an e-mail,' she promised.

I thought she would be too tired, but before I went to bed that night I checked to see if she had sent me an e-mail. She had.

> Ethel's right. George and Olivia both dislike
> Phoebe. Ethel did a brilliant job of pretending
> she didn't know me. She saw me enter and
> came over doing her spiel about being the
> secretary and asking me what I wrote and if I'd
> ever been published. She took me over to
> Phoebe and introduced her as the president.
> Phoebe was being very welcoming. She smiled
> and said hello to people when they arrived.
> Then her manner changed. An overweight,
> balding man who looked mid to late 40's, just as
> Ethel described, came over to the table where

Phoebe was sitting. I heard Ethel call him George.

Phoebe asked him where he'd been. That was odd because she didn't ask anyone else. A few said they were sorry they hadn't been there last week, and she was normal about it. But when George said he'd been ill, she didn't look as if she cared. Now this bit's strange. He gave her a five pound note. Instead of her giving him three pounds change, she said he was a pound short. He said he didn't have it.

She said, 'We agreed.'

He looked around as if he was frightened someone would hear. 'I've been ill.' He was whispering.

She said, 'I'm sure if you look in your pockets you'll find another pound.'

He looked, and I think he was desperate to find some more, but couldn't. Then Phoebe said, 'Remember that you owe seven pounds next week.'

I thought it might be a good idea to befriend him, so I said I'd give him a pound. He was very grateful.

Not sure what to make of that, but she seems to have some hold over him. I think he was telling the truth about being ill. He did look pale. Ethel was right about his work too. He wrote some story that I couldn't understand. It was full of long and unusual words. He sounded as if he'd swallowed a dictionary. Someone else read it out for him. The comments were fair, but George said that it didn't work because of the way it had been read. Phoebe said that the way it had been read was the only good thing about it. Harsh but true. I'll go along next week and see if I can find out more.

We went to the pub afterwards. Not wanting to be too obvious that I wanted to talk to George, I sat next to Olivia, who spent a lot of time moaning about the smoking ban. She drank a lot and was unsteady on her feet by the time we left the pub.

I gave her a lift home. She's almost certainly an alcoholic, which is a shame because she's a fantastic writer. She lives in a housing association flat. She has a son, but he left home as soon as he went to college. He never visits, which upsets her. She doesn't even know where he lives.

She left her handbag in my car. Thinking she wouldn't be able to get inside I was going to run after her, but she must have had her key in her pocket because by the time I'd got out of the car I saw her going inside. I'll return her bag sometime today – it'll be a good excuse to get to know her better. If you're free, do you want to come with me? I'll introduce you as my boyfriend. I'll ring her first. Be prepared – her clothes are bizarre.

The next morning Vanessa sent me a text. Olivia hadn't missed her handbag. She was in bed when Vanessa rang and sounded as if she had a hangover. They'd arranged for us to go to her flat in the evening, which saved me the trouble of having to slip away from Sharon on some pretext.

Olivia's flat looked as if it had been burgled. It was hot and it stank of cigarette smoke. Vanessa had not exaggerated when she'd said Olivia's clothes were bizarre. A black lace skirt dotted with sequins was worn with fishnet tights, white trainers and a skimpy yellow vest that showed grubby bra straps. The hotchpotch made her look as if she'd started to dress for ballroom dancing, had changed her mind and decided to go for a walk. The cheap perfume she wore failed to mask her body odour.

As soon as we arrived she offered us a drink.

'Thanks,' I said. 'Coffee would be good.'

'Haven't got any.'

'Tea will do just as well.'

She giggled and pointed toward the kitchen. 'See if you can find any tea bags. There might be some.'

From the kitchen door I saw the overflowing bin. Empty wine and gin bottles lay on the floor. Foil food containers had gone mouldy. I didn't go in. I went back to the lounge. 'It's okay, I can do without. We only came to return your bag.'

'You must stay for a chat,' she insisted.

'Only if it's no trouble.'

She pushed papers and books off the sofa onto the floor. 'Sit down.'

'Thanks for making Vanessa so welcome at the group last night. She's been trying to get the confidence to – '

'It was a great poem,' said Olivia. 'Very original.' She gazed at me and smiled flirtatiously. I wondered if she'd forgotten that Vanessa said I was her boyfriend, or if she didn't care. She poured gin into a glass, filled it with tonic and sat in the armchair.

'I was telling Robert how fantastic the group was,' said Vanessa. 'What's the president's name – I've forgotten.'

Olivia took a large swig of her drink. 'Phoebe. Little Miss Perfect. Never does anything unconventional. Not like me. She'll never take risks. Plays it safe. Always has done. Even when we were at school. I was good at school too. Had to be. They were strict. My parents were too. Never put a foot wrong, I didn't. Then I went to university. It was me, Phoebe and Margaret, another of our friends.'

I guessed it was the same Margaret who worked in Medical Records.

'We were all so excited about going to Exeter together and we were all doing the same history and English degree. But they didn't change. They were the same as they were at school. Now me, I changed. I grew up. But not them. I started smoking and then . . . ' she looked as if she was about to cry. After taking a swig of her drink she went on. 'I fell in love. Phoebe and Margaret didn't. They were too busy working and studying. They became so dull. They started a homework club. How tedious can you get? They wanted me to join. Me? Join a homework club? No, I had fun.

'He was a lord, the man I loved. Well, the son of a lord. He was like me. He wanted fun too. We smoked. We went to parties that went on all night. We drank. All sorts of stuff. Sometimes I was so drunk I couldn't stand up and I'd have to stay in bed the next day.'

Olivia talked as if being drunk was an achievement.

'That sanctimonious Phoebe said it was a waste of a day. But you have to try out all these things, don't you? One of the tutors was furious with me. Threatened to write to my parents. He knew them. I did try and get back on track. I never needed to study at school, but I only just passed the first year exams. That was a bit of a shock. Phoebe said it was because the cannabis was destroying my brain.

'The next year our tutor insisted that I join Phoebe's homework club. It was so dull. Phoebe had to structure everything. She's a control freak. There were ten of them in the homework club. We met at a different member's place three nights a week. 'We've all got to help each other,' Phoebe was forever saying. Drove me mad it did. She still says it and it still drives me mad. It's her mantra. She's always preaching.

'We'd have tea and coffee or water when we were working and then two hours later, when we finished, we

179

were allowed to have food. We all had a rota for bringing something. The food was the best bit. When it was my turn to bring food, I was supposed to bring some sort of dessert, but I forgot. You should have heard the fuss. They all got so cross you'd think they were going to starve to death. I didn't last longer than one term.'

'Did your work improve?' Vanessa asked.

'I suppose it did,' Olivia admitted reluctantly. 'But my social life was dying. And I was dying of boredom. I think the homework lot were glad when I didn't come back. Just before the next exams the tutor read me the riot act. Threatened he'd write to my parents, he was so angry when I left the homework club.

'My boyfriend and I went to a party a week before the exams started. It went on all night. I thought I'd better go to the lecture, the grumpy tutor was holding, but I didn't have time to go home and have a shower and change my clothes, so I went straight to the lecture room. I was the first one there . . . that was a first for me. Phoebe's face was a picture when she walked in and saw me. She looked amazed and then really pleased. She came over and sat next to me. Then she saw I was in my party gear. She was all scrubbed and clean. You could tell that she'd gone to bed at a respectable time, and got up early, had a shower and a healthy breakfast – she was always going on about eating properly. She looked like the Virgin Mary in her navy trousers and white polo necked jumper.

Vanessa smiled. 'That sounds like an interesting title for a book.'

'What does?' asked Olivia.

'The Virgin Mary in a white polo necked jumper.'

Olivia laughed so loudly I was sure the people in the flat upstairs could hear her.

'What happened to your boyfriend?' I asked.

'We were in love. Real love. It wasn't his fault what happened. We did things that were really exciting at first. Didn't realize the dangers. Phoebe warned me, but not in a friendly way. She was condemning. 'Cannabis first and then you'll need something stronger, Olivia,' she said. The bitch was right. Oh, I never did heroin, but he did. He died. I found him dead. I was pregnant.

'His parents didn't want to know about the baby. Nowadays, with DNA tests, I could have taken them to court. They blamed me for his death. But they were the ones who made him do wild things. His nanny was the one who gave him all the love. And when he went to boarding school he never saw her again. It had a bad effect on him. He felt rejected. I don't suppose they considered him to be important. He had five older brothers who were married with sons to inherit the estate and keep the family name going. They had seven legitimate grandsons, they didn't need any more.' She put her hands over her face and wept. 'Phoebe's right. I've wrecked my life.'

'It's not too late,' said Vanessa firmly.

'It is. My son's ashamed of me,' she sobbed. 'Phoebe was right about that too. I should have had him adopted. I was going to, but when I saw him, I couldn't. I should have. He only loved me when he was little. When he grew up he said I embarrassed him.' She made an effort to stop crying. 'Look at this . . . if I can find it.'

She went to the stack of books in the corner. While she searched I wondered if her tears were really for herself. Was she stricken with guilt because she had set fire to the wrong house and killed an innocent man and a baby?

She found a photo album, which she gave to me. 'My parents were so proud of me. They liked Phoebe and

181

Margaret too. We were inseparable when we were at school. My parents bought me a camera and this album so I could record my experiences.'

Vanessa looked over my shoulder as I opened the album. The first photo was of three smiling girls standing in front of an ancient looking building. Phoebe and Margaret were easily recognizable. I guessed the other girl was Olivia, but she looked so different it was hard to tell. Dressed in classical clothes of a dark skirt and white blouse with well cut hair that shone. The contrast between what she had been and what she had become was tragic.

'Margaret – she's in the writers' group too, isn't she?' said Vanessa.

Olivia nodded.

'It's unusual that the three of you not only went to school together, but are all writers,' said Vanessa.

'It's what drew us together. There was a creative writing club at school and we were all in it. We all wanted to be writers. Phoebe's made it, but I haven't and Margaret writes short stories, which are not commercial enough on their own, even though they're brilliant and she wins most of the competitions she enters. She's made a lot of money in prizes over the years. She's trying to write a historical novel, but she's finding it difficult.' She saw me looking at the photo.

'Yes, that's me. You wouldn't have known if I hadn't told you, would you?'

'No,' I said softly.

Olivia wiped away her tears with a sodden tissue. 'I always cry when I look through this album.'

I turned the pages. One photo had been enlarged and under it Olivia had written, *Margaret, Phoebe and me in the front garden of our home for the next three years.* She'd even put the address. Her writing was neat and cursive. The house in the background was large and imposing and had three floors. There were probably about eight bedrooms.

'Lovely looking house,' I said.

Olivia dropped her tissue on the floor and pulled another one from the box. 'It belonged to our lecturer and his wife. They didn't have any children and took a parental interest in their students. My dad was friends with Lloyd Kerslake the lecturer – they'd been at university together. I only lasted in the house for a year – they chucked me out. Phoebe still keeps in touch with them and so does Margaret.'

'Why did they make you leave?' asked Vanessa.

'Always coming home at, what they called, an unearthly hour, forgetting my key and having to ring the door bell and waking everyone up and being drunk. If I had one wish it would be to go back to that day and do things differently.'

Vanessa looked at the photos and then back at Olivia. 'You could look like that again,' Vanessa said.

Olivia looked at her in disbelief. 'Oh yeah. How?'

'You haven't put on any weight if the photos are anything to go by. Have you kept any of your old clothes?'

'They're here somewhere. I never throw anything away – just my life and chances. When I had the chance to get friendly with Phoebe again, I fell for George's big ideas.'

'He can't write,' said Vanessa. 'His stuff was so boring.'

'He thinks he can. He tries to fool everyone. Tells people he's a freelance journalist, says he's got an agent. When I used to go to his flat to talk about this new writers' group he wanted us to set up, he was always on the phone – but I don't think he was really – just pretending he was talking to his agent. But he was always saying the same thing.'

'Did you set up another writers' group?' Vanessa asked innocently.

'No. No one came. Phoebe said then, in her disappointed

voice, 'You always follow the loser, Olivia'. She was right.'

'You're a very good writer – '

'That's kind of you, Vanessa, but what good's that going to do me? It's not finished. It'll probably never be finished.'

'How far are you?' I asked.

'Fifty thousand words.'

Vanessa looked impressed. 'How many for a full novel?'

'Seventy-thousand or more.'

'Well that's not far to go. If you've written fifty, surely you can write another twenty thousand.'

'Who's going to want to publish it?'

'You don't know till you try. Olivia, the people in the writers' group are fierce critics. I know I've only been once, but they don't give false praise and they were enthusiastic about your novel. Finish it. Send it to publishers.'

'No one's going to want it.'

'Lucky JK Rowling wasn't a defeatist like you,' I said.

'She's not an alcoholic.'

Her self-awareness surprised me. 'You can get help. Go to the AA.'

She smiled. 'Why? I don't drive.'

Vanessa laughed.

'Yeah, I know,' said Olivia. 'Alcoholics Anonymous.'

'Will you go? I'll drive you to the first meeting if you like,' Vanessa offered.

'Would you?'

Vanessa nodded.

'Why are you helping me?'

'Because . . . well, I hate to see someone wasting their life.' She picked up the bottle of gin. 'The first thing is to get rid of this. Lucky it's nearly empty.'

Olivia looked as anguished as if we were going to kill a cat.

'It's the first step,' I said. Every time you do something towards achieving your goals, write them down.'

Although I'd never taken to drink, I had become lethargic, careless of my appearance and happy to lose my days asleep in bed. Now, I remembered the words of my parents and grandparents and Vanessa, as they chivvied me back into living.

'Your goals, Olivia,' I said, speaking in the same tone they had used to good effect on me, 'are to become a writer and give up drinking. When you write one paragraph you're stepping towards your goal. When you write one page you're even further. When you go to your first AA meeting, you're making progress. Have you got a job?'

She shook her head. 'Who'd want to give me a job?'

'You've got to get this place tidy and clean,' said Vanessa. 'No, don't look at me as if I've said you've got to climb Mount Everest. Give me one reason why you can't get it tidy and clean?'

'It's too untidy and dirty.'

'One room at a time. You don't go to work, so you've got lots of time. Start with the kitchen. Then you'll be able to cook yourself proper meals. If you eat properly and stop drinking you'll have more energy.'

'I haven't got any cleaning stuff.'

'Then go out and buy some tomorrow.'

'I haven't got enough money.'

'But you've got enough money to buy cigarettes and gin.'

'I need them.'

'No. You want them. You don't need them,' Vanessa said firmly. 'What you need is nourishing food and a clean house. I'll call for you tomorrow morning at nine and take you shopping.'

'I'll still be in bed. I don't get up till – '

185

'You'll get up at eight and have a shower. I'll be here at nine. Don't get dressed. We'll go through your stuff and find all your old clothes, then we'll buy you some decent food and cleaning things. I'll help you to begin with, but then you're on your own.'

As Vanessa outlined Olivia's tasks for tomorrow, I asked myself if we were helping rehabilitate a murderer.

I'd memorized the address written in Olivia's photo album and the name of her lecturer. I rang directory enquires from my car, praying it wasn't an unlisted number. We were in luck. I rang the number. A young sounding female answered the phone. Lloyd was out and so was his wife, but she'd leave a message for him. I gave my home number. An hour later he phoned. I briefly told him why I wanted to see him and his wife, and we arranged for Vanessa and I to visit them the next day after six in the evening.

The front of the house in Exeter looked much the same as it had in Olivia's photo. Not only did Lloyd and his wife remember Phoebe, Margaret and Olivia very well, we discovered that Stuart had also been their lodger and that's how he and Phoebe had met. I'd assumed that Phoebe had married Margaret's brother, but it was Margaret who had married Phoebe's brother. After I'd discovered she was one of eight children I should have checked to make sure. It probably wasn't important, but one of my rules was never to assume anything.

Lloyd had given a speech at their weddings, they kept in touch by e-mail and saw each other a couple of times a year.

'That class was the most memorable I've ever taught,' said

Lloyd. 'Nineteen eighty-eight. It was completely divided down the middle into positive and negative – to use the politically correct terms. Those days I called it good and bad. Phoebe was a beacon of the positive. She was not the brightest in the class, Olivia was, but she was intelligent and hard working. She started a homework club, she worked in a hotel restaurant to supplement her grant, she drank little and didn't smoke. She made good use of her time, spent her money wisely and didn't get into debt.

'Margaret was the same. She worked nights in a supermarket stacking shelves. Both good solid workers. They had to study hard to pass their exams, unlike Olivia who was brilliant.'

He saw my look of surprise and asked, 'Will you let me guess what she's doing now?'

I nodded.

'Unemployed? Unmarried? Hoards of children?'

'Only one child,' said Vanessa. 'He left home as soon as he left school. She never sees him. Says she's a fantasist.'

'Do you think she is?'

I didn't say we were wondering if she was a killer.

Vanessa gave a wry smile. 'Well, she says that she'd be the daughter-in-law of a duke if fate hadn't taken away the man she loved.'

'Fate.' He snorted. 'Charles. He wasn't the son of a duke.'

'I thought it was a fantasy,' said Vanessa.

'He was the son of a lord.'

'Oh. Actually, now I remember she did say lord. I didn't believe her.'

'He was the negative force. Sixth son. His parents last desperate attempt to have a daughter. Ignored through his childhood, sent to boarding school where he was expelled for taking drugs. He was good looking, charismatic and corrupt.

He abhorred Phoebe and her group – they despised him. Olivia fell in love with him a few months into the year. She went to his parties and got drunk and stoned. Her work suffered. Instead of coming top of the class at the end of her first year she just scraped through. In their second year Charles took some bad heroin and died. It was Olivia who found him. She sobered up and tried to be more sensible, but then discovered she was pregnant.

'By that time she looked rough. She wore odd clothes and I'm sad to say she could have been easily mistaken for a prostitute. She'd dyed her hair blonde and the dark roots were showing, which added to the effect. She went to the lord and lady who said that by the look of her the baby could have been anyone's. They accused her of leading their son astray and they wanted nothing to do with her or the baby.

Phoebe and Margaret attempted to put things right by going to visit them. They were adamant, but they treated Phoebe and Margaret with more respect than they treated Olivia, who didn't even get inside the house. They were taken into a room and allowed to sit down and were able to plead Olivia's case.'

'She said you told her to leave here.'

He grimaced. 'We did. She'd been given plenty of warnings that if she didn't stop making a noise when she came home late – '

'What sort of noise?'

'She'd either forget her key or loose it, and ring the doorbell. If she did remember her key she'd bang the door and come up the stairs singing at the top of her voice or shrieking with laughter. The night we said she had to leave, she was very drunk, staggered into Phoebe's room and vomited all over her. Poor girl was fast asleep, she woke up and screamed. It took us an hour to get things cleaned up.

We couldn't take anymore, so we gave her a weeks notice. She left the next morning and moved in with Charles. From then on she went completely bad.

'It was difficult for me. Her father and I were friends. Eventually I knew I had to do something so I told her that if she didn't start coming to lectures I'd have to tell her father. I also said that she had to join the homework club Phoebe and Margaret had started. She gave me cheek and said was I sure I wanted her in my house again. I told her I was doing it for her father. This was before Charles died.

'She caused disruption in the homework club, but her work did improve. She started handing things in on time, but her earlier brilliance had evaporated. The first essay she ever handed in was so exceptional I read it out to the class. It was the best essay I'd ever read. It was better than anything I could have written. What happened to her was a tragedy, but it was mostly of her own making.'

His wife took up the story. 'It started off so well. Three attractive and jolly girls who were close friends. Olivia and Phoebe worked at the same hotel. One night, not long after she started going around with Charles, a customer clicked his fingers at Olivia and she swore at him. He complained. She was sacked on the spot. Phoebe took over his table and he gave her a fifty pound tip. When she told Olivia, Olivia sneered and said she had no pride if she grovelled to such a rude man. Phoebe argued that she would never have to see him again and that fifty pounds would come in very useful. I think she spent some of it on new clothes. She bought us wine and smoked salmon and she treated Margaret and Stuart to a trip to the cinema.'

Vanessa arrived for dinner two nights later looking pleased with herself. After giving me a bottle of wine, she bounded into the lounge and produced a book from her bag. 'Phoebe's novel. I went to the book signing. Lots of people there – had to wait in a long queue to get it signed.'

I opened it.

To Vanessa,
I'm looking forward to hearing more of your poetry.
Best wishes,
Phoebe Harris

'No wonder there was a long queue if she wrote personal messages for people she knew,' I said. I began to read the first page.

It was twenty years since we'd seen each other. We'd reconnected through Face Book. I was the one who'd looked for her. It was curiosity really. I wanted to see if she'd fulfilled her dreams. She'd wanted to be an actress. I'd never heard of her, but I never went to the theatre so she might have been on the stage, but just never made it as a movie star. My ambitions had been to get married and have children and be loved and cherished. I've never married, never had children and no one loves me. I was one of those people no one would ever miss. When I left a job, no one cried or bothered to buy a card or say goodbye.
We met in Bushy Park. Even without the YSL logo on her yellow cashmere jumper the signs of success were evident – the well cut hair, beautifully tailored navy trousers, suede brogues and crisp white shirt. I already knew she was married and she wore a big diamond engagement ring. And she smelt of expensive perfume. I swallowed my envy and we talked while we had a

picnic. The picnic was my idea because one of those cafes or pubs that she'd be sure to want to go to, would be too expensive for me.

It was six months later that I discovered she cut her own hair, bought all her clothes from charity shops, went into department stores and used one of their perfume testers at the Dior counter, and she and her husband were in danger of losing their house.

But by then it was too late to undo the damage.

'Can I borrow it?'

Vanessa grinned. 'Searching for clues?'

'Yes. Were George or Olivia there?'

She shook her head. 'But yesterday Olivia and I went through all her old clothes. She's got some really nice things. We washed her jumpers by hand and took her shirts, jeans and skirts to the launderette. She does own an iron – an old one, but it works.

Vanessa and I were having lunch in The Crown pub near Bodmin on Sunday afternoon. It was one of those places that were becoming increasingly rare, where there was no TV or music. They served wholesome British food and real ale. I was sitting opposite Vanessa with my back to the doorway and bar.

Suddenly she nudged me with her foot. 'George has just come in.'

'Is he alone?'

'As far as I can see. He might be joining someone. Shall I see if I can get him to sit with us?'

Much as I disliked the thought of putting up with his company instead of having a relaxing afternoon, it was too valuable an opportunity to miss.

'He's coming our way. Looking for a table.' Vanessa waved. 'George!'

He looked at her blankly.

'Remember me? I'm from the writers' group. Would you like to join us?'

He put his pint of beer on our table and sat down. His clothes reeked of cigarette smoke. 'Yes, I remember now. Sorry, I was deep in thought. Let me see if I can remember your name.' After a few moments he shook his head. 'Sorry.'

'That's okay. I'm Vanessa.'

'That's it. I would have got it eventually.'

'This is my boyfriend Robert.'

George was pale. His eyes were bloodshot and he looked desperately unhappy, which would make sense if he'd accidentally killed a baby and an innocent man. His teeth were discoloured and his breath was stale.

'Hi, Bruce,' he said to me. When I looked puzzled he said, 'Bruce as in Robert the Bruce.'

'Ah, I see.' Remembering Ethel's description I smiled.

'You don't mind, do you? I can tell.' He looked at Vanessa. 'And I've got a good name for you. Monster. Vanessa. Nessie. Nessie the Lock Ness Monster.'

Vanessa put on a good show of allowing him to think he was clever and original.

'Are you feeling better?' she asked.

'How did you know I'd been ill?'

'I heard you telling Phoebe.'

'Oh, right. I'd forgotten. Thanks for lending me the money.'

Vanessa smiled. 'That's okay. I hope it was nothing serious.'

George looked sorry for himself. 'It could have been. I had a slight heart attack. Lucky I was in a shop when it happened and they called an ambulance.'

I knew that many people who had suffered heart attacks were left with depression. I wondered if this, rather than guilt and remorse, explained George's unhappy manner.

'How terrible for you, but I'm glad you're feeling better,' said Vanessa. 'I can't tell you how excited I am about the writers' group. I'm so pleased I found it.'

George grunted. 'It could be tons better. It's badly run.'

'Is it? How? I've only been once, but it all seemed to go smoothly.'

He looked bitter. 'You think so?'

Vanessa widened her eyes. 'Yes. What's wrong with it?' She began to look worried and doubtful.

He drank his beer. 'I shouldn't say this, with you being new and all.'

But you will say it, I thought.

'It's okay, George. I won't tell anyone. If anything is dreadfully wrong I'll leave and find another group. I don't want to get mixed up in anything dubious.'

'It's Phoebe. She's the big problem.'

'Phoebe?'

George nodded. He launched into a tirade similar to the e-mails he'd sent Ethel. I yawned. He didn't even notice.

'But she seems very popular,' Vanessa said when George paused.

'Oh yes. We were friends once. I used to like her. I thought she liked me, but she was just using me for ideas. She didn't want to be the president at first and I helped and supported her, but as soon as she got used to the power she thought she was indispensable. Cunning. That's what she is. She's made the group social so members depend on it for friendships. Christmas dinners, summer picnics, parties – '

Suddenly I was no longer bored.

'Parties?' said Vanessa, succeeding in looking nonchalant. 'Does Phoebe give the parties?'

'Yeah.'

'Are they any good?'

He frowned. 'If you like that sort of thing.'

'What sort of thing?' Vanessa asked, looking as if she hoped he was going to reveal something scandalous.

'You know, standing around talking. No music or dancing, just talking, drinking and eating.'

I looked at him with disapproval. 'So you like her enough to go to her parties.' I wanted him to say he didn't go to them, but he'd heard about them and thought they sounded boring.

'We used to be friends and I helped her before I realized she was just – '

'So you have been to her parties.'

'Yeah. Used to go to all of them. Not any more though. I'm on the black list. Don't get invited now.'

I had to make sure. 'Does she have the parties at her house or hire a hall or something?'

He wasn't fazed by what was an odd question. 'At her house. Otherwise I might do what you're suggesting and gatecrash!' He grinned. 'That'd serve her right.'

That left us with Olivia. Vanessa was visiting her every morning to make sure she got out of bed and had a shower. The next time I saw her was the Monday after I'd taken George off our list of suspects. Vanessa had kept me informed about her progress, but I was nevertheless surprised by how different she and her flat looked. Her hair was clean but messy and she didn't smell of body odour. She wore a dark green polo necked jumper and jeans. The flat was cleaner and tidier, although she still had a lot to do. She must have turned down the central heating, because it was no longer stiflingly hot.

Olivia led us into the flat. Suddenly she turned to Vanessa. 'I need a drink. I need a cigarette.'

'No you don't,' said Vanessa. 'What have you eaten today?'

'Nothing.'

'What have you had to drink?'

'Nothing alcoholic. Just coffee.'

'Then no wonder you're miserable.'

'I wouldn't be miserable if I had a drink and – '

'Yes, you would,' said Vanessa. She went in the direction of the kitchen. 'What food have you got?'

'Don't know.'

'Olivia, you've got to make an effort. Spend the money you save on booze and cigarettes on decent food.'

We followed Vanessa into the kitchen, where she opened the fridge. Apart from a carton of milk it was empty.

She took Olivia by the arm. 'Right you're coming with me to the supermarket. Where's your purse?'

Olivia found her handbag and Vanessa marched her out of the flat leaving me behind. Unsure how far away the supermarket was I quickly searched the flat, but found nothing that could have been used as an accelerant.

They returned half an hour later with a ravioli microwave meal. Vanessa stood over Olivia while she heated it and ate it. Then she put an orange in her hand. 'Peel it and eat it.'

Olivia obeyed.

'Well?' Vanessa asked when she had eaten the last segment.

'Thanks. I do feel better.'

'So in future you'll eat properly, won't you,' I said deciding to add encouragement.

She nodded.

'Good,' said Vanessa. 'So instead of buying cigarettes what are you going to buy?'

'Food.'

'Right. But it can't be any sort of food like hamburgers, can it?'

'No.'

'And it would be cheaper and better if you prepared it yourself rather than buying meals you can just bung in the microwave.'

Olivia nodded. 'A chop and two vegetables, with an apple or some fruit for afters?'

'Yes. And what are you going to drink?'

'Coffee, tea, water and fruit juice.'

Reminded of what one of my friends in London did when they were giving up smoking, I said, 'And put what you spent on fags and booze in a jar, and at the end of the month count it and spend it on something special.'

Olivia smiled and stood up. 'I'll make some coffee.'

'No, it's okay, we have to get going,' I said.

Her dismayed expression made me realize that Olivia craved company.

'We'll stay for a quick coffee,' said Vanessa.

'What strikes me about this case,' Vanessa said later, 'is the number of people who used to be Phoebe's friends and are now her enemies. Bridget, Olivia and George. It looks as if she can't cope with them changing. And she is their enemy too.'

'She and Margaret are still friends. Close friends.'

'Yes, but – '

'Let's take them one at a time,' I said. 'Olivia first, because they were friends at school. When they went to university

Olivia started drinking, doing drugs and not bothering to study. Phoebe tried to help her, but was rejected. Strong reasons for the disintegration of their friendship.

'With Bridget, they were work colleagues who became friends. The friendship ended because when Bridget got into a position of power she bullied her workmates. Bridget ended the friendship, because she wanted to get on. She had the choice of siding with her colleagues and being bullied by Elaine at best, and losing her job in the worst case scenario, or siding with Elaine and getting on. And she did get on. She grew up on a council estate, so did her husband, and they ended up owning a lovely house in a respectable area. Both were ambitious. Declan's colleagues at the garage speak of his dedication and hard work. Their ambition paid off financially.'

Vanessa nodded.

'Now George. He's the one that said they were friends. We've not got Phoebe's side of things yet.'

'From what I've seen they're certainly enemies. He hates her.'

'What's her attitude to him?'

Vanessa thought for a moment. 'Hard. Unyielding. He was trying to get her sympathy – no that's the wrong word – he was trying to get her to understand something – no that's not it either. Soften. He was trying to get her to soften, but she wouldn't.'

That night I read the first chapter of Phoebe's novel, searching for any reference to Bridget or Elaine or any clues to the murder. I couldn't see any.

When Vanessa and I called on Olivia a few nights later we hardly recognized her. The long bleached hair that had looked like straw, had been cut off. The remaining dark hair was very short and silky. Her skin looked clearer and the dark circles under her eyes had almost gone. Her eyes were no longer bloodshot. She was bubbling with excitement. Her flat had also undergone a transformation. It was tidy and smelt clean.

'You look terrific,' Vanessa said. 'And so does the flat. Who cut your hair?'

'I did. Phoebe, Margaret and I all used to cut our own hair. We helped each other to do the back. And I've done some more writing today.' She thrust some pages at me. 'Do you want to read it?'

I did. I sat down and Vanessa sat beside me.

Today I became a criminal. Or was I a criminal from when I planned all this? If I am, that makes my parents and my sister criminals too. It's all gone well so far. But no one was looking for me then. They'll start investigating now. But they'll be looking for me in Sydney not in Melbourne. They'll be looking for a Jonathan Grey, not a John Gray. And I've moved the month of my birth forward 3 months. I kept the right year of birth. 1945 was the year the war ended. It was a lucky year and I didn't want to go against that luck. And if they look for my parents they won't find them in Sydney either. I feel guilty that they've uprooted themselves and moved to Brisbane for me, but as my dad said, I'm doing this because of the way they brought me up.

I've got a job. I live in the same block of flats as my sister. Her flat is my official address. She was the one who said if I was being followed, I needed a flat with an inside communal staircase. My parents' letters for me

are addressed to her in blue envelops. Hers are in white
ones. Between us we've got all the possibilities covered.
From the outside the block of flats are bland, but in the
three months I've been here I've managed to make mine
look like a home. I've put dark green sheets over the
horrible grey lounge suite and I've hung up matching
curtains. I bought second-hand rugs for the floor. My
parents gave me money to buy sheets, blankets and a
bedspread.
At first I was reluctant to make friends, but no one
seems to suspect anything so I've relaxed. I've got a few
friends at work and I've even got a girlfriend,
something I always thought was too dangerous. But if
everything goes the way I pray it will, after 1973 I
won't have to worry about anything.

It's six months since I started this diary. I knew it was
all going too smoothly. A party. Who would have
thought that an innocent party might wreck everything.
And I didn't even go to the party. My sister did. I'd
considered all the things that could go wrong. I'd
thought of every possibility except this.

'You certainly know how to end something on a cliff-
hanger,' said Vanessa.

Olivia looked at us anxiously. 'Is it any good?'

'More than good,' I said. 'It's excellent.'

'Can you guess what it's about?'

I shook my head.

'It's based on what happened to one of my uncles who
went to Australia in the fifties with his parents. They were
ten pound Poms. Conscription was compulsory, like it was
here, except not everyone was called up – it depended on

when your birthday was. My uncle and his parents were like the characters in this story. They did exactly what I've written about. Breaking the law was easier then – no computers and I don't know about now, but in those days they didn't have any National Insurance Numbers in Australia.'

'What was the bit about 1973?' I asked.

'The general election. The Labour Party won and released draft evaders from jail unconditionally.'

'Did your uncle get away with it?' Vanessa asked.

'Yes. But I started thinking about what if they hadn't. And all the things that could have gone wrong. Sometimes things go wrong because we make the wrong decisions, but sometimes it's just fate. Good fate or bad fate. Do you believe in fate, Robert?'

Fate. Right decisions, wrong decisions. Olivia was right. Sometimes it's just fate. I'd never thought about it till fate dealt me a crushing blow.

Two months before Judith's maternity leave came to an end, she agonized. To return to work meant leaving Hannah. She'd booked her into the hospital crèche, until being told that parents' visits during the lunch times were discouraged because they unsettled the child. We talked about the alternatives. A live-in nanny was rejected. A non-live-in nanny would disrupt our work if she was late or unable to come because she was ill. My parents and Judith's parents worked. My grandparents lived in Cornwall. Judith's lived in Oxford. She wanted to continue her work as a paediatrician, but she wanted to spend as much time with Hannah as she could.

'I could defer my career till she starts school,' she mused. 'but I want a consultancy. Am I being selfish?'

'No,' I assured her.

Judith was respected and liked by her colleagues. Screaming babies calmed when she cuddled them. Fraught mothers listened to her advice, and praised her methods. I put Hannah's easy childhood down to Judith. Her nursery was pink and white with lots of mobiles and pictures and a radio tuned to Classic FM. When she was a little older Judith put up diagrams of the skeleton and respiratory systems. The breakfast room had a diagram of the digestive system on the wall. Judith let Hannah ask the questions first. 'What's that?'

'That's what we look like inside,' said Judith. 'It's where our food goes after we swallow it.'

The diagram of the skeleton fascinated her even more.

By the time Hannah started school she could pronounce oesophagus and duodenum.

Although a wonderful mother, Judith was hopelessly undomesticated. She hated cooking, cleaning, ironing and gardening. If she tried to paint a wall she got covered in paint. If she used a roller she'd drop it. If she used a paintbrush she'd drop that. Non-drip paint dripped when Judith applied it. While she had been on maternity leave the house was always untidy. She rarely finished anything. If she started to wash up she'd get bored and start to vacuum, but get fed up after doing one room. Nothing, apart from being in the car with me, made her more bad tempered.

I came home one night to find her crying. 'I've decided to have a career break. I can't leave Hannah with strangers and I'll miss her too much. If I could see her at lunch times it'd be okay . . . '

I put my arms around her. 'What about leaving her with me?'

'What?'

'Me taking a career break instead.'

She gazed at me. 'Would you?'

'Yes.'

'Could you?'

'Yes. I asked about it the other day.' I looked around the chaotic dining-room and wondered how long it would take me to sort it out.

Judith's parents were ecstatic. My mother was amazed, but encouraging. I'm sure my father was disappointed, but he didn't voice his opinion, just as he hadn't tried to persuade me to join his law practice instead of being a policeman. Although the law interested me, I was passionate about languages. For a few years I had toyed with the idea of being an interpreter, but when I returned from Europe and began looking for a job in London the only ones were for multinational corporations and banks. I was fluent, but my lack of a formal degree in languages was a barrier. I became a tourist guide with a travel company, but frustrated by the petty complaints from people who should have been enjoying themselves, I only lasted one season. I did a stint with my father and it was then that I knew I didn't want to defend or prosecute, I wanted to solve crimes.

I enjoyed being a house-husband. I did things I hadn't had time to do when I worked. I landscaped our small garden. I finished painting the rest of the house. My grandmothers gave me recipe books and I taught myself to make pastry, pizzas and lasagne. I couldn't do anything elaborate, but I made sure we had plenty of variety. When it was cold I made fruit pies or crumbles for pudding and in summer we had strawberries, blackberries, raspberries, bananas or peaches with cream, yoghurt or ice cream.

Hannah was a happy child who never had tantrums. Even teething hadn't been much of a problem. She loved being bathed. She enjoyed going for walks and loved her playgroup and got on well with other children. Vanessa, who lived in the next street, visited most days. I took Hannah to the hospital three times a week to have lunch with Judith.

'Why,' I asked my feminist grandmother, 'did women fight to give up all this for the drudge of an office job?'

'This is only temporary for you, Robert. As soon as Hannah starts school you'll go back to work full-time.' She looked around the clean and tidy kitchen in wonder. 'Are you good at housework because you like it, or do you like it because you're good at it?' Her smile was rueful. 'I loathed it and hated being financially dependent on my husband. I was lonely. I missed talking to people. I talked to other mothers, but it was always about domestic things never about politics or world events. I can't believe you actually like ironing.'

'I don't like it, but listening to CD's or the radio makes it bearable. Doing Hannah's stuff is the worst – it's so fiddly.'

Judith came home after work to, what she described as, domestic bliss. The house was always clean and tidy, the washing and ironing done, preparations for dinner underway and Hannah gurgled with glee when she saw her mummy. While I got on with the dinner, Judith played with Hannah, fed her and put her to bed. Our dinners were leisurely and we shared a bottle of wine three times a week. We talked about events in the news, told each other about our day and planned our weekends and holidays. While I did the washing up, Judith had a shower and checked her e-mails.

Hannah went off to school on her first day with no fuss or tears. After school she rushed out to meet me babbling with excitement. She was popular with the other children and the teachers. My return to work went smoothly. Vanessa collected Hannah from school and took her to our house where they played together until Judith and I got home.

We employed a cleaner. We were happy. We were lucky. It's not that I took anything for granted or thought I deserved it. When I read the papers, or when any of our friends or colleagues were having problems with their relationships, I'd thank God I was so fortunate.

'You're a lucky bastard, Trevelyan,' one of my friends said in the middle of his acrimonious divorce. 'How come you've been allocated such a good deal for so long?'

Until then I'd never thought about happiness, misery or other fates in those terms.

In 2005 my happiness allocation expired.

Vanessa e-mailed me after the next meeting of the writers' group.

> I called for Olivia early tonight and helped her choose what clothes to wear. We decided on jeans, a white shirt and a red jumper that she wore with desert boots. She found a locket that the boyfriend had given her for her birthday. It was heavy, looked Victorian, or even older, and was probably at least eighteen carat gold. The ruby in the middle looked real. She told me he'd taken it out of his mother's jewellery case.
> You should have seen Phoebe's face when she saw Olivia. She was astonished, but genuinely happy. So was Margaret. Ethel thought she was someone new, which was funny. Olivia told them that it was all thanks to me, and afterwards in the pub Phoebe thanked me and admitted that she and Margaret had failed to help Olivia when she needed it most.
> Now, although this is all good news on a personal front, it's done nothing to help solve the crime. I really don't think Olivia is capable of murder no matter how angry or aggrieved she felt. She's more self-destructive and would

harm herself rather than anyone else. And with George having been to Phoebe and Stuart's house, it's back to Bridget being the intended victim. The only thing I can think of is that George was drunk and got the wrong house. Shall we meet at Farrier Way tomorrow night say at about 11?

Vanessa and I stood on the footpath in front of Phoebe and Stuart's house.

I shook my head. 'No matter how drunk George was he'd remember that the front door of Phoebe's was to the right of the windows not the left. And Bridget's house has a huge tree in the front and Phoebe's hasn't.'

It was after midnight when I got home. Before going to bed I made a few notes. Now that George and Olivia were eliminated as suspects, I focused on Bridget and those who hated her. Suddenly my thoughts jumped to Elaine. Had the anonymous messages caused a serious enough rift in their relationship for her to want to kill Bridget? To me she sounded unhinged. If she thought that the messages were true, was she unhinged enough to kill?

14

SHARON

I fought my way out of sleep and finally woke from the nightmare. Not that it was a nightmare, more of a replay of my experience. I still feel battered when I remember that day. I'd been visiting my mum and dad. I'd left their flat and was walking to my car when I heard someone scream. I took out my mobile and ran in the direction of the screaming. I turned a corner and saw two men trying to rob a girl who looked about the same age as me. She had a toddler in a push chair. He was crying. Food had fallen from her carrier bag. Tins of baked beans, tomatoes and soup rolled on the path.

One of the men was holding a knife at the girl's neck. After phoning 999 I charged towards her attackers.

'Police! The rest are on their way,' I yelled.

The skinny one, who was holding the knife, froze. The taller, stronger looking one ignored me. He grabbed the girl's handbag. 'Money. Where's the money?'

'Haven't got none left!'

He tipped her bag upside down. Tissues, keys, make-up and a purse fell out. He bent down to pick up the purse. I grabbed him and yanked him into an arm-lock. 'You're under arrest!' I heard the sirens.

The knife going into my shoulder hardly hurt. The pain was excruciating when he pulled it out. He raised it above his head. I saw the flashing blue lights of the police cars as they

206

drove onto the estate. The knife was heading towards my chest. The girl picked up a can of baked beans and smashed it over his head. Deflected, the knife tore into my upper arm. I felt it hit the bone.

The rest was a blur. I was taken to hospital by ambulance. I had two operations to repair the damage to the tendons and muscles in my shoulder and arm. I'd lost a lot of blood, but the knife had missed my artery.

After intensive physiotherapy I was fit for work, physically at least. But I'd lost my confidence. I saw danger everywhere. Being alone in my ground-floor flat in Hackney unnerved me. Walking down the street in daylight frightened me. Counselling helped, but not enough. To try and make light of my experience I often told myself that I owed my life to a can of baked beans.

I was determined not to let my nightmare wreck the day. It was five when I woke, so instead of going back to sleep I had a shower and got dressed. I made coffee and toast and sat at my computer trying to work out how we could solve this case without getting a confession. When Robert arrived I made him coffee and then he outlined his new theory about Elaine. I agreed she needed investigating.

'I don't think she's unhinged,' I said, 'but I do think she's a bully, confrontational and has no idea how to manage people. We certainly need to find out more about her. She should be out of hospital by now. I'll e-mail her and ask if we can visit.'

Robert looked thoughtful. 'We could say that we want to talk to her about the chap who punched her – throw her off guard. I want to know what sort of a place she lives in. She seems to have zero social life. Her mother might be like Mrs Bradley. Or she might live alone. If she's as unpleasant at home as she is at work she's probably got no friends.'

'What about family?'

'They might all be like her – or if they're not they probably don't see much of her.'

To make it official, we sent the e-mail from my computer at the station. She replied immediately. She was at home, but her jaw was still wired up. She gave a long list about her liquid diet and the way she had to suck her food through a straw. She didn't say whether or not we could visit. Sounding sympathetic I replied that she wouldn't have to talk to us, but we wanted to tell her personally. She agreed that we could visit that afternoon. On the way to her house we stopped at the hospital and asked the ward clerk if Elaine had had any visitors. She hadn't, which didn't surprise us.

Her terraced house in St Austell was in a dreary treeless street. The front of her house was paved, there were no bushes or grass, and a car that was about a year old was parked outside. It was as polished and clean as if it had just come out of the showroom.

Elaine's face had been covered in blood the last time we had seen her, and now I was surprised to see that, even with the fading bruises and missing teeth, she was attractive. Her eyes were deep blue. Without the grey streaks in her hair she would have looked younger, but I put her age at early forties. She was overweight, but not fat.

We followed her into the lounge and sat on the sofa. The colour scheme was beige and brown. Her clothes were beige and brown, although unlike the uniforms she had made her staff wear, they were good quality. The furniture was modern with a real leather sofa and chairs. Her television was huge. The walls were bare and there were no photos or ornaments on the surfaces. I thought how much Robert would hate the lack of character and books.

He was charming and sympathetic. 'You don't have to speak, just nod or shake your head. This must be an ordeal for you. Do you live alone?'

She nodded.

'Do you have any family who could help you until – '

She shook her head.

'While we're here is there anything we can do for you? Can we get you a cup of coffee or tea?'

She nodded, giving us a reason to go into the kitchen. She led us into the modern and immaculate kitchen and gave him a jar of instant coffee and a mug. When the coffee was made she put a straw in the mug and we went back to the lounge.

'Did you visit Bridget in her new house?'

She nodded.

'Did you see Phoebe?'

She nodded and held up three fingers.

'Three times,' said Robert.

She was looking impatient, so I said, 'We've no news about the whereabouts of Leslie Hooper yet, I'm sorry to say. But we'll let you know as soon as we do.' I stood up and, as if I'd just thought of it, I said, 'A few of the medical records staff mentioned that Bridget was taking a lot of time off work when she returned from maternity leave. Is that true?'

She nodded.

'They also said you were angry with her and – '

She made sounds of protest and her face went red.

Robert said calmly, 'They just said that you had berated her in front of them. Don't worry about it now. E-mail us. It might not be important, but could you also give us details about the anonymous messages you were getting.'

We got into the car.

'That provoked a response,' said Robert.

'Do you think she looked guilty?'

'Hard to say, but she certainly didn't like it. I've just had a thought. Can we try something?'

'What?'

'The neighbours. See what they think of her.'

He got out of the car and I followed him up the neighbour's path. A woman with a baby in her arms answered the door. A little girl aged about four stood next to her.

Robert smiled. 'I just wanted to let you know that Elaine, your neighbour, has a broken jaw, she was in an accident – '

'Good,' snapped the woman. 'Hope it hurts like hell.' The vehemence was startling. 'Always picking on my kids, she is. Complaining they make a noise. Of course they make a noise. They're kids – it's what they do. She even rang the police once.'

'Well,' said Robert. 'You won't hear much from her for a while – her jaw's wired up.'

The woman giggled. 'Serve her right. Are you her friends?'

'No, we're the police investigating the accident,' I said.

'Figures. Didn't think she's got any friends. Never seen anyone visit her.'

We got a similar response from the neighbour on the other side of Elaine. We went back to the car.

'Is she obnoxious because she lives alone or does she live alone because she's obnoxious?' Robert said.

'You're on dodgy ground there, Sergeant. We both live alone.'

'Yes, but we're younger than she is.'

'Do you think living alone is bad for our mental health?'

He nodded. 'That's why there should be more places like Pengelly House – company when you want it and privacy when you don't. Humans weren't meant to live alone.'

I really wanted to ask him how long he'd lived alone, but hesitated. Then I decided to risk it. 'How long have you lived alone?'

'Too long.'

'You don't like it?'

'I hate it.'

'Then why do you?'

He pulled away from the kerb and avoided my question by asking, 'Where to now?'

'Bridget's. And I hope her mother's out.'

She was in, and as belligerent as ever. 'Have you arrested Phoebe?' she asked as soon as she saw us.

'No, Mrs Bradley,' said Robert.

She folded her arms. 'Why not?'

He barely hid his surprise when I said, 'Phoebe has been eliminated from our enquiries, because she was miles away in the company of dozens of people when the fire started. We need to ask Bridget some questions. You can stay and not interrupt or we can do this somewhere else. What is it to be?'

Looking furious, Mrs Bradley went into kitchen and slammed the door. Bridget looked pale and even more thin. We all sat down.

'Bridget,' I said. 'Your colleagues told us that there was a disagreement between you and Elaine over the amount of sick-leave you were taking when you returned to work after having the baby. Is that true?'

'Yeah. She told me off in front of everyone. She shouldn't of done that.' Her voice was weary and disinterested.

'How did they react?'

'They enjoyed it. I could see them all smirking.'

'What happened then?'

'Elaine went into her office and left me standing there

211

with all them looking – '

'I mean – did your relationship with Elaine deteriorate – go wrong?'

'Yeah. I started looking for another job then. One closer to home. But it would of been hard.'

'Hard? Why?'

'She wouldn't of given me a good reference.'

'Why ever not? It's perfectly reasonable that you'd want to find a job closer to home.'

'She'd never see it like that.'

'How would she see it?' asked Robert.

'She'd say I was letting her down.'

And unlike Phoebe you had no one you could ask for a reference, I thought.

'I suppose that with you gone she would no longer have anyone to back her up,' said Robert. 'Did you ever visit Elaine at home?'

'Before I was married I did.'

'How many times?'

'A few times. Can't remember how many.'

'Is she married?'

'No.'

'Has she ever been married?'

'No. She lived with her dad. When he died she got everything. She didn't have no brothers or sisters. Always saying how lucky she was to have no mortgage.'

'How long ago did he die?'

'Not sure. Before I knew her.'

'Was she single by choice?'

'Don't think so. She pretended she were, but she fancied some of the men at the hospital, you could tell. But they wasn't interested in her. She really liked one of them who worked with us, but he hated her. She tried to get him on her

212

side, but when he made it plain – he were very crude about it – that he weren't interested, she went the other way and picked on him. He were the one that went crazy.'

That Bridget had said something against Elaine for the first time since the investigation was interesting.

'How did you get on with Leslie Hooper?'

'Okay – till I got promoted. We all got on okay till I got promoted.'

'Are you on compassionate leave?'

'Yeah. Elaine wouldn't let me have longer than a week, but I went to the doctor and got a certificate for a month. He said I can have one for another month when that runs out.'

'Are you going back to the hospital?'

'Don't think I will. When I get Declan's life insurance money I won't have to work.'

'The house Elaine lives in now – is that the one that belonged to her father?'

Bridget nodded. 'She were born there. Never lived anyplace else. She told me she spent lots doing it up when he died. There was lots of rubbish to chuck out.'

I wondered if ornaments and photos had been what Elaine classed as rubbish. Although I had no ornaments or photos I hadn't lived in my house very long. And I'd certainly never get rid of any photos my parents had.

'Did she get on well with her father?' Robert asked.

'Don't know. She never said.'

'Do you know what happened to her mother?'

'She died. Cancer. Why do you want to know all this?'

'Bridget,' Robert said carefully. 'During our investigations we've discovered that you have a lot of enemies.' He held up his hand to quell her protest. 'It's also clear that many people are very fond of you. Your colleagues at the hospital liked you before Elaine became the manager and promoted you.

But in view of your dwindling relationship with Elaine we have to consider that she is a suspect.'

Bridget look shocked. 'Never thought of that. I still think it's that Phoebe – even if she did – '

'Let's consider all the aspects,' Robert said. 'You visited Elaine before you were married. You no longer do. That's understandable, but she may see that as a rejection. I'd say she's lonely. And there are the anonymous messages she was receiving. All the staff knew about them. Margaret said Elaine held them up and even threatened to call the police.'

'Bet it were Margaret who sent them – trying to turn Elaine against me.'

I decided to ignore the fact that she'd originally said it was Phoebe. 'Did it work?'

'The first one didn't. She showed it to me and we laughed about it. She called a meeting and demanded to know who had sent it. No one said nothing. But she got more upset about the others, when they kept coming. She went right off me – got cold with me. Stopped telling me things. That's why I took lots of sick-leave. It were them letters making her go off me. And the others – they was so happy about it – I couldn't stand the looks they was giving me – Margaret were the worst. Elaine stopped sitting with me in the canteen – that was the worst bit – had to sit at a table alone and watch them all giving me funny looks.'

'So you weren't really sick?'

'I were sick of Elaine and the way she treated me. And I'd worked lots of unpaid overtime so it's not as if – '

'Elaine told us the unpaid overtime was voluntary. Is that true?' I asked.

Bridget frowned. 'Depends what you mean by voluntary. If I'd said no she would of punished me.'

'Like she punished Phoebe?'

'Yeah.'

'So she would have made you redundant?'

She nodded. 'Or she would of got me promotion took off me – the first year was . . .'

'Probationary?' Robert supplied.

'Yeah. Or she might of sacked me.'

I couldn't resist the opening she offered me. As gently as I could I said, 'In siding with Elaine you gave her excessive power. You lost your friends – '

'What else were I to do?'

'Well, if you'd fought against her like the others did her position would have been weak. If everyone had complained about her she might have got sacked or at least disciplined. Her methods of managing staff seem to have been draconian.' Realizing that she probably wouldn't know what draconian meant I went on, 'Threatening people with the loss of their jobs goes against modern ethics. Especially, if what we've heard is true, the medical records department had previously been well run and there were no complaints.'

Bridget looked sullen.

'Before Elaine came, had there been complaints?' Robert asked.

Bridget was trapped. 'No,' she finally admitted.

Robert warmed to my theme. 'Inspector Richardson is right. If the department had been badly run with missing files and uncooperative staff and a new manager improved things then complaints would have been ignored. But from what we've heard it was well run and managed. If all the staff, including you, had formally complained, your grievances would have been taken seriously. I'm not criticizing you, Bridget. I'm sure your position was difficult and the prize she was offering was tempting.'

'Did you like Elaine? I mean really like her?' I asked.

Bridget looked guarded.

'Did she visit you in Farrier Way?' Robert asked.

His question surprised me until I realized he wanted to see if Elaine and Bridget's stories tallied.

'Yeah. I never invited her – she said she come to see the baby. But she never come with any presents for him. And she kept asking me when I were coming back to work.'

'So you didn't really like her,' I said. 'I can understand that. Everyone else we've spoken to hates her. You've done very well for yourself. You were an ordinary clerk who ended up as the assistant manager. It has been said, by more than one person, that you only became friendly with Elaine to safeguard your job and get a promotion. You dumped Phoebe as a friend because she would have hindered your progress. Is that true?'

'Phoebe were jealous – the rest of them – '

'Bridget,' I cut in. 'This is serious. You are still alive, which means the person who tried to kill you might try again. Who else knows this address?'

'Phoebe.'

'Anyone else?' Robert asked. 'Does Elaine know?'

'Yeah.' Bridget burst into tears.

Mrs Bradley flung open the kitchen door. 'What are you doing? I'm going to complain about you to the papers. We're victims! Stop treating us like we done it.'

Robert stood up.

'Mum,' wailed Bridget. 'They think Elaine could of done it.'

'If you think of anything else you'd like to tell us, just send us an e-mail,' I said to Bridget.

'Why did you say Phoebe had been eliminated as a suspect?' Robert asked as we went back to the car.

216

'I had to say something to shut Mrs Bradley up.'

'Is Phoebe still top of your list?'

I sighed. 'Near the top with Yves. Instead of eliminating suspects were getting more and more.'

'Do you think Elaine is a serious suspect?'

'Unfortunately I do now.'

'So do I,' he said. 'In my estimation she's possessive and lonely, which makes things worse, and when crossed she turns vicious. And her house – it belonged to her parents – she's lived there all her life, but it's totally devoid of anything personal like photos – you'd think she'd have at least some photos of her parents.'

'Yes, that struck me too. They could have all been in her bedroom, but I doubt it. Do you think she just lacks sentiment or is it something deeper?'

He didn't reply till we got to the car. 'It could be something sinister . . . '

'Such as?'

'They might have been abusive. They might have been like Mrs Bradley and objected to any boy she bought home. She's attractive – when she was young she would have been even more so. Elaine said she was interested in men – did her parents object to her boyfriends?'

'If she was a bully that would have turned most men off,' I said.

He nodded. 'She either lacks empathy and always has, or her parents might have made her the way she is.'

'Robert, do you think it's possible that she might have murdered one, or even both, her parents? I know Bridget said one died of cancer, but that's what Elaine told her. Do you think we ought to check and make sure they died of natural causes?'

'Yes,' he said. He made a sound halfway between a laugh

and a grunt. 'We're not only getting more suspects – we might have uncovered even more victims.'

'It's interesting that she was romantically interested in the man whose nervous breakdown she caused.'

He frowned. 'Do you think it's true or is Bridget twisting the truth?'

'We'll have to check up on it – perhaps ask Margaret Fox. And the messages she was getting about Bridget – well she must have suspected they were true.'

When I got home I went into my study and thought about the way Robert did things. He said he always wrote by hand because it helped him concentrate. I took a clean sheet of paper out of the printer began to write.

Elaine – an obsessive bully with no friends or family. No one we've spoken to likes her. No it's worse than that. They hate her. How important are the anonymous messages she was getting? Although she was older than Bridget she was more attractive to look at. Was she jealous because Bridget was married and had a baby?

Bridget – variable behaviour depending on the circumstances. At best she's a friendly outgoing person with lots of friends. At worst she's a schemer who takes any advantage on offer with no thought for anyone else. She only became friendly with Elaine to further her chances.

Mrs Bradley – Possessive, demanding and a bully – a bit like Elaine. Unpopular.

Phoebe – Obsessive about clothes. Every time we've seen her she's been well dressed, except the day she was gardening, but even then the clothes she wore were good, just old and worn. Shirts and jumpers for every day of the fortnight. Is that excessive or is it just me? Is her passion for clothes even relevant?

I went to my wardrobe and chest of drawers and counted my shirts and jumpers. I had seven shirts and six jumpers. Was Phoebe's interest in clothes abnormal or was my lack of interest abnormal? Was one shirt and jumper for everyday of the fortnight obsessive or practical? The elbows of my jumpers wore thin quickly. Phoebe's would last a lot longer. Since seeing how clothes improved my appearance I chose them more carefully, thinking about how I would look as well as their suitability for the job.

I went back to my desk and thought about Yves.

Yves – Secret homosexual. Desperate to keep it from his parents. Bridget was a threat. Even though he'd stopped going to the same church as Bridget, she could have told his parents when they came to visit. She would have known when they were there, because she spies on people.

I threw down the pen. This was going nowhere useful. Nothing new had occurred to me when I was writing.

The next morning I went into a bookshop in St Austell to look at Phoebe's book. I'd only wanted to read the blurb and the first page to see if Bridget's allegation that it was rubbish and full of long words was true. The blurb was compelling and the first page was written in clear prose. If Bridget had failed to understand it then she was even more unintelligent than I had thought.

By page three I was hooked. I took the book to the counter and bought it. I read another two chapters in bed that night. The plot was complex, but easy to follow. Bridget was the name of the nasty protagonist. Was that the extent of Phoebe's revenge?

The next day Robert and I went to the hospital and asked Margaret Fox if she thought that Elaine had been romantically interested in any of the male staff.

'Yes, she was. So much has happened since, I'd forgotten. She was particularly interested in the chap she bullied so much he had a breakdown. Bridget helped her torment him. They'd both appear and order him into Elaine's office and shut the door. He'd come out half an hour later distressed and humiliated. They'd stand over him when he was working and said he was too slow or doing it incorrectly. I guess that was her way of paying him back for rejecting her.

'And I suspect Elaine fancied Leslie Hooper too, but she was more subtle about it that time.' Margaret looked scornful. 'When ever a male doctor came into the department she went all girly – it was comical, but also repulsive. She had no idea how she looked. It gave us satisfaction to think of her as a frustrated and repressed old maid who lived alone. If we hadn't hated her so much we might have felt sorry for her.'

'Why do you think she made you wear uniforms?' Robert asked.

'So we'd all look plain – there are some very attractive, single girls in the department and she didn't want any competition. And that's why she wore a different uniform – it was royal blue, in a good fabric and her blouses were silk.'

'Bridget wore the same uniform as Elaine?' I asked.

'Yes, and it was an improvement on the clothes she used

to wear.' Margaret grinned. 'Bridget's so plain that Elaine didn't look on her as a rival. Elaine, although she's middle-aged, is quite attractive – shame she's so vile.'

The death certificates showed that Elaine's father had died from a stroke and her mother had cancer. If our list of suspects was getting longer at least we didn't have any more victims.

15

ROBERT

The e-mail from Elaine was sent only to me and she had called me Inspector. Sharon smiled when I showed her. I was expecting her to be furious, so I was relieved.

'She fancies you, Robert.'

'What?'

'She's man mad. You're a man and not bad looking.'

'Good God. Just what I need.'

'The way she's addressed you is deliberate – she's trying to flatter you.' Sharon grinned. 'Perhaps you could visit her alone and coax a confession out of her.'

'No thank you.' I turned my attention to the e-mail.

> Bridget changed after having her baby. She was no longer dedicated. She took full maternity leave and when she finally came back she took lots of sick-leave. Running the department without her was arduous. The staff were more uncooperative than ever. They would talk when they were working and I had forbidden this. How can they concentrate on what they are doing if they are talking?
>
> When I first made Bridget my deputy I told her we should stop friends going to lunch breaks together, because lunch breaks were where they could plan their revolts, and she agreed. Phoebe and Margaret and others disobeyed and I had to have them disciplined. They got the union involved, but the man who tried to defend

them had a stammer. Bridget and I saw him in
private first so we could put our side of the case
to him without Phoebe and the others butting
in. I told him I hoped he never had to make
long distance calls and that made his stammer
worse – he couldn't wait to get away from me.
Bridget and I told him that when friends went to
lunch together they always came back late, and
he agreed that work, not pleasure, came first.
Of course, they all denied they came back late,
but it was Bridget's and my word against theirs.

Sharon expelled her breath. 'She's so spiteful. And Bridget
encouraged her. Stopping people going to lunch together!
She's almost admitted she lied about them coming back late.
No wonder someone lost their temper and thumped her.'

When Bridget was on maternity and sick-
leave the staff went on whatever lunch breaks
they wanted. Without Bridget to back me up I
was powerless to do anything. The staff became
increasingly cocky and insolent. So yes, I was
angry with her. Yes, I did reprimand her in front
of the staff because I wanted to teach her a
lesson. She had to know that if she defied me
she would be punished.
As far as the anonymous letters were
concerned, I'm certain that either Phoebe or
Margaret sent them, or knew who sent them.

The rest of her e-mail was rambling and contained
nothing else that was relevant. Sharon and I composed a
reply. We asked her if the letters had affected her
relationship with Bridget and did she think they were true.
We received her reply an hour later.

I showed Bridget the first anonymous letter
and she told me it wasn't true. She was upset

223

and I believed her. When the others arrived I began to wonder. She looked guilty as well as upset.

A long rant against Bridget followed.

'Not once has she expressed any sympathy for Bridget's tragic loss of not only her home, but her son and husband,' said Sharon.

'Elaine used her,' I said. 'She promoted an unintelligent, ignorant girl to a position of power so she had someone to unquestioningly support her nasty schemes and back her up with the management when the staff protested.'

Now Olivia was friends again with Phoebe and Margaret, and neither she or George were suspects, I assumed Vanessa would stop going to the writers' group. I was surprised when she said she had to visit our grandmother to get more poems.

'Robbie, I've got something to tell you,' she said when I queried her. 'There's a chap there that I like.'

I was pleased. Vanessa hadn't had a boyfriend since the break-up of a five year relationship eighteen months ago. The break-up had come at the time when everyone in the family was expecting them to announce their engagement. He had met and fallen for someone else, and Vanessa had been distraught. I'd liked him and we'd got on well. I hoped this new man would be good for her and not hurt her.

'What does he write?' I asked.

'Science Fiction. It's very good and even though it's not a genre I like, I've really enjoyed the parts he's read out. Last week he told us that he'd finally got a publisher interested. He's had an agent for about six months and just when the agent said she didn't think she could place it, a publisher said they enjoyed his novel so much they were willing to take a chance on an unknown writer.'

'Has he shown any interest in you?'

'Sort of. Tentative. He's not the sort to rush into things – and that's okay because neither am I. He sat next to me in the pub and seemed a bit, well, flirty. He lives at Pengelly House, so you might have seen him when you went there. He and Phoebe have been friends for years.' She smiled. 'So I need some more poems.'

We visited our grandmother on Sunday for lunch. After giving Vanessa a whole folder of poems, she said, 'I need your advice. This house is too big for me now. I'm lonely. I'm thinking of moving. I know exactly where I want to move to, but there's a problem.'

I thought she was going to say she wanted to move to Italy – she'd never stopped talking about her trip, so her next words surprised me.

'I want to move into Pengelly House.'

I was relieved. 'Perfect. Ethel said there might be an apartment coming up – is there competition for it?'

She shook her head. 'Not yet.'

'What's the problem?' asked Vanessa.

'Me.'

'Why? It's ideal,' I said.

Vanessa nodded. 'Much better than a retirement village. And Ethel's there.'

My grandmother sighed. 'We all had the preconception about communes. Hippies, drugs, orgies. When we heard the plans for Pengelly House the whole village was of the same opinion. I led the movement against them. But we were powerless to stop their arrival. It was all there for me to see if only I hadn't been so narrow-minded. The house was restored before they moved in. It had to be. No one, not even hippies high on drugs, could have lived there with the dry rot and the damp and squalor. Part of the roof had caved in.

'But instead of being delighted that it wasn't being pulled down and replaced by a housing development that squashed as many houses onto the site as possible, I became fixated about the ruin hippies would bring to the area. It was a year before they could move in. Busybody and trespasser that I was I went regularly to look around. I was blind to the sensitive restoration. Blind to the . . . everything.

'When they all moved in, people's attitudes changed. I was blind to that too. One by one the villagers who'd vowed to campaign against them, changed their minds. The antique dealer said they'd come into his shop and spent more money in a day than he usually takes in a month. They'd bought a lot of the furniture in Pengelly House and they had it restored. The organic shops and free range butcher reported soaring profits. Even the vicar liked them. Ethel took the trouble to call on them and told me she liked them. That they were decent and hardworking and respectable.

'But me? Oh no, I had to go stomping up to the house. What did I see? Seven people working in the garden . . . digging, hoeing, pruning. No psychedelic Rolls Royces or tatty caravans. No wild orgy. No unruly children. One little girl was earnestly raking up leaves with a miniature rake. A boy was wheeling a barrow. There was a pram on the lawn. From the house I could hear music. The Beatles? No. Heavy rock? No. Reggae? No. It was Chopin.

'Oh, I'm so ashamed about what I did next. One of the young women greeted me and asked me if I needed help. I told her that she needed help if she thought we were going to sit by and watch degenerates like her ruin our village. They all looked at me. They were bemused. They could have been abusive and told me to clear off. They could have had a wonderful time making fun of me. But they were polite. They invited me up to the house and showed me around. They introduced themselves. They explained why they'd all joined together to buy the house. They told me what they wanted for the future. I slunk away in shame.

'The next day I made a cake and picked roses from my garden and visited them. A little girl answered the door. Her mother, the same women I had been so obnoxious to, came up behind her. I held out the flowers and said, 'I neither deserve or expect your forgiveness, but I hope you will accept an apology from a foolish old woman.'

She smiled and said, 'Come in and have a cup of tea.'

'At the next church meeting I made a speech saying how wrong I had been. I resigned as chairman. They refused to let me go. The vicar made a speech supporting me and thanking me for my apology. They all applauded. I felt very grateful. Again their forgiveness and understanding was more than I deserved.'

'Everyone's forgiven you, but you can't forgive yourself,' I said.

'Pengelly House is perfect,' said Vanessa. 'It's full of life. You'd never be lonely. You've got a lot to give.'

'Such as?'

'Knowledge. Wisdom. Good advice. Experience,' I said.

Vanessa had been out with her new boyfriend twice when I met him. She arranged for us to meet in The Crown pub one evening. I was late and apologized.

'That's okay.' He stood up and shook my hand. 'Leslie Hooper. Vanessa told me about your work. Guess your time's not your own.'

Disguising my shock, I sat down. My thoughts were

chaotic. While previously I had sympathized with his plight, I now worried that my cousin was going out with a man who had lost his temper and resorted to violence. He didn't look aggressive. His face was sensitive and his voice was cultured.

'What's the matter with you?' Vanessa asked when Leslie went to the bar to get more drinks.

Telling Vanessa first would have been unfair. I suddenly had the thought that perhaps this was a different Leslie Hooper.

'Don't you like him?'

'It's okay, Vanessa. I'm sorry.'

'Sharon been giving you hell?'

I nodded. 'And so has her boss.' This was true. The superintendent had summoned us and made us go through every aspect of the case. He agreed that it was difficult, but still demanded a result, which made Sharon start harping on about Phoebe again.

When Leslie came back with our drinks, I asked, 'I've heard about your book and how good it is. Do you write full time?'

'I had a job when I wrote this one, but I've left now. I'm working on my second one already. But my advance is tiny so I have to get another job until I can make enough money to write full time.'

'Where did you work?'

'For the NHS.'

Hell, I thought. 'A pharmacist?' I asked as casually as I could.

He shook his head. 'A clerk. I used to be a teacher. That's how I know Phoebe – we worked at the same school and left for the same reasons – out of control children and some were aggressive too – no support or back-up from the head or the board of governors. She found a job at the hospital and when a vacancy came up she told me about it. I applied and got it.'

For the rest of the night I wondered how to handle this new development.

When Vanessa went to the toilet he said, 'You don't approve of me, do you?'

'We have to talk,' I said. 'About Elaine Dunn.'

'Oh. I see. You're investigating the fire at Bridget's house?'

'Yes. I'm not judging you, but we need to talk. Did you punch Elaine Dunn?'

'Yes. Do you want to arrest me?'

'No. Definitely not.'

'But you quite rightly don't want a violent man going out with your cousin.'

'I don't think you are violent – not under normal circumstances,' I said, remembering what Phoebe had told us about Bridget and Elaine trying to provoke her into hitting one of them.

'Thank you.' He sipped his beer. 'I was wrong to loose my temper, but . . . no I'm not going to make excuses. I was wrong. I'll tell Vanessa and let her make the decision.'

'I have heard that you were provoked,' I said.

He nodded. 'She humiliated me in front of everyone.'

'What did she say?'

Leslie took a deep breath. 'That I was a pathetic specimen of a man, who failed at everything I did and how on earth had I become a teacher when I was so thick and slow. What pushed me too far was when she asked if I'd had a sex change that went wrong.'

I winced. Leslie was thin with fine features and a thick head of hair, but there was nothing effeminate about him. 'She wanted you to hit her so she had the excuse to sack you.'

'I know.' His smile was grim. 'But I don't think she wanted me to punch her as hard as I did.'

I saw Vanessa coming toward us and changed the subject.

The next night I was about to get into bed when someone pounded on the door. I ran downstairs. It was Vanessa.

'How dare you!' she spluttered.

'What?'

'Leslie. You've ruined everything.'

Vanessa and I had had childhood quarrels, but never since we'd grown up, so her fury shocked me.

'Vanessa, I – '

'Don't make excuses.'

I laughed, which increased her fury.

'Have you forgotten you might have actually killed a man?'

I pulled her inside and shut the door. 'Sh. And have you forgotten what they were going to do to you? Leslie Hooper thumped a woman so hard he knocked out some of her front teeth and broke her jaw. '

'He was provoked.'

'I know. But his life wasn't in danger.'

'It was a culmination of things. Elaine was always picking on him.' She paced the room. 'Look, it's his ambition to be a writer. The previous day his agent had told him that she didn't think they'd be able to find a publisher. He was already upset and Elaine berating him in front of everyone else and then saying he looked as if he'd had a sex change that hadn't worked, made him flip. Can't you understand?'

'Yes. Just listen to me. Elaine Dunn is demanding that we find him and arrest him. I have no intention of doing so. I think it's at the bottom of Sharon's list of priorities, but I'm not going to tell her that I know where he lives. We've got a murder to solve. So, what's all this about?'

'He feels threatened.'

'Not by me.'

'His mother told him the police were looking for him.'

I didn't tell Vanessa that his mother had told Sharon and me that she didn't know where he was.

'I knew there was something wrong last night. You were really off with him.'

'I wasn't. I was a bit shocked. Now what did he say? Why are you so angry?'

She sat on the sofa. 'He said it's best if we stop going out together.'

I sat opposite her. 'Vanessa, what you need to do is talk to him.'

I wondered if she would tell him that she and I had once taken on six rapists and beaten them insensible. Would she tell him that I didn't know if I had killed one? Suddenly his violent act provoked by a deeply unpleasant woman seemed mild compared to what Vanessa and I had done.

'If he's been sacked from the hospital, what's he doing for money?'

'He's got three interviews. He's desperate to get something before Elaine comes back, because he's given Margaret's name for a reference.'

Vanessa went home, still angry with me, but she had agreed to talk to Leslie. I told her if she needed me to be there I would.

Then I had a terrible thought. Had Leslie Hooper set fire to Bridget's house? Sharon and I had never considered him a serious suspect. But neither of us had known what Elaine had said to him. He seemed a sensitive man. If he had murdered a baby his conscience would have tormented him.

I went to bed, but couldn't sleep. I went into the kitchen and made a mug of coca. It worked, but I woke up at four in the morning, feeling fully awake. I went into my study and switched on the computer. I decided to go with one suspect at a time. Because Elaine was the newest I thought about her carefully. I re-read her e-mails in the order that she had sent them. They were dull in places and full of irrelevant details, but I was looking for clues, so I read every sentence instead of scanning them as I had done previously. That's when I saw it – the paragraph about Phoebe in the second e-mail.

> Bridget had no idea that Phoebe lived in the house next door before she moved in. When they were friends Phoebe and her husband had lived in a smaller house. Phoebe ignored Bridget when they became neighbours and she must have poisoned the other neighbour's minds against Bridget too. It's not as if she'd lived there very long herself, but she behaved as if she'd been born there.

I cursed myself. I was a stickler for believing seemingly irrelevant statements could sometimes be vital clues, but I had missed this one because most of Elaine's e-mail was a self-important, boring ramble. But that was no excuse. It was now five in the morning. I showered, dressed and made breakfast. At seven o'clock I rang Sharon and said I couldn't come in till later. She demanded to know why. I wouldn't tell her. Understandably she was furious. I ended the call and drove to Farrier Way.

Phoebe came to the front door in her dressing gown. She looked at me in terror and burst into tears.

Stuart came to the door. He was also in his dressing gown. 'What the hell is going on now? What do you want?'

'I need to ask you something.'

He put his arm around Phoebe. 'We've told you all we know.'

I smiled. 'I'm looking into something else. Any

information you have could help solve this case today.'

Stuart grudgingly let me inside. We went into the kitchen.

'I was just making coffee,' he said. 'Do you want some?'

'No thanks. How long have you lived here?'

'Why do you want to know?' asked Stuart. 'What's it got to do with anything?'

'It might have a great deal to do with this case,' I said quietly. 'I'm investigating a new line of enquiry.'

'Four years,' said Phoebe.

'When did you become president of the writers' group?'

'In two thousand and three – five years ago. I don't understand what –'

'I want to ask you about George –'

'George?'

'George Wilson – at your writers' group.'

She looked astonished. 'Why?'

'You've got something on him. What is it?'

'I haven't got anything on him. I don't like him –'

'He hates you. Why?'

She looked bewildered. 'How did you know? I don't understand what this is about. George doesn't know Bridget. She's never been to the writers' group.'

'Tell me why you charge him more than you charge other members at the meetings.'

She shook her head. 'I didn't report him. How did you find out? Has something happened too him?'

'Like what?'

She looked concerned. 'Is he okay?'

'As far as I know. What did you think may have happened to him?'

'He's unhappy.'

'Do you know why?'

She nodded. 'He's divorced. His ex-wife is Italian. She

took their baby daughter to Italy about seven years ago. She says George can see her anytime, but he hasn't got much money. He's unemployed. He's unstable. He tries things, but they never work out. I thought he might have taken an overdose or something.'

Suddenly I knew what had happened. 'When he was the treasurer did he steal money from the writers' group?'

'Yes,' said Phoebe. 'It went on for years. There was a great president who left five years ago. The group was large and had some published authors. No one noticed George was helping himself to the money.'

'Why not?'

'People wrote their names, and what they were reading, in the register and left their money on the table. When I became president I sometimes had difficulty reading names and titles, so I sat at the table and wrote in the register myself. I wanted to compile annual anthologies of short stories and poetry written by members. I got quotes from printers and kept a total of what money we should have had. A year later at the AGM George's treasurer's report fell way below what I knew we should have. I asked him about it, and he blustered and said that maybe people forgot to pay sometimes.

'I knew it was impossible, because I was taking the money and giving out the change. He said that it happened when I was on holiday and the vice-president had taken the meetings. We're talking about over a thousand pounds, so I knew he was lying. Finally he broke down and told me all his problems. I told him he'd have to pay it all back and that if he didn't I'd go to the police. He resigned as treasurer and I made it look as if it was voluntary. At an emergency general meeting Margaret was elected as the new treasurer.'

'Did she know he'd stolen money?'

'No. I told her that George had borrowed money for an

emergency and was paying it back.'

'Has George ever been to this house?'

'No. Why?'

'Does he know your address?'

'I don't think so. Why?'

'Have you ever invited him to this house?'

'No.'

'Never? Are you sure?'

I saw Stuart looking at me as if I were crazy.

'Oh yes,' said Phoebe. 'Once. Just before I found out he'd been stealing. Then I told him not to come.'

'So he must know your address?'

'Yes. I'd forgotten.'

I stood up. 'Thank you.'

'Has he stolen money from somewhere else?' asked Stuart. 'Is that what this is about?'

'I can't say anything at the moment.' Although I was sure George was too shattered to make another attempt on Phoebe's life, I took the precaution of saying, 'Please be careful,' before running out of their house and jumping into my car.

When I parked in front of George's house I tried to ring Vanessa, but her phone went to messages. Praying George would be at home I rang his doorbell. He came to the door with his mobile phone in one hand and a cigarette in the other. He recognized me and gestured for me to follow him upstairs. Inside his flat, which was almost as untidy as Olivia's had been, he paced up and down with the phone. He was in a shabby towelling dressing gown.

The only things he said were, 'Yes, no, okay, that's right, that'll do.' He repeated them about six times.

I remembered what Olivia had said. As well as being a bad writer, George was a bad actor. It was obvious that no one was on the other end of the phone.

The flat was hazy with cigarette smoke that made my eyes sting. George could have saved a lot of money if he had given up smoking, but he had chosen to steal from the writers' group instead.

Finally he ended the call. 'Sorry about that,' he said. 'My agent's just checking on an article I've written for a magazine. You're Monster's boyfriend, aren't you? Nice to see you.'

'George,' I said. 'I'm a police officer. I'm – '

His colour changed from white to grey. 'She promised she wouldn't say anything to anyone. Okay I'm late with payments, but I've been ill – I had to spend a few days in hospital – you can check their records. It was my heart. I had a mild heart attack. I have to be careful. I'll pay it all back . . . I'm trying. She knows I've got money problems.'

'I take it you are referring to Phoebe,' I said.

'Who else?'

'I'm not here about the money. I'm part of the team investigating the death of Phoebe's neighbours. A toddler and his father. The houses in Farrier Way are numbered consecutively. Someone who saw number one in the dark would think the next house was number three where Phoebe and Stuart live. But it's not. It's number two.'

George sank onto the sofa and put his head in his hands. 'Oh, God.' His shoulders shook.

'You made a mistake, didn't you?' I said quietly. 'You knew Phoebe's address, but had never been to her house.' To make sure that George had intended to kill Phoebe and not just burn her house down, I said, 'She wasn't at home that night. She was at a party to celebrate the publication of her book. Did you know?'

He shook his head. 'No one tells me anything and she

makes sure I'm never invited anywhere.'

'So you intended to kill Stuart too?'

'Yes. He's just as cold and unforgiving as she is. They don't know or care what it's like to have money problems. They don't know what it's like to be divorced. They don't understand how it feels not to see the child you love because she's been taken to another country.'

When George took his hands away from his face and looked at me, I realized he was seriously ill. His blue lips indicated he was about to have another heart attack.

'Have you got any aspirin?' I asked as calmly as I could.

He nodded.

'Where?'

'Bathroom,' he mumbled.

I raced into his bathroom, which stank of mildew. Damp towels and clothes were on the floor. I yanked open a cupboard, found the aspirins, tipped one into my hand and went back into the lounge. He was clutching his left arm.

'Take this,' I said holding out my hand.

He shook his head. 'Let me die.'

I grabbed his head, held his nose and when he opened his mouth I forced the aspirin under his tongue. Even though he spat some of it out, gradually his breathing eased and his lips returned to a more normal colour. He still looked ill, and I knew I had to get a signed confession out of him as quickly as I could. His computer was on a desk in the corner. Its screensaver of exotic fish was on. I moved the mouse and sat down. Keeping my eyes on George I typed a confession. When I finished I read it to him.

'Is that correct?'

'You haven't put she was blackmailing me.'

'She wasn't blackmailing you. She told you that unless you paid the money back she would go to the police. That's not blackmail.' I printed it out and looked for a pen. I couldn't see one. 'Where's your pen?'

'Don't know. Don't care.'

Plunging my hands into my pocket I searched for a pen.

George laughed weakly. 'A dying man, a confession and a pen. It's no good unless I sign it, is it?'

'It is under certain circumstances. And I've been recording this conversation,' I lied. 'A signature just makes things easier.' I threw things that were on his desk onto the floor, then searched his drawers and finally found a pen. 'Please sign this, George. Innocent people, who have nothing to do with this crime, are under suspicion. Lots of them. I'll phone an ambulance as soon as you sign this.'

'Then I won't sign it. I'll only sign it if you say you won't call an ambulance.'

'Okay. I won't call an ambulance.' Praying he wouldn't tear it up I handed it to him.

His hand shook, but his signature and the date were clear. I folded it, put it in the pocket of my jacket, took out my mobile phone and called an ambulance.

George looked appalled. 'You promised you wouldn't.'

'No, I didn't promise, I said I wouldn't, but I lied. They're on their way.'

George closed his eyes and lay on the sofa. 'I want to die,' he gasped.

'I understand. I would too.'

Now the case was solved I was in no hurry to return to the station. As soon as the ambulance left with George, I went home and typed out a summary of how I'd solved the case. I also typed a letter of resignation. Then I drove to Farrier Way.

Stuart opened the door and scowled. 'What is it now?'

'I've got some news. You can relax. You are no longer suspects.'

He let me in and called for Phoebe who came running up the stairs from the basement.

'George Wilson set fire to the house next door,' I told them.

'But he didn't know Bridget,' said Phoebe. 'Or did he?'

'No. But he knew you.'

16

SHARON

Robert's absence forced me to tell Superintendent Venning that he was being uncooperative. If I hadn't been summoned into his office I would have dealt with Robert myself, but Mrs Bradley had made a formal complaint against us. She had also written to the papers, and two reporters wanted a statement about the harassment allegations she had made. Hoping Robert would show up with a plausible excuse, I listed all our suspects and their motives.

'So Phoebe Harris is your top suspect?'

I nodded.

'What's she like?'

'She's not your typical murderer and I don't think she's a danger to the public, but I think Bridget provoked her and she cracked. Her flaunting the baby when ever she had the chance was the final blow for Phoebe.'

'And what does Trevelyan think?'

'He disagrees.'

'Mrs Bradley claims you and Trevelyan are hounding them.'

'We're not. And Mrs Bradley is also a suspect.'

He studied the list. 'My chief suspect would be Yves,' he said. 'I'd discount Phoebe Harris because she was not in the vicinity. I think your theory about her biking through the forest in the middle of the night is far fetched. Yves was there. Strong motive too. Concentrate on him.'

'Sir, I – '

'You're no further forward than you were the night the fire started. I had high hopes that you and Trevelyan would work well together. You have both disappointed me.'

'Sir, if Bridget hadn't been so hated, I think we would have put this down to a random arson attack. And it could still be the case. Our difficulty is that most of the people who hated her said they were in bed asleep. Whether they were or not is almost impossible to prove. The only people who were not in bed at the time are Margaret, Phoebe and her husband Stuart. They were all at the party at Pengelly House. No one saw anything – '

Robert opened the door and strolled in. Without being invited he sat down.

'Where have you been, Trevelyan? Inspector Richardson has told me you are obstructing this case – I'm taking you off it,' Superintendent Venning snapped.

'Good,' said Robert. 'It's solved.'

'Solved?' we said together.

He nodded. He took a sheet of paper out of his pocket, unfolded it and placed it on the desk. 'The confession – signed and dated.'

Superintendent Venning read it and checked my list. 'There's no George Wilson on here.'

'George Wilson?' I echoed, sounding, and probably looking, stupid.

'Is he under arrest?'

'No, Sir, he's in hospital in the intensive care unit. He's had a heart attack.' Robert took an envelope out of his pocket and put it on the desk. 'My resignation and a summary about how I solved the case. And far from being obstructive I was working with an inspector who is an irrational bigot and was

241

determined to persecute the wrong person, who was actually the intended victim.' He stood up and left. He closed the door quietly.

Reeling from Superintendent Venning's lecture and the threat of being demoted, I got into my car shaking with rage. I drove to Robert's cottage. The front door was open and I went inside without knocking. There was a man sitting on the sofa in the lounge with a glass of wine and a bowl of peanuts on the coffee table in front of him. Robert was about to go into the kitchen. He had his back to me and hadn't heard me enter.

'You bastard!'

He spun round.

'You stuck up, supercilious bastard. Happy are you? I bet you are now you've shown me up and made me look incompetent.'

'You are incompetent. You're also a bigot.'

'And what are you?' I looked at the man on the sofa who was looking stunned. 'A queer? Or worse? Someone who likes little girls?'

I saw an old lady standing in the doorway of the kitchen. She looked horrified. I heard someone running down the stairs. It was the blonde. She rushed at me, held me in an arm lock and dragged me outside. I tried to get out of her grasp, but it was impossible. She pulled me down the street to a blue car and opened the door.

'Get in.'

I tried to struggle free, but my self-defence techniques were futile.

'I'm a karate black belt and if you don't get in the car I'll break your arm.'

I got into the car.

She slammed the door and ran to the driver's side. 'Put your seat belt on.'

'What if I don't?'

'I'll break both your arms. Try and get out of this car and I'll break your legs as well.'

I fastened the seat belt. 'Who are you?'

She ignored me and put the car into gear. She was a good driver. In spite of her aggression towards me, she drove calmly.

'Where are we going?' I asked.

She didn't reply. Wondering if I was in danger I thought about what I could do. She didn't look mad, but her calmness was more worrying than her anger. She drove carefully down narrow lanes and she gave way to a few other drivers and acknowledged their waves of thanks. I considered pulling frantic faces, but guessed the people in the other car wouldn't notice. I was just feeling reassured by the knowledge that I had my mobile phone and might be able to press 999 if things got dangerous, when she turned into a church yard and turned off the engine.

'Get out.'

Thinking she was going to dump me there, I got out and waited for her to drive away, but she got out of the car, took my arm and pulled me into the church.

'You're going to look around for something specific. When you find it come outside. I'll be in the graveyard.'

'What am I looking for?'

She went to the door. 'You'll know when you see it.'

My fear evaporated. She must know I'd have a mobile phone. She wouldn't have left me alone in the church if she meant to harm me. Even if she intended to lock me in, I could survive a night in a church. I spent five minutes wandering round trying to see something significant. I couldn't. I went outside.

She was looking at a lichen encrusted headstone. 'You didn't find it.'

I shook my head, wondering how she had known.

'Go back inside and look again. Look higher this time.'

'Am I looking for divine intervention or forgiveness?' I asked unable to keep the sarcasm out of my voice.

She went back to looking at the headstone. I went inside and resumed my search. There were brass plaques in memory of people I've never heard of. There was a roll of honour covering the two world wars. Most of the windows were clear glass with diamond panes. Apart from around the altar, there were only a few stained glass windows. One looked newer than the rest. I looked at it and read the plaque underneath.

In memory of Judith Trevelyan 1975 – 2005
And her daughter Hannah Trevelyan 2000 – 2005
Killed in an avalanche in Switzerland.
Beloved wife and daughter of Robert.

There was more, but unable to read further I sank to my knees. I don't know how long I'd been like that when I heard the door creak open. A cool wind gusted in.

'You found it.'

I managed to speak. 'Yes.'

'I'll drive you back.'

We had almost reached Robert's village, when I spoke. 'Please will you tell Robert how sorry I am?' The words were trite, but I didn't know what else to say.

'You should tell him yourself.'

'I don't think he'll ever want to see me again.'

She said nothing.

'Are you his girlfriend?' I asked.

'No. His cousin. Judith was my friend. The man you saw on the sofa is my boyfriend.'

'I'm sorry I wrecked your evening.'

'His name's Leslie Hooper.'

It took a moment to register, and if she hadn't sounded so challenging I would have missed it, I was so wrapped up in shame and misery. 'Oh. Ah – '

'Yes, that Leslie Hooper. Elaine told him he looked as if he'd had a sex change that hadn't worked – she said it in front of everyone. So are you going to arrest him?'

'And have you break my legs?'

'Are you going to report him and get someone else to arrest him?'

'Why are you telling me?'

'Because he wants to give himself up. He hates skulking about, worried that one day they're going to find him. He thinks there's a chance that if it goes to court he'll get a fine or a suspended sentence. Margaret told him that while he'll have lots of character witnesses, Elaine won't have any. Well she'll have character witnesses, but they'll be there to say how vile she is and how she wanted him to hit her so she could sack him. I don't think anyone will say anything good about her. So, Leslie's at Dolphin Cottage if you want to arrest him now, or he lives at Pengelly House if you want to do it later.'

'Why? What's he done?'

She smiled. 'Thank you, Sharon.'

'I'll write to Robert. I owe him that at least.'

'A face to face apology would be better – but not just yet.'

She dropped me in the village and I went back to my car. On the way home I decided to call in at Elaine's and tell her where Leslie Hooper was.

She answered the door and gestured for me to go inside.

'No thanks, Elaine. I just wanted to tell you that we've found out where Leslie Hooper is. He's gone to Australia.'

At home I looked at the card I'd bought. On the computer I drafted the letter I wanted to write. After six attempts I found my gel pen and copied what I written onto the card.

Dear Robert,

My profound apologies for my appalling behaviour and vile accusations. I do not expect you to forgive me, but I am asking you not to resign. You are a far better detective than I am and your resignation would be a terrible loss.
I am going to Australia. In view of my failure I am giving up police work. Please apply for my job. You deserve it. It should have gone to you in the first place. My sincere sympathy for the tragic deaths of your wife and daughter. I hope you will find happiness one day.

Sharon

I addressed it, put a stamp on it and ran to the letter-box. When I got home I e-mailed my brothers. Then I applied for an Australian visa.

17

ROBERT

For a long time I wished I'd been with Judith and Hannah that day. Sometimes I still do. The last time I saw them they were sitting on a ski lift. As the lift took off up the mountain they turned and waved. Judith in a blue ski-suit. Hannah in a red one with her blonde curls lifting in the breeze. We had arranged to meet at the top for lunch. The only reason I hadn't been with them was that I had hit a patch of ice the day before, skied into a tree and dislocated my shoulder. Judith, skiing behind me, had watched in horror.

'Thank God it wasn't worse,' Judith said that evening when the shoulder had been put back and my badly bruised arm had been supported in a sling. 'You could have been killed.'

Remembering her words at their funeral service I thought, I wish I had been killed, Judith. I wish I had been.

After Vanessa had stormed off with Sharon, my grandmother, shocked by Sharon's allegations, set about trying to get our evening back to normal. She began by pouring a large brandy and telling me to drink it. So she could fill us in on the progress of her move to Pengelly House and meet Leslie, I had invited them all round to dinner.

Vanessa had been away for just over an hour when she returned. Leslie was in the bathroom. She told my grandmother and me where she had taken Sharon. 'She is very upset.'

'So she should be,' said my grandmother.

'She asked me to tell you how sorry she is.'

Considering the dreadful start to the evening the dinner went well and I managed to relax. In retrospect I knew that I should have told Sharon I was sure who had set fire to the house and asked her to meet me at George's address. She might have refused, but I hadn't given her the chance. There had also been times when we had discussed the case without friction between us and I should have let her know what I suspected.

The best time to tell her would have been when we were having lunch in the pub in Blissland. George was still in my frame as a suspect and I should have told her then. It wasn't her fault that I hadn't. It was mine. I don't know what she would have said, but she might have taken the suggestion seriously. We had been discussing psychology and I should have used George's distressed manner to at least convince her that he was worth investigating. When I discovered how the houses were numbered I should have tested my theory on Sharon not Vanessa.

Because I had refused to tell her where I was going, and she had no idea when I was coming back, she was justified in telling Superintendent Venning that I was being obstructive. I was less justified in claiming all the credit for solving the case and had effectively jeopardized her career. Her fury, but not her accusations, had been understandable.

That night I dreamt that I was back in St Margarets with Judith and Hannah. When I woke up I felt the excruciating pain of loss. Having resigned I faced an empty day. I rang Vanessa and asked if she was free for lunch.

'Aren't you at work?'

'No. I've resigned.'

'Why?'

'I'm coming in with you.'

'Oh, hell! Go and unresign.'

'What's wrong?

'Oh, no . . . I've – '

'You asked me, remember? Have you changed your mind? I thought – is it because of Leslie?'

'No. It's all gone wrong.'

'What, you and Leslie? You were okay last night.'

'I'm coming over.' The line went dead.

When she arrived at Dolphin Cottage she looked upset. 'I'm sorry. I was going to tell you – the credit crunch has caught up with me. The woman I went to *The National Archives* for, e-mailed me a few days after I got back from London. She's being made redundant and told me to cancel the investigation. I hadn't started to write the report, thank goodness, but I wasted money on the trip to London. She said if she gets another job she'll be able to go on with the investigation, but – I don't know. I can't see things getting any better soon. And normally I've got quite a few enquiries, but I've had nothing for a month. I'm sorry, Robbie.'

'Are you okay for money?'

She nodded. 'I'm cutting down a lot. It's amazing how much little things add up. I've stopped buying the papers, and I go to the supermarkets late and get lots of things near their sell-by dates cheap – and no, don't even offer to help – I got myself into this mess – I'll have to get myself out of it.'

'The credit crunch and collapsing banks aren't your fault.'

'But I should have listened to my parents advice and got a proper job in the civil service or NHS or something.'

'You did what you wanted to do – it was the right choice.'

'It doesn't feel like the right choice now.'

I knew that, apart from her mortgage, Vanessa didn't have any debts. That was one thing we'd both listened to our parents about. We'd heeded their advice, 'If you can't afford it – go without. If you really want it – save up for it.' Neither of us had any credit cards – just debit cards.

'Have you got enough money to pay your mortgage?'

'At the moment.'

'You can always rent out your house and move in with me.'

'If things get really bad, I might have to do that. I was going to tell you. I didn't expect things to happen so quickly.'

'Neither did I.'

I wondered what to do. I didn't need a job financially. I'd paid off the mortgage on our house in St Margarets with Judith's life insurance money. Dolphin Cottage had been far cheaper, which meant I had plenty of money, most of which I'd invested. I could live off the interest, but I wanted a job.

The following morning Sharon's card arrived.

18

SHARON

The newspapers were full of the story about George's arrest. He was in hospital, under guard and out of intensive care. Mercifully they were more interested in the personalities and motive involved than the time it had taken the police to find the murderer. If they had known about my bungling of the investigation they would have torn me to pieces. As it was the team was praised for solving, what the papers called, a complicated case.

Phoebe and Stuart were hounded by reporters demanding statements and full stories, which they refused to give in spite of being offered substantial sums of money by several papers for exclusive rights to the story.

Bridget and her mother made the most of it, but Phoebe, a beautiful novelist and Stuart a handsome artist, were more interesting subjects and their pictures appeared more often than Bridget's who looked even worse in the photos than she did in real life. In one of her statements she blamed Phoebe for the murder of her husband and baby.

'She never lit the fire, but if she hadn't made enemies my family would still be alive and happy,' she said, ignoring the fact that she had made far more enemies than Phoebe.

When all the staff in the medical records department defended Phoebe and condemned Bridget, the story died.

Shaking with nerves I walked down the hill to Dolphin

Cottage, just in time to see Robert come out. I watched him walk to the beach. Keeping some distance between us I followed. The tide was out so far the boats were sitting on the sand. He went to one of the boats and climbed inside. I stood with my heart thumping, tempted to just leave. I didn't know if he'd received my card or not. I hoped he had as he would know my intentions were not aggressive. I had no idea what his cousin had told him. Apart from Robert the beach was deserted.

Wanting to get it over with as quickly as possible I went to his boat. 'Robert.'

He looked up. His expression was surprised when he saw me, but not hostile.

I took a deep breath. 'You deserve an apology in person. My accusations were filthy and unfounded.'

He jumped out of the boat. 'I got your card. Thank you.'

'I'm sorry about . . . everything. Good luck with your future. I hope you get the inspectors job.' I turned away.

'Sharon.'

I turned back.

'Best of luck in Australia.' He held out his hand.

I took it and we shook hands. I began to cry. Embarrassed by my weakness, I pulled away and ran along the beach.

He caught up with me and took hold of my arm. 'Shall we have a cup of coffee together?' he asked. 'And talk as friends not adversaries?'

Getting a visa to live in Australia was so difficult I thought that getting out of jail would be easier. The forms were long and if it hadn't been for my brothers I'm sure I would have been rejected. I had to prove my financial status, which fortunately, was excellent. Desperate to get my parents out of the council estate that was becoming so violent they felt they were entering a war zone every time they went out, I gave them a choice. Either come to Australia with me, or live in my house in St Austell when I go. They chose Australia. My brothers had to guarantee that they would look after my parents if they got into financial difficulties.

The day after I got my Australian visa, Robert was promoted to inspector. I bought him a bottle of champagne. We went out to dinner with Vanessa and Leslie to celebrate. Thanks to Margaret's reference Leslie had found a job stacking shelves in a supermarket. It was a lowly position for someone who had been a teacher, but he said he had plenty of time to think about the new novel he was writing. To give himself time to contemplate he walked the two miles to work.

He told us that Phoebe and Stuart had put their house in Farrier Way on the market and were buying an apartment in Pengelly House. He also took great pleasure in telling us that all the staff in medical records had put in written complaints about Elaine Dunn. After an investigation she was sacked. Margaret was the new manager.

'Why not see if you can get your old job back?' Robert asked.

He shook his head. 'Elaine wrote to Human Resources and they wrote to my mother's address and asked me to attend a hearing to defend myself. I didn't turn up and they sacked me.'

The following morning I found out what it was like to wake up in Dolphin Cottage to the sound of the waves and the view of the sea, with Robert's arms around me. And I was right about the romantic dinners with candles burning and classical music playing on the CD.

The photographs of Judith and Hannah were back in place. Looking at them made my throat ache. Hannah had blonde curls just like the little girl we'd seen at Pengelly House. No wonder Robert had looked at her with longing. A family group, obviously taken by a professional, showed a happy trio all blessed with good looks.

Instead of diminishing, my guilt grew. My judgment had been way off. A more astute person would have realized Robert was tormented by loss and struggling to rebuild his life, rather than arrogant and sullen as I had thought. The conclusions I had jumped to were wild. I, who hated it when people assumed I was the sergeant and Robert was the inspector, had assumed that the paediatrician Robert had mentioned was a man. Just because he didn't flirt with women and didn't have a girlfriend I'd wondered if he was a homosexual.

He tried to persuade me to stay in England. But having told my brothers and parents I was going to Australia I felt committed. My brothers had found me a flat in Perth. And although Robert had forgiven me, the memory of what I had said was too shameful for me to dream we had a future together. On two occasions I had been guilty of causing him terrible hurt.

And my attitude to Phoebe had been caused mostly by envy, which was unforgivable and compromised my ability as a detective. Even after discovering she'd had miscarriages and a baby who'd died shortly after being born, I had still felt envious of her beauty and the way she dressed. No man would ever look at me admiringly when I walked into a room.

Before my parents left for Australia I made them go to the dentist. My father got new dentures. All my mother's decaying teeth were extracted and she was pleased with her dentures, which looked good and didn't hurt like her old teeth had. I made an appointment for her to go to the hairdressers. It was the first time for thirty years that she'd had her hair professionally cut and styled. She used to hack at it herself. The new style made her look ten years younger. I made my father go to the barber. I failed to persuade him to give up smoking. He was more willing to let me teach him how to use e-mail and do basic internet searches.

I didn't go to London to see them off. I'd be seeing them in three weeks. My brothers had found them a one bedroom flat and bought them a computer. My dad bombarded me with e-mails from Australia. They loved the flat, they loved the beaches and the weather and they were absorbed in their grandchild and looking forward to arrival of the second. Most importantly, they got on well with their daughters-in-law. That they had settled down so well made it more likely that I would stay in Australia. I already had an appointment for an interview, but not with the police. If I got the job I would be a civil servant.

After a lot of thought I decided to rent out my house rather than sell it. If things didn't work out in Australia I'd have something to come back to and the rental would give me income. A week before I was booked to fly to Australia, Robert and the team threw a surprise leaving party for me in a private function room in a pub and presented me with a state of the art digital camera.

The following day we received the news that George Wilson had died.

'The best thing for him,' Robert said. 'It's what he wanted.'

'And the best thing for the country too,' I agreed. 'Spared the expense of keeping him in jail.'

My cases were packed and the estate agent had organized the letting of my house to a young married couple. I spent my last night in England with Robert. We. left at six in the morning to drive to Heathrow. Just before we drove out of Cornwall we stopped. at a motorway service station for breakfast and Robert bought a local paper. There was a photo of Bridget on the front page. When her house in Farrier Way was repaired she was going to sell it and move to Ireland with her mother.

Robert shook his head. 'Poor girl.'

After I'd checked in Robert and I had a cup of coffee.

'You will come and visit me?' I said keeping my voice steady.

He reached over and took my hand. 'Of course.'

'You taught me a lot,' I said.

'And you taught me a lot too.'

I grunted. 'What? It sure wasn't how to be a good detective.'

'In my disappointment about not getting the promotion I was arrogant. I thought you'd been promoted over me because of political correctness. But it wasn't, was it?'

'I think it was, actually. They needed to promote a woman to counter the claims of sexism.'

He shook his head. 'No. It was because you had great courage.'

Talking about it embarrassed me so I'd never told him. But one night after we'd made love he'd asked me about my scars. Even then I'd brushed it aside and told him they were caused by an accident.

'Courage?'

'You went to the help of a girl who was being attacked by two men, one of whom was armed with a knife.'

I blushed. 'How did you find out?'

'Superintendent Venning told me. He didn't want to loose

either of us. I think he even wanted us to work together again, so he used that to try and persuade me. I think he was right. We could work together again – we both know where we went wrong and we've learnt valuable lessons.'

'I made too many mistakes,' I said, fighting the temptation to rush to the check-in and tell them I'd changed my mind. 'If it hadn't been for you the case would never have been solved. Phoebe and Stuart would have had suspicion hanging over them. Even worse, George might have burnt their house down.'

'I doubt it,' said Robert. 'The stress would have been too much for him. Knowing that he'd killed a baby and an innocent man made him ill. I don't think he would have had the will to try again. Desperation drove him to want to kill Phoebe. He was too weak to solve his financial problems any other way. He was a heavy smoker, he ran a car when there was no need to – he lived close to the town and should have walked, but was too lazy. Instead of stealing money from the writers' group he should have got a job, but he thought he was too good for anything as menial as working in a supermarket.'

'Bridget might have burnt Phoebe's house down – she was so certain that she was the murderer.'

He grinned. 'You're determined to make yourself look as incompetent as possible.'

'Being a detective is too important to – '

'What would you have done if I'd told you my suspicions when I saw how the street was numbered?'

I laughed.

'What?'

'It would have depended on my mood at the time. And that's another reason why I'm giving up being a detective. I'm a victim of my hormones. If you'd told me when I was in

257

a good mood, I would have agreed that we should investigate that aspect. In a bad mood I would have told you to stop being stupid and accused you of trying everything to get Phoebe off the hook because you liked her.'

'You're very honest, Sharon. I'll miss you. If things don't work out in Australia please come back.' He smiled. 'You might hate all that sun and the beaches . . . ' His smile faded, leaving him looking lost and unhappy.

I'd finished my coffee. I didn't want to cry, so I stood up. 'I'd better go through now.'

Hand in hand we walked to the doors. Neither of us spoke again. We hugged. We kissed. Then I turned away and walked through the doors.

I don't know if he'll come to Australia. I don't know how long I'll stay there. Maybe forever. Maybe not. But I'll give it a chance.

42130333R00150

Printed in Poland
by Amazon Fulfillment
Poland Sp. z o.o., Wrocław